"I am not yo[u]

Madeline said softly. "[I] did to your family, and [...] an my heart I could restore them to you."

"I know you are not responsible," he replied, wishing she would go so that he could dress.

"Is the water very cold?"

"Yes."

To his astonishment, she began to remove her clothing.

"What…what are you doing?" he demanded huskily.

"I am going to wash, too."

When her garments fell on the ground and she stepped forth naked, he could only stare as she took a deep breath and walked into the river.

Here, now, she would choose a man for herself. This man, this warrior, protector and comforting companion whose family had suffered so much at the hands of her countrymen.

When he took her in his arms, she leaned into him gladly.…

Dear Reader,

As promised, this month we are very pleased to bring you *The Welshman's Way*, award-winning author Margaret Moore's sequel to *A Warrior's Way*, which earned a 5★ rating from *Affair de Coeur*. When a Welsh outlaw sets out to rescue a Norman maiden from an attack, he unwittingly saves her from an unwanted marriage and sets into motion a series of events that will change their lives forever. Don't miss this extraordinary story!

Bestselling author Theresa Michaels hits her stride this month with *Once an Outlaw*, the second book in her new Western series featuring the infamous Kincaid brothers. *Romantic Times* calls this delightful love story "an engrossing, not-to-be-missed read."

For Love of Rory is Barbara Leigh's new medieval story of a young woman who forces a wounded Celtic warrior to help her find her kidnapped son. And from Carolyn Davidson, her first book for Harlequin Historicals, *Gerrity's Bride*, a Western marriage-of-convenience story with plenty of fireworks.

Whatever your taste in reading, we hope Harlequin Historicals will keep you coming back for more. Please keep a lookout for all four titles, available wherever books are sold.

Sincerely,

Tracy Farrell

Senior Editor

Please address questions and book requests to:
Harlequin Reader Service
U.S.: 3010 Walden Ave., P.O. Box 1325, Buffalo, NY 14269
Canadian: P.O. Box 609, Fort Erie, Ont. L2A 5X3

Margaret Moore

The Welshman's Way

Harlequin Books

TORONTO • NEW YORK • LONDON
AMSTERDAM • PARIS • SYDNEY • HAMBURG
STOCKHOLM • ATHENS • TOKYO • MILAN
MADRID • WARSAW • BUDAPEST • AUCKLAND

ISBN 0-373-28895-6

THE WELSHMAN'S WAY

Copyright © 1995 by Margaret Wilkins.

Books by Margaret Moore

Harlequin Historicals

*Warrior Series

MARGARET MOORE

confesses that her first "crush" was Errol Flynn. The second was "Mr. Spock." She thinks that it explains why her heroes tend to be either charming rogues or lean, inscrutable tough guys.

Margaret lives in Scarborough, Ontario, with her husband, two children and two cats. She used to sew and read for reasons other than research.

Prologue

Moving as quickly and quietly as he could, Dafydd adjusted the girth of the saddle on the roan horse. His injured shoulder ached from the effort, but he ignored the pain. He had to get away before he was discovered in the stables of the monastery of St. Christopher.

Although most of the monks were sleeping, Father Gabriel often chose to keep a vigil in the chapel, and Dafydd had seen the pale, thin light of a candle shining from the window of the infirmary.

He was nearly healed and to stay longer would be foolishness. He had been relatively safe while Abbot Peter was alive and in charge of the Dominican monastery; unfortunately, the new abbot was an ambitious man who made no secret of his interest in worldly affairs of state. If Abbot Absalom realized they were harboring a Welsh rebel, he would not hesitate to turn the man over to the nearest Norman overlord.

Abbot Absalom had left that morning to attend a wedding that would unite two Norman families, apparently planning to pay visits to certain important lords and clergy along the way. No one would dare to enter the abbot's cell during his absence, except perhaps a thief who needed to get back his sword, acquire some money for a long and difficult journey, and some clothing. If his luck held, it wouldn't be until the abbot's return that anyone would realize anything was missing.

The good brothers had saved his life, and he regretted rewarding them with thievery, but there was no help for it.

Nearby, one of the monastery's placid donkeys shifted and a horse stamped its foot. Overhead, a mouse scampered through the hay, reminding Dafydd that he must not tarry.

Dafydd finished tying his meager pack to the back of the roan and led the beast from the stall. It was not an impressive animal, but he had chosen it more for stamina and strength than beauty, for he intended to ride north and west into Wales, to where the roads were not good and the way not easy, avoiding towns or villages or fellow travelers. He would also take care to skirt the land of Lord

Trevelyan and his son-in-law, Morgan, who had good cause to remember Dafydd's face.

Dafydd ap Iolo was going to get as far as he could into the most remote part of Wales. He would find a quiet, simple Welshwoman and have lots of children. He wanted no more of fighting and death and deprivation.

He simply wished to be left alone.

Chapter One

Gloucestershire, 1222

Madeline de Montmorency stared at the Mother Superior as if she did not believe her ears, which was indeed the case.

"I am sorry to have to inform you of this so bluntly," Mother Bertrilde said, her voice as cold as the stone walls of her small, spartan chamber in the convent. "Your brother's epistle has only just arrived."

"I am to be married in a fortnight?" Madeline asked incredulously, hoping somehow that the notoriously serious Mother Superior was making a jest.

But no, she was not. "So your brother writes."

Madeline shifted uneasily, trying to digest this unbelievable news. She had not seen her brother in ten years, ever since their parents died of a fever within days of each other. For months she had been expecting word from him, anticipating the day he would come to take her home, away from this convent and back into a world of freedom, color, laughter—not to another prison as the wife of a man she did not know. "Surely he would not decide such a thing without one word to me," she protested. "Does he speak of a betrothal or—?"

"Unless I have lost the ability to read," Mother Bertrilde said sternly, "I am certain the contract has already been signed. Since you are your brother's ward, you should prepare to obey him."

"But who is this Lord Chilcott? I have never even heard the name!" she cried, aghast at the horrible sense of finality in Mother Bertrilde's face and voice.

"I have no idea, but I suppose he is of a wealthy family of noble blood. What more need you know?"

"Surely there must be a mistake! My brother has to be talking of a betrothal, not a wedding. I need more time—"

"Your brother writes that he will be arriving soon to take you to his home to prepare for your wedding," Mother Bertrilde reiterated frigidly.

Madeline realized she had made a major error in even hinting that Mother Bertrilde could have made a mistake. "But this marriage is impossible,"

Madeline pleaded, taking a different tack. "I thought to take my vows in a fortnight and I have been waiting longer than any of the other novices."

While this was not strictly true, Madeline said it anyway. She had studied and pretended a deep interest in the contemplative life, if only to keep the curious sisters from speculating at her brother's tardiness in sending for her.

Mother Bertrilde looked at her with an eyebrow so slightly raised that only a person who had been studying her expressions for years would have noticed the sign of severe displeasure. "I had hoped to tell you of my decision regarding that at a more appropriate time," she said, without one ounce of genuine solicitude. "However, your brother has left me little time for tact. Madeline, I would not have allowed you to become a nun. Did it not occur to you that I was delaying because I was not certain of your vocation? The convent is no place for a woman of your temperament—"

"*My* temperament?"

Mother Bertrilde's expression would have been a scowl if she was not so adept at smiling when she felt anything but happy. "You are demonstrating your lack of suitability at this very moment. You are not humble. You will not submit your will to obedience. You are *much* too interested in worldly things.''

"But I—"

"Therefore, Madeline," Mother Bertrilde continued, "I would suggest you prepare to leave with your brother and abide by the provisions he has made for you."

"To further his own ends," Madeline replied. How dare this reproving, unfeeling woman and her brother plan her life like this? She was no longer a child!

"Whatever his reasons, it is your duty to obey."

"My duty is to marry a man I have never even seen?" she asked, venting her anger in sarcasm.

"What other choice do you have?" Mother Bertrilde demanded, clearly unmoved. "I cannot keep you here against your brother's will."

"Very well, I will leave," Madeline said with a severity that did credit to the teacher standing before her. "If my piety and devotion and patience are to be rewarded by being cast out as if I were a leper, if you think I have no choice but to obey like some sheep, then I will gladly go—but not with my brother."

Still Mother Bertrilde remained unimpressed. "With whom do you intend to travel? I assure you, I will provide no escort."

"Then I will go without one." Madeline took a step toward the heavy door.

At last Madeline's determined words seemed to penetrate the Mother Superior's facade of stone. "You are speaking nonsense, Madeline," she admonished. "You cannot leave here by yourself. Not only would you be acting like a common peasant, but you would surely be killed, if not suffer a worse fate. The lands hereabouts are full of thieves and rebels."

Madeline's lip curled with haughty disdain. "What would be the difference, Mother, between being raped by an outlaw or by a man to whom I have been married against my will?" With that, she spun around and stepped toward the door, only to collide with a man's broad, solid chest. Two strong hands reached out and pushed her back.

Madeline stared up at the man whose dark eyes glared at her and whose lean, hawklike face was reserved and forbidding. Indeed, he was a taller, broad-shouldered, harsher version of herself, without the softness of femininity to smooth his rough edges. "Roger?" she gasped.

"Madeline?" Roger de Montmorency, who was not known for the sweetness of his temper, looked over his sister's head toward the black-garbed bulk that was the Mother Superior. "What is the meaning of this? She was to be ready to leave."

Mother Bertrilde, who was more known for her strict adherence to the rules of her faith than a soft heart, glared back. "I regret," she said insincerely, "that your messenger was delayed. He only arrived this morning."

Roger turned to the nobleman standing behind him. He had iron gray hair and a careworn face, but there was youth in his eyes, and some sympathy, too. "Albert, find out what happened with Cedric. Then have one of the nuns gather up my sister's belongings." With a nod, the man moved to obey.

"I am not going with you," Madeline announced, crossing her arms and frowning.

Roger looked at the sister he had not seen in so many years as she stood in the middle of the room. She was taller than he had expected, prettier, too, even in the plain habit of a nun. But those eyes, those angry, defiant bright blue eyes belonged to the Madeline he remembered, without a doubt. To think he had hoped that the nuns would have made her placid and pliable! "The arrangements have all been made. Prepare your things, Madeline," he ordered. "We leave at once, for it will take some days to reach my castle." He pulled a bag of coins from his belt. "This is to thank you for your trouble," he said to the Mother Superior.

Mother Bertrilde frowned reproachfully. "I suggest you keep your money and give it to a priest to say intercessions for your immortal soul, since I must remind you that this is a convent, and in this convent, it is *I* who tell the nuns what to do. *Not* you and not your men."

Roger de Montmorency was not impressed by the Mother Superior's words or the angry expression on her face. He turned toward Madeline. "Come."

"I told you, Roger, I am not going with you. I will not marry at your order, and certainly not a man who is a stranger to me."

His sister's anger made no impression on him, either. "I have not met Chilcott myself," he said dismissively. "My overlord, Baron DeGuerre, wants our families to be united. You are my responsibility and you have no choice but to obey, in the same way that I strive to obey the baron. What *my* lord orders, I assure you, *will* come to pass."

"I will leave when I am ready," Madeline insisted, "and I will go anywhere *but* your castle."

"Enough!" Roger bellowed. He had no time for arguments from Madeline or empty courtesies with the Mother Superior. His departure from his castle had been delayed, the torrential rains of early April had made the journey a nightmare and it was only a fortnight until the wedding was to take place.

Abruptly he grabbed Madeline's arms, pulled her toward him and threw her over his shoulder. "You are ready now and you are going to my castle." He turned toward the door, then, ignoring his sister's struggles, he glanced back at the Reverend Mother. "One of my men will wait until her goods are prepared for the journey. Good day."

Carrying his squirming sister as if she were a sack of grain, Sir Roger de Montmorency marched stoically from the room.

"Roger, stop!" Madeline demanded as he carted her along the stone corridor and out into the convent's yard. To add to her humiliation, Madeline caught glimpses of curious women whispering together like little clusters of birds. "Let me go at once!"

Roger finally put her down. Flustered, Madeline straightened her belt and glared at him. "How dare you! How dare you treat me this way!"

"I dare because I am your elder brother," he retorted. "How dare *you* try to disobey me!"

"You can't simply order me to marry this Chilblain—"

"Chilcott. And yes, I can."

Madeline became aware of the sudden silence and glanced around the yard. Several of the sisters were unabashedly staring, their eyes wide and their mouths open.

Perhaps the best thing to do would be to wait until they were away from this place, where she could argue with Roger in peace. "We shall continue this discussion later, dear brother," she said, smiling sweetly.

His expression grew hard and was completely without sympathy. "There is nothing to discuss, Madeline. Not now, and not ever. I have given Chilcott my word that you will be his wife."

With that, he turned and left her standing in the courtyard while he bellowed for his men.

Dafydd was finally beginning to feel that he would not get caught and be condemned to death as a thief. At first, he had kept in the forest, riding parallel to the road, where the going was not easy. This morning, he had decided to risk the easier travel along the road, at least for a little while.

He was even feeling somewhat happy for the first time since he had awakened to find himself weak and helpless in a Norman monastery. He had no clear idea how he had managed to get so far from the Welsh border. He vaguely remembered crawling and stumbling away from the place where Morgan had left him to die. At the time, he certainly had no care for what direction he took, as long as it was away from Morgan's land. He knew, from listening to Father Gabriel and the others at the monastery, that he had been found near death by a traveling monk who brought him to the monastery on the back of his donkey. Over time, Dafydd had come to believe that he was several miles to the east of the border, and not nearly as far from Morgan and Trevelyan as he could hope.

Still, he was free, and getting closer to Wales with every step.

The scent of wet earth and damp foliage filled his nostrils, a pleasant change from the medicinal smells of the infirmary. He ran his hand through his shoulder-length hair, enjoying the feel of the warm spring sun upon him although the woolen dalmatica made him swelter and wish for other garments. Surely he would fool no one into believing he was a holy brother, even if was wearing one of their robes, with his hair and his build and his wound that could only have come from battle. However, he had had no alternative, except to go nearly naked.

He glanced up at the sky and saw a gathering of dark clouds, which signaled a change in the weather. There had been many storms and much rain of late, and the roads were muddy and treacherous. Still, he would welcome these clouds if they heralded a cool breeze.

On the horizon, he could see the beginnings of the higher ground that was the first hint of the terrain he knew. In a couple of days, he would be nearer to the mountains of Wales, although he had other hills and valleys to cross first.

He tried to recall what he had heard the holy men saying about the lands surrounding the monastery. At first, he had not understood their language, but eventually he had come to be able to guess at most of what they said. If they surmised he was not a Norman or a Saxon, they kept their suppositions to themselves, while he had used the time to learn as much as he could of their language, in order to protect himself. However, he never actually said a word and, wisely, the brothers allowed him to remain silent.

He thought about the villages and manors the brothers had talked of. There was a village not many miles away, in the northerly direction he was taking. He thought it was small, from the way they spoke. It was tempting to go there, to get some more appropriate clothing and food, and yet this horse he had taken was rather distinctive looking, in a homely way.

While he was still trying to make up his mind, he came to a fork in the road. What was obviously the main road went straight on ahead; another, narrower and less-used way veered to the west. He was tempted to turn along it, until he recalled that a Norman manor belonging to someone named Sir

Guy was said to be slightly to the north and west of the monastery. Dafydd gathered the holy men did not like the Norman nobleman. Lustful, he seemed to recall they said of him. Well, what Norman wasn't, whether for women or power or wealth?

Still, he had no wish to encounter any noble Normans. Most of the overlords in this area, the border lands between Wales and the rest of England, were harsh and brutal men, given a free hand from the king to do whatever they felt necessary to subdue any Welshmen who dared to rise against them. Dafydd knew all too well what they would do to him if they caught him.

He passed by what appeared to be an abandoned farm. Two burned shells of buildings gave evidence of some disaster, and Dafydd's lips curled in disgust, for he did not doubt that he was looking at some Norman's handiwork. Perhaps the poor peasant had been unable to pay his tithe, or had once been of an important family and could not mask the pride that he still bore. Maybe he had had a pretty daughter who was not flattered by a Norman's attentions,

Dafydd shook his head to clear it of such thoughts, and instead wondered just how far away lay the castle of Lord Trevelyan and the manor of Morgan, the Welshman who had married Trevelyan's daughter. He would have to find out, and take great care that he came not near there. If he was recognized, his freedom would not last long beyond that moment.

Dafydd decided he would stay on the road until he drew near to the village. It was a bit risky, but the way was much easier on the road, and the air cooler. Once near the village, he would take greater care, although he did hope that he would be able to venture into an alehouse to get a better grasp of which way to go and purchase some other garments.

The road entered a narrow valley, heavily forested. Fallen leaves from years gone by made a thick covering on the road, which deadened the sound of his horse's hooves. Young ferns were appearing at the edge of the way, and wildflowers provided a splash of yellow and pink. A slight breeze stirred the newly budding branches, and despite the springtime beauty, Dafydd's first thought was that the dead leaves and rustle of the branches would effectively mask the sound of creeping men. In fact, this place was an ideal spot for an ambush. He had little enough to tempt thieves, but he knew there were many men who had even less. They would not care who they robbed and murdered, either, whether Norman or Welsh, noble or peasant.

Dafydd scanned the trees, trying to discover by senses too little used of late if he was being watched.

He never should have remained in the monastery as long as he did. He had grown too soft.

Suddenly he paused, cocked his head and listened. From somewhere up ahead came the familiar sounds of metal on metal and the shouts of men in battle.

Sliding from his horse, he pulled his sword from the scabbard tied onto his saddle. The road curved off to his right, around the wooded rise. If he went straight up the rise and through the trees, he might be able to see what was happening on the other side without being noticed. It was not his desire to interfere, simply to see who was fighting and how it might affect his own progress. He led the horse into some covering underbrush and began to move cautiously through the trees.

His long, cumbersome woolen robe got caught on a bramble bush. He paused to untangle it, and it was then he heard the woman's terrified scream. For an instant, he was paralyzed, powerless like the boy he had been. An image, a name on his lips...and then he felt the hot blood of anger burst into his heart. With a curse, he tore off the garment, threw it onto the ground and dashed toward the top of the rise clad only in his linen breeches. When he was near the top, he began to creep forward slowly and stealthily, scanning the road below, his pulse throbbing through his body, gripping his sword so tightly his knuckles were as white as a lamb's fleece.

He could see what looked like a band of thieves attacking a small group of mounted travelers. The ragged, rough men on foot had surrounded two noblemen, one mounted woman—a nun, it seemed—and some armed soldiers. The nun's horse pranced nervously, but she controlled it very well while the noblemen, surely Normans, fought with great skill and determination. He could tell from the calls, shouts and orders that the attackers were Welshmen. Dafydd did not think these men had any motive other than robbery, as three of them were swiftly making off with the pack animals and leaving the guards alive. If rebellion was their motive, they would have killed the soldiers.

Nor did he think the lady and her escort had much to fear. The Normans were skilled fighters and well armed. The thieves were only holding them off as best they could until the packhorses were gone.

With a shuddering sigh, Dafydd moved back, still watching, more from an interest in seeing the Normans' fine swordsmanship than concern for any of the combatants.

And then one of the ragged band grabbed hold of the bridle of the nun's horse before swinging himself onto the animal behind her. The woman screamed and one of the noblemen twisted to look at her as the outlaw kicked the horse to a gallop, back along the road in the direction from which Dafydd had come.

What did that fellow want with her? Ransom, perhaps, or something more?

Quickly Dafydd sprinted through the woods, ignoring the brambles scratching his naked chest, legs and arms. He ran as fast as he could to where his horse waited and then he stood perfectly still.

He heard something off to his right. A struggle. Harsh commands. Once more he plunged into the forest, following the noises. The achingly familiar noises, from the day his sister was raped and killed by the Norman soldiers who had murdered their parents. How Gwennyth had tried to fight them! They had not seen the boy hiding in the trees, alone. But Gwennyth had. In the moments before she died, she had turned her head and looked at him. He would never forget her pain-racked eyes, or that her last effort had been to mouth his name.

Dafydd came to a glade. The thief was there, the woman on the ground and struggling beneath him, screaming curses and trying to scratch the outlaw's face.

Dafydd had been helpless to protect Gwennyth and his parents that terrible day. He was not helpless now, and whether this woman was Norman or

Welsh did not matter, and whether this fellow merely wanted to hold her for ransom or not did not matter.

Dafydd ap Iolo, Welsh rebel and outlaw, a man who had been fighting the Normans since he was ten years old, forgot that he had decided his fighting days were finished. With a ringing battle cry, he raised his weapon and attacked.

Chapter Two

"How dare you lay a hand on me! My brother will kill you if you hurt me! How much do you want? Roger will pay!" Madeline cried as she struggled against her captor. Despite her fear and panic, she knew she was worth much more alive and unharmed than shamed and dead. She also realized that he was only slightly taller than she was, and although he was stronger, he was not much bigger.

He gripped her flailing arms tighter. "Useless it is to fight, woman," he snarled in barely understandable Norman French, his Welsh accent strong and his voice guttural. "Or killing you I will be. Worth a lot, you are."

Suddenly a bloodcurdling cry rent the air. For an instant, Madeline saw surprise in the outlaw's face before he rolled off. Desperate to get away, Madeline twisted and crawled as quickly as her shaking legs would let her toward some large bramble bushes. If she could but get out of sight!

In her haste, she ignored the clang of sword on sword, the exchange of curt, unfamiliar words and what she was sure was Welsh profanity until she was in the cover of the bushes. Only then did she turn to look at who had come to her rescue.

It was not Roger. Or Sir Albert. Or anyone she had ever seen before. Her savior was dark, tall and nearly naked, well built, muscular and, by his stance, a man who knew how to fight. His long, black hair hung to his shoulders, obscuring much of his face. She felt as if some ancient warrior god of the Britons had come to life to save her.

Then, as he circled his foe, she saw that his broad right shoulder was marred by a massive scar and he bore the mark of another serious wound on his left side. Yet the most startling thing about him was the intense concentration and hard line of his mouth as he stared at his opponent. Even Roger had not looked so completely determined when the outlaws had attacked.

Whoever he was, wherever he came from, she had never been happier to see anyone in her life.

Her rescuer continued to circle the outlaw, his stance wary like a cat couched to spring. The outlaw, whom she now saw was but a youth, was on his feet and snarling like a cornered rat. The two opponents swayed from side to side, swords held in both hands low to the ground, waiting. Watching.

Abruptly the man raised his sword. The outlaw did likewise and the clash of the weapons resounded through the trees. The outlaw's sword slid along the other's blade, seemingly direct for the man's chest. Madeline opened her mouth to shout a warning, but before she did, the man twisted his hands, disengaging his weapon, stepped back and swung his sword in a great arc, striking the outlaw in the leg, the whole action accomplished before she could make any sound. Both men cried out and fell to the ground at the same time, the outlaw clutching his bleeding leg and the other his shoulder.

The outlaw's wound was not a severe one, however, and he lifted his sword and ran straight at his adversary as the man staggered to his feet. The man moved to avoid the blow, then swung his sword again.

He missed. But as the outlaw ran by, he stuck out his foot, tripping the fellow, who sprawled in the dirt. When the outlaw tried to get up, the other man lifted his sword and struck him on the head with the hilt. With a low moan, the outlaw slumped unconscious to the ground.

The other man dropped his weapon and stood panting heavily, his hands on his knees. Sweat dripped from his forehead and muscular chest, and his shoulder-length hair still shrouded his face.

Madeline crept out of the underbrush. Unsure what to do now, she tugged her wimple back into place, adjusted her disheveled clothing and tried to regain some measure of self-possession. She kept her eyes on the stranger, however, wary of him. Mother Bertrilde had painted the world outside the convent walls as filled with all manner of evils and evil men, and after what had just happened, Madeline was not so inclined to view Mother Bertrilde's ideas with as much skepticism as had been her wont.

After a long moment broken only by the man's panting, he raised his eyes and looked at her. Suddenly her heart started to pound as if she had been the one doing battle. What a strange expression was in his dark, piercing eyes! As if he were surprised to see her there, and yet, had he not deliberately come to her rescue? Risked his own life for hers?

She quickly told herself that she felt so oddly because she had never seen such a man in all her cloistered life. What was it about him that affected her so? He was undeniably handsome, with his dark, searching eyes, and his relaxed lips had a sensuous quality she had rarely seen before. But there were handsome men in her brother's entourage. He was possessed of undeniable strength and had wielded his sword with what she knew had to be great skill. Yet her brother and other men had strength and skill.

He had more than all that. In a way, he seemed almost savage in his ferocity, but he was too controlled to be brutally cruel. She did not doubt that he could have killed the outlaw with ease, yet he had not.

Perhaps it was only that he had come to her aid. No, there was something more, something personal in the intense dark eyes that moved her beyond admiration for a handsome face, strong body and battle prowess, and gratitude.

His expression changed, altered into something that made her curious and excited and overwhelmed, all at once. Then she knew, without any doubt and although she had spent the last years of her life in the exclusive company of women and the old priest who came to say mass at the convent, that this man, this warrior, was looking at her not as a student or a novice, or as a highborn noblewoman. He was regarding her simply as a woman. It was so new, so intoxicating...so wonderful. "Who...who are you?" she asked, unable to bear the silence any longer.

He blinked, rose slowly until he stood upright and started to walk away. His dismissive action recalled her attention to her perilous situation, although she found she no longer feared him. After all, he had helped her and was prepared to leave her, so he obviously had nothing to do with the attack.

"I thank you, sir, for your aid," she said, hurrying after him. "My brother will be happy to reward you."

He kept walking, as if he intended to leave her there, with the unconscious thief and who knew how many conscious ones lurking nearby. She grabbed his arm. He glanced at her, then her hand and she flushed and stepped away. "I have to get back to my brother."

He made no answer, although his dark gaze didn't leave her face.

"Will you not help me? I...I do not know where I am and there may be other thieves about."

He started to walk again.

She quickly circled around him. "What about that outlaw? We cannot leave him there like that. He should at least be bound, should he not?"

The man only shook his head and kept going. She trotted after him, puzzled by his behavior. Surely he had not saved her only to abandon her to her fate.

They reached an incredibly ugly roan horse placidly tearing up grass near a large oak as if nothing of any significance had happened. The man reached down and picked up a garment, which he pulled over his head.

Her nerves strained, her breathing coming in labored pants, Madeline had had enough. "Sir! I am Lady Madeline de Montmorency and I demand that you assist me to return to my brother and his men. I am very grateful to you, of course, but truly—" She finally noticed what he was wearing. "You are a *priest?*"

He did not respond, except with another silent stare.

"Or a lay brother, perhaps. Yes, that's it, surely. A lay brother. No priest could wield a sword like that. You must have been a soldier. But why...oh, I understand!" she surmised, calling to mind some stories she had heard in the convent. "You are under a vow of silence. For penance?"

When he made no sign of giving her the courtesy of an answer of some kind, Madeline bristled. "Sir, I do not know who *you* are, but I know full well that *I* do not deserve to be ignored in this manner. However, do not answer if it suits your purpose and I will assume I have surmised correctly." She ran her gaze over the horse and the pack tied onto it. "And I believe you are going on a pilgrimage as part of your penance. Whatever it is you are doing, sir," she went on with great formality, "I will require your assistance to return to my brother and his men, who I'm certain would have rescued me if you had not.''

Dafydd regarded this astounding woman standing before him. As he had raced to help her, a part of him had been impressed that she had the strength to fight and the will to curse her attacker. Then, when he had won his battle and had time to really look at her, he had been startled by two things. The first was her beauty; the second was that this beauty was encased in the vestments of a novice in a convent.

For a moment, he had feared she had been injured or was going to faint, for her complexion was unnaturally pale. When she did not, he credited her with more inner strength and ability to recover quickly than most noblewomen possessed, until it had become quite apparent that she was not only recovered—if her sharp tongue was any guide—but she was ungrateful, too. Apparently she accepted his rescue as a natural right, and not only that, he should be willing—nay, anxious—to take her back to her brother.

He had to be on his way, out of Norman territory and on to Wales. He had no wish to play nursemaid to some Norman noblewoman, especially not the haughty sister of Sir Roger de Montmorency, a man who was notoriously ruthless with

Welsh rebels. Next to Morgan, he was the one man Dafydd knew he should avoid at all costs.

God's holy rood, who would have guessed that he would find himself in such a predicament? There was no way under God's heaven that he could go anywhere near Sir Roger de Montmorency. Nor could he leave her alone in the forest, tempting though it was. There were too many dangers for a lone woman.

His shoulder ached fiercely and he was dead tired. He never should have interfered. The poor young fool who lay unconscious on the ground back there surely only wanted some ransom money and wouldn't have really hurt her. Nevertheless, he supposed he could take this woman some-where...neutral. Sir Guy's manor, perhaps. It would be risky, but certainly less dangerous than riding up to Sir Roger de Montmorency.

Lady Madeline began to tap her foot impatiently. "Will you please be so kind as to accompany me back to my brother's party?" she repeated insistently, glaring at him with enormous blue eyes that betrayed every emotion like a signpost. "I am quite sure he has sent the rest of this rabble packing as easily as you dispatched that miscreant."

Dafydd frowned, even though he agreed with her. The Welshmen would be long gone, although they were probably not very far away. They would be waiting for the young fool who had taken it into his head to try for ransom. A Norman lady would be worth a great ransom, and so the risk.

Yes, as an object for ransom, she was quite valuable. To him, too. Why, he could get enough silver to live as well as any nobleman. He turned away, in case his eyes were no more inscrutable than hers.

"Roger will pay you for your trouble, or at least see that you have a decent horse."

Reward money was less risky than a ransom, he realized. Still, any contact at all with Normans was to be avoided. He decided to follow his original plan and see that the lady got to the nearby manor, then he would be on his way.

Without speaking, he grabbed Lady Madeline around the waist and hoisted her onto the beast she spoke of so scornfully.

No doubt she would not be so quick to insult it when she realized the only alternative was to walk. Dafydd mounted behind her and reached around to pick up the reins, his arms encircling her shapely body. He turned his horse in the direction from which he had come and nudged the horse into a walk. At that precise moment, he realized something else.

It had been *much* too long since he had had a woman. The whole time he had been in the monastery, he had not so much as seen one, let alone touched one.

He was certainly touching one now. Not just *any* one, either.

Lady Madeline de Montmorency was extremely lovely, with her rose-tinted cheeks, large corn-flower blue eyes beneath shapely brown brows, a delicate nose and finely formed chin, the edge of which he could see if he leaned slightly forward. Her lips were lovely, too. He leaned forward again, enjoying the subtle contact that sent a rush of hot blood through his veins.

She even smelled good. Like fruit. What would happen if he tried to take a little taste....

This arrogant Norman creature would surely snap his head off if he so much as touched her cheek, but she was as beautiful as she was proud. Maybe the aftermath would be worth the kiss.

No, he should just ignore her, with her beautiful Norman face, her scornful Norman blue eyes, and her Norman lips.

He wondered about her clothing. She was at-tired as a nun, but she acted nothing like the nuns he had ever seen or met. Perhaps her clothing was some kind of disguise to ward off unwanted atten-tion. Yes, a brother might think that way, espe-cially if the sister was as lovely as this.

Lady Madeline de Montmorency. Her name seemed slightly familiar. Because of her more famous brother? No...the marriage the abbot was attending...was not de Montmorency one of the parties? Yes, that was it.

So, this woman was due to be married soon. Heaven help the man she wed! He would have a shrew on his hands.

A low rumble of thunder sounded in the sky. He glanced upward. It would soon be night, and the sooner he got Lady Madeline de Montmorency off his hands, the sooner he could be on his way.

"This is not the right way." Madeline twisted in the saddle to look into the man's inscrutable face. "We passed this way some time ago, my brother and I. I recognize that ruined building. You have made a mistake. My brother is the other way," she said firmly.

The pilgrim frowned and shook his head.

Although she had no wish to return to her brother's castle or obey his edict about her future, she had no idea where this pilgrim was taking her, if pilgrim he was. Perhaps she had exchanged one abductor for another, the garment only a sham, her mind clouded by the comeliness of the fellow. She could not believe that whoever or whatever this man was, he posed any direct danger, or he would have acted before this. Nevertheless, it could be that in revealing her identity, she had made an incredible blunder. As an object for ransom, she would be worth much. "I am right," she insisted.

He shook his head again. Suddenly the strong arms around her that had made her feel protected moments before seemed to be a cage.

"Sirrah, I appreciate your willingness to assist me, but I must insist that we go the other way," she said, trying not to sound as panic-stricken as she felt.

Cursing herself for a stupid fool, she tried to think of a way to escape and return to Roger. Whatever she did, it would have to be soon, before it was dark, when it would be impossible for her to find her own way. To think she had lived not many miles from here for so long, and this was the first time she had been on this road. If only Mother Bertrilde had not been so strict about staying within the walls of the convent.

When they rode beneath the first trees of what seemed a dark, nearly impenetrable wood, she heard the soft babble of a stream and immediately said, "I am thirsty. May we stop and refresh ourselves at that creek?"

The man nodded and pulled the horse to a halt. Trying to appear calm, Madeline slipped from the horse and headed for the stream. She took a drink of the cold, clear water and watched out of the corner of her eye as the man also dismounted and walked toward her.

"I...I will go into those bushes," Madeline said, hoping she sounded not frightened but filled with maidenly modesty. She sidled toward the shrubs. When the man bent down to drink, she dashed for the horse as quietly as she could and clambered into the saddle. She kicked the beast, which leapt into motion.

At the sudden sound of his horse breaking into a gallop, Dafydd spun around. What was she doing? Where did she think she was going? He sprinted to the road, to see Lady Madeline and the roan disappear around a bend.

A host of colorful Welsh epithets came to his mind as he stood in the middle of the road now completely defenceless. She had everything he possessed, including his sword as well as the money he had taken from the abbot. Then, swiftly, apprehension replaced his anger. The horse belonged to the monastery. If anyone happened to see it and recognize it, they would know where it had come from, and not only that, they would discover the stolen coins in his pack.

Sir Roger would make certain somebody came looking for him. If they found him, Sir Roger would surely guess that the former guest of the good brothers was no simple soldier or religious pilgrim. He would be hanged for a rebel, as well as a thief.

Dafydd realized that he could forget the horse, the money and his sword and run away, or he could follow Lady Madeline and try to get them back before anyone recognized the beast. Perhaps if he hurried, they might be too preoccupied with their reunion to open the pack, and he could steal that back, too. He had to get his sword, at the very least. It had been in his family for generations.

With a grim face, Dafydd hitched up his heavy robe and marched down the road after Lady Madeline de Montmorency.

Chapter Three

Sweating profusely, anxious and angry, Dafydd once again cursed the impulse that had led him to interfere as he hurried along the trees that skirted the roadway, listening for the sounds of anyone approaching along the muddy track. Without his sword, he was helpless against the Normans, or any outlaws, for that matter. He did not really expect to be accosted by outlaws, however. They would not think one lone, empty-handed man worth the effort and he believed the ones that had attacked Sir Roger's train would be far away by now, rifling the packs and deciding how to divide the profits.

The Normans were more worrisome. If they were uninjured, they would surely pursue their attackers, who would disappear as rapidly as dew on a hot summer's day. If they found him instead, the Normans might not listen to his protests that he was not one of the outlaw band. He would be Welsh, and that would be enough to condemn him.

He smiled sardonically at the idea that he might be hanged for a crime he did not commit, rather than the ones he had.

The sun was nearly on the horizon, he realized as he finally reached the place where he had halted when he had heard the attack. He cut through the woods and reached the top of the hill. There he easily spotted Lady Madeline de Montmorency. She was alone, crouched in the mud, examining the ground. The untethered roan stood at the side of the road, the reins dangling. Although he did not move cautiously, she did not hear him approach, but continued to stare at the trampled and muddy road, the signs of the fight all too obvious, and at one spot in particular, stained red with blood. Her shoulders rose and fell with a ragged sigh, and a choked sob escaped her throat.

Lady Madeline did not seem so arrogant now. Indeed, it struck him that she had a mixture of pride and vulnerability such as he had never encountered before. Except, perhaps, within himself.

Dafydd ignored the small pang of pity and understanding in his heart and surveyed the area. At the same time, Lady Madeline realized she was not alone. She started up, staring at him with fear in her eyes, clutching something in her slender fingers. "What do you want?" she asked, wiping at her tear-dampened cheeks. Nevertheless, he could see the dread in her eyes.

That fear disturbed him far more than anything else that had happened. "Not hurting you, me," he said slowly and reassuringly, trying to make his accent as much like a Norman's as he possibly could.

"You spoke!"

He nodded his head.

"Then tell me who you are," she demanded, her tears and dread forgotten, or submerged beneath an incredibly strong will and brave heart.

He did not reply, but pointed instead at her hand.

Lady Madeline held out her open palm and he could see something glinting in the waning light. "This is my brother's cloak pin," she said quietly. "It was my father's. He would never leave this behind."

Dafydd recalled the younger man who had fallen and realized it might have been Roger de Montmorency. He had assumed the gray-haired man would be the famous knight. "Your brother," Dafydd said firmly, "he will not be dead."

She eyed him warily. "How can you be so sure of that?"

"Too good a fighter, he is. Hurt, maybe, but those others were not good enough to kill him."

"Do you really believe that?"

"Said it, haven't I?"

"You are not a Norman."

It was a statement, not a question, so he did not try to deny it.

"You are not a priest, either."

Again there was no point to lie. He did not look like a priest, and he knew it.

Her eyes narrowed even more and she backed away. "Are you a pilgrim, at least?"

"Yes." It was close enough, and he didn't want to frighten her. He took a step toward her, willing her not to be afraid of him. He hated Normans, but she was a woman first. "I am going to Canterbury," he added for veracity.

"Then you are going in the wrong direction," she observed suspiciously.

It was all he could do to keep from smiting himself on the forehead. He should have kept in his mouth shut! In truth, all he knew about Canterbury was that it was holy and somewhere in England. "Other places first," he replied after a long moment while she watched him expectantly. "I give you my word that I will not hurt you."

"I must find Roger. Will you help me?"

"No."

His blunt refusal both startled and upset her, but he couldn't help that. Better she should know right now what he meant to do, and what he would not do.

"But you must!"

"No."

"You're not going to leave me here! What if those thieves come back?"

"I will take you to help."

"Help? What help?"

"There is a manor, back there." He gestured back along the road and wondered if he was making another foolish mistake offering to help her. Still, she was quite right. He could not leave her where she was.

"I suppose I should be grateful for that," she muttered, managing to sound arrogantly ungrateful. "But I must find Roger."

"To get to your wedding?" he asked impertinently.

"Yes, to get to my wedding," she answered defiantly, as if she thought he would doubt her urgency.

Before he had any time to wonder at her reaction, there was a loud crack of thunder and a torrential rain began to pour down on their heads. The horse whinnied and shied nervously. Dafydd managed to grab hold of the dangling reins before the roan ran away. Clutching the animal's bridle, he hurried to her and swiftly, and without so much as a word, lifted her onto the saddle and started to run through the mud, along the road and then through the trees toward the ruined farm he had noticed before. He soon reached it and hurried to the one hovel that still stood intact. The wide doors were held on by one hinge each and some of the timbers had fallen down, but the roof looked sound enough, and the horse would fit inside, too.

He paused to shove open the door and Lady Madeline quickly dismounted, immediately dashing inside. He followed, leading the horse through the entrance.

He scanned the tumbledown building composed of cob and thatch. A few parts of the roof were leaking, but otherwise it was quite dry. It smelled of hay and animals still, and he saw that the large room was divided into two by a partition.

He led the horse farther inside, surreptitiously making certain that the pack on the back of the saddle had not been disturbed.

She stood at the door, looking out at the steadily falling rain. "I must find my brother," she announced again. "As soon as the rain ceases."

He glanced at her, a little regretful that the vulnerable woman had disappeared, to be replaced once again by an arrogant noblewoman. She drew off her wimple. A cascade of long, thick, curling hair fell down her slender back nearly to her waist. God's blessed blood, he had never seen hair like that. What would it feel like, what would it look like spread about her naked body?

Without the cloth bound around her face, her beauty was even more apparent. Her cheeks looked smooth and soft, her eyes clear and bright with intelligence, her lips inviting. It was no wonder Sir Roger would try to hide such beauty in the drab robes of a holy order.

Beautiful she was, yet there was something about her mouth suggestive of a strong, stubborn will. She had the proud carriage and demeanor that belonged to the conquering Normans, too. She had probably had her way in everything all her easy life. She would make some Norman a fine wife and together they would make a lot of little Norman children to control the land.

Dafydd brushed the horse with quick vigorous strokes. She might just as well be a nun for all he would ever have to do with her or her kind.

"I think the rain is getting worse," she said accusingly, as if he were responsible for the weather. "We may have to stay the night."

He pulled off his wet dalmatica and spread it out to dry. He had slept in worse places, and in worse weather, too. At least they had a roof over their heads.

He untied his pack and set it at his feet. Reaching inside, he pulled out a flint with which to build a fire. There were the remains of a round hearth in the other part of the building. He gathered some of the straw and a few pieces of wood that lay in the corner, all of which was extremely dry and caught easily. He grabbed his bundle and found the pieces of bread he had hidden in his bed during the last few days before he left the monastery.

She turned and looked at him as he bit into one of the small, round, stale loaves. The only noise disturbing the silence was the sound of the rain. It was late now, and the darkness outside had as much to do with the setting sun as it did with the clouds. Soon it would be too dark to travel, especially over wet roads.

As she stood there illuminated by the flickering flames of the fire, he became very aware that he was half-naked and alone with her.

She came toward him, eyeing him warily. Clearly she was no longer certain what kind of man he was, whether pilgrim or soldier or outlaw or peasant. Suspicious, yes, but not afraid, and he was pleased, although he knew it should not matter.

Still, she was, without a doubt, the most beautiful woman he had ever seen and he enjoyed the play of the light on her face and the intimacy of the moment.

She sat on the dirt floor opposite him. He handed her a piece of the bread and saw with some amusement that she was not pleased to be offered stale bread. Surprisingly, however, she said nothing, but started to eat, averting her eyes demurely as if he were a suitor and she a coy maiden being wooed.

That thought amused him greatly. He could not imagine a Norman wooing a woman, or certainly not properly, with eloquent words, or a love song, perhaps, and kisses begged in the dark shadows of a summer's night. It was a pity, in a way, because he thought this woman might deserve such a wooing.

He had never actually wooed a woman himself. His life had been one of battles and skirmishes and hiding in the woods, his times with women frenzied moments of passion with a willing wench who thought it the height of excitement to make love with a rebel. He could barely remember most of them.

He noticed Lady Madeline was shivering and wondered if he should suggest she remove her damp clothes. An interesting idea, that.

"I have to find my brother," she repeated defiantly, fortunately calling his thoughts away from contemplation of her as a woman to the necessity of helping her.

"Not on *my* horse," he said.

Even her pout had a certain loveliness about it. "I assure you, whoever you are, that you will be suitably recompensed for that beast and your trouble. My brother is very wealthy. And very powerful."

"Your betrothed is wealthy and powerful, too, no doubt."

"Yes."

Despite the lift of her shapely chin, he thought she was not quite sure about that. Interesting. Unimportant, but interesting.

He held out another crust of bread and Madeline gingerly lifted it from his fingers, then sat down as far away from the fellow as possible while remaining as close as she could to the heat of the flames. To her chagrin, the nearly naked man grinned at her. A devilish grin it was, too, and she wondered how she could ever have surmised that he had taken holy orders.

She looked away, determined not to look at his face anymore, or that horrible scar on his shoulder, or wonder how anyone could survive to bear such a mark. She wished he would put his robe back on.

She forced herself to think about what to do next. She had no idea how to proceed in this particular, strange and foreign situation. For the past ten years, every moment of her life had followed an established pattern and been lived among the same people whose habits, likes and dislikes were as well-

known to her as her own. Then, there had been the
news of her impending marriage, Roger's arrival
and her abrupt departure from the convent, the attack, her rescue and now here she sat, afraid to be
so close to this muscular stranger who was not
Norman, yet more afraid to leave this fellow's
presence and go out into the rain and the unknown.

But should she, perhaps, be so ready to believe
his reassurances about Roger? The outlaws had
outnumbered them, after all. Perhaps Roger was
lying wounded somewhere, bleeding and in pain....
Just because she had not been able to convince him
to at least postpone the wedding until she had met
her future husband did not mean that she had
ceased to care for her one and only living relative.

Indeed, if Roger was *not* hurt, why had he not
come to find her? Surely he would be searching for
her, if he was able to. Even if he cared for her only
as an instrument to fulfill his plans. Or *especially*
if he considered her in such a light.

She suppressed a sorrowful sigh at the notion
that time and training could make her brother so
coldhearted. Why, this man sitting across from her,
this total stranger, was showing more concern for
her than Roger had.

Who was he? Where had he come from? Why
had he helped her? Some things about him she

could guess with some certainty. She knew he was Welsh, despite his attempts to mask his accent, for there had been Welsh servants at the convent, which was rather close to the borderlands.

He must have been trained as a soldier, for he wielded his sword with considerable skill. He might be a rebel, or someone who saw the chance for ransom, but he did not try to bind her, or curtail her movements in any way. If she wanted to, she could run away at any moment.

She could ask him, of course, but he would probably answer with that disquieting stare, or even worse, that grin.

He caught her looking at him and pointed to a pile of straw in the corner. "Go to sleep."

"Where?" she asked cautiously. Thus far he had proven trustworthy, but she was a woman and he was a man. A young and vital man.

He gestured again at the pile of straw. "There."

"No." She shook her head decisively. After all, they were alone here, and he was half-naked.

"Not touching you, me" he said, obviously and quite honestly insulted by her reluctance.

"There might be . . . rats," she confessed with a very real shudder. All her life she had had a horror of the small furry creatures, and she was absolutely certain this shell of a building was a rat's idea of paradise. Where there was one rat, there would be hundreds. And she thought it a very good excuse.

He started to laugh, a deep, rolling sound that was surprisingly pleasant to hear. With appropriate catlike grace, he rose quickly, grabbed his sword and swung it through the straw. "No rats."

He crouched back down beside the fire, laying the sword beside him. She saw him wince as he did so. "Does it hurt, your shoulder?" she asked without thinking.

"Not now." He gazed at her intently, and for a long moment, she simply gazed back, trying to read his dark eyes and quite determined that he could not outstare her. The only person whose scrutiny she had never been able to bear was Mother Bertrilde, and he did not frighten her as much as the Mother Superior in an angry mood.

And yet she was the first to look away, because she suddenly realized, as the heat of shame replaced the pleasant warmth, that she was actually enjoying his scrutiny in the most unseemly fashion.

"Where are you from?" she asked innocently, although she already knew the answer.

"Cornwall."

"Ah." His lie disappointed her. Did he think she was a fool? His dark hair and complexion gave his country away, as well as his accent. "Have you been a soldier?"

He nodded, and she hoped that this was not a lie, too.

"You are a fine fighter. Perhaps you could serve my brother. He is always seeking good soldiers."

The man's face darkened into a scowl and she suspected he would not answer any more of her questions. Rather than let him ignore her, she went over to the straw and lay down.

"Sleep now," he said, settling against the wall of the building, stretching his feet out until they were nearly in the fire.

She rolled onto her side, so that her back was to him. As if she could sleep in this situation, with a man who lied to her and fought like a demon and sat there unabashedly half-naked and unashamed.

For once she was grateful that Mother Bertrilde was so strict. She had spent many a night on a vigil and had long ago learned how to rest without falling into a true sleep. If the man came anywhere near her, she would be fully awake instantly and on her guard.

Every part of Sir Roger de Montmorency's body seemed to ache, his head in particular. Where in the name of the Blessed Virgin was he? A candle flickered on a plain bedside table that held a plain clay cup from which a medicinal smell emanated. The rest of the room was shadowed. The walls nearest him were almost painfully white and very smooth. A large crucifix hung over the bed. He could hear singing. Low, deep—men's voices, sonorous and comforting. Chants.

It was night, and he was in a monastery.

What had happened? There had been a skirmish, with outlaws. Madeline had screamed....

"Madeline!" he cried, sitting up abruptly. The pain that shot through his temple made him flop back onto the coarse pillow.

Sir Albert Lacourt bent over him, and his anxious face looked to be floating in a mist.

"Where...?" Roger whispered.

"You are safe at the monastery of St. Christopher, Roger. You were wounded."

"St. Christopher? Then we are nearly back at the convent! Where is Madeline?"

"We...we do not know. Everything has been done to locate her, Roger," Albert said quickly.

"I must find Madeline." Roger tried to get up, but he felt as weak as a newborn kitten.

Albert glanced over his shoulder at someone standing in the shadows, then bent over him again. "You have lost much blood. Father Gabriel says you must not try to get up."

"Who in the name of the saints is Father Gabriel to order me!" Roger exclaimed weakly. Once more he struggled to sit up.

Instantly there was a pair of very gentle but very forceful hands pushing him back. "My lord, I must insist. Or you may die."

Roger glared at the man holding him down. His gray eyes were kind but held a certain firmness of purpose that Roger had seen before, when he had been practising his sword skills and his teacher had been adamant that he keep practising. Still, this fellow had more of the scholar than the soldier about him, although he was surprisingly strong for a priest, or else, Roger thought, I am even weaker than I thought. "I have to find my sister. The wedding's in a fortnight and we are still far from my castle."

"Please, my lord, do not exert yourself!" Albert said. "We have Bredon out with the dogs."

Roger felt some slight relief. Bredon was the finest huntsman in England. He was in charge of Roger's hounds, which were also the finest in England. If anybody could find Madeline, it would be Bredon.

Albert cleared his throat and looked again at the anxious priest. "Unfortunately, it has been raining since near evening and we cannot search as we would like."

"You must have faith, my son," the priest said softly.

Roger de Montmorency's lip curled skeptically in his dark, handsome face. He had faith in only three things: God, his sword and his ability to wield it. Unfortunately, God seemed to have turned his face from him, and from Madeline, too. As for his sword, he would soon have his strength back, and then he would wield it. By God, if anyone had touched her, he would ply it with no mercy. "Find her, and I want those outlaws. Alive."

"Capturing those rogues may be difficult. Other Welshmen will surely give them sanctuary," Albert replied. Roger's glower was all the answer Albert got, and all he needed. "Very well, my lord. We will search for them, too."

Father Gabriel cleared his throat deferentially. "My lord, please recall that there may be other factors at work here. If these men are simply outlaws, as you believe, try to understand that there are other lords, less wise than yourself, perhaps, who are harsh with their tenants and so create—"

"If men break the law, they must be punished."

"Be that as it may, a little mercy—"

"They will get precisely what they deserve, Father. No more, no less." Roger looked at Albert and tried to focus on his friend. "I don't think they were rebels."

Albert shook his head. "Nor I, my lord."

"What of ransom?"

"We have heard nothing."

"I pray Chilcott does not hear of this. Or Baron DeGuerre."

"Should your concern not be for your sister's safe return?" Father Gabriel asked softly.

Roger saw the rebuke in the man's eyes. "Of course I am worried about her, man! Leave me now!"

The tone of command was unmistakable, and Father Gabriel wisely did not linger.

"Surely there will be no need to inform your sister's betrothed," Albert said placatingly. "At least we have not found her body. It may be that she managed to escape and is now—"

"Lost in the forest? Small comfort there, Albert! I will lead the search for her myself." Roger threw off the bedclothes, set his feet on the ground and stood up.

Then Sir Roger de Montmorency fell back onto the bed in a dead faint, his face so pale that Albert ran down the corridor shouting for Father Gabriel.

Chapter Four

Madeline inched her way forward, hardly daring to take a breath, although the rise and fall of the Welshman's broad, naked chest gave her assurance that he still slept. When she had first awakened and realized he was sleeping and that the rain had ceased, she had been tempted to run away, until she realized she had no idea where she was. She might find herself lost in the woods, the very same woods that harbored the outlaws who had attacked their party yesterday. Therefore, she had decided upon a different course of action.

Ever so carefully, she pulled the sword away from the Welshman's loosened grip. There! She had it! She lifted it cautiously, amazed at the weight and the beauty of the design, and wary of its sharpened edge. Then, taking a deep breath, she placed it against the Welshman's collarbone.

He opened his eyes—and was instantly awake. "What are you doing?" he demanded, his accent strong in his surprise. He shifted ever so slightly.

"I want you to answer my questions. I want to know who you are." She shoved the tip forward a little to show that she expected answers, not grins.

"David," he replied. "My name is David."

"Very well, David, if that is truly your name and I do not fully believe it is, what are you doing dressed in a priest's robe?"

"I told you, a pilgrimage I am making."

"To where?"

"Canterbury."

"Why then are you not heading south?"

"I . . . visit family first."

"And you are from Cornwall?"

"Yes."

"You are lying to me, David."

He didn't reply.

"We had Welsh girls serving us in the convent. I recognize the accent. What else have you lied about? That you mean me no harm?"

"That is the truth. I will not hurt you."

Whatever else he said, she believed this. She saw the truth of it in his eyes and heard the sincerity in his voice, utilizing the several subtle skills developed in the convent, where some tried to gain superiority by claiming extraordinary piety or to gain favor with the Mother Superior. Madeline had learned to detect hypocrisy and deceit. She saw none of that when he said he would not harm her.

Even more importantly, there was something else in his eyes when he looked at her. Not fear, because she held a sword at his throat, but a kind of grudging respect, all the more rewarding because she suspected he did not give that easily, not to a Norman, and not to a woman, probably, either. "Shall I tell you what I think, David?" she asked, her tone lighter than before although still serious. "I think you are a soldier of some kind, or you were. You are no longer, because of that wound to your shoulder, or else you are traveling in disguise. I also realize that you do not like Normans. So, you are a Welshman who can fight who doesn't like Normans. Are you, by any chance, a rebel?"

"If I am," he said with a mocking smile, "do you think me stupid enough to admit it?"

She rose, her hands still wrapped around the grip of the sword. He rubbed his throat, watching her. "I am telling you what I suspect to prove a point. I do not care who you really are, or what you may have done. I have no interest in the truth about you beyond its pertinence to my safety." That was not strictly true, but there was no point in letting him know that she was curious about him. "Nothing about you matters to me, as long as you assist me."

"I said I would, but I will not take you to your brother. He hates the Welsh."

Madeline did not respond to his blunt observation, because she didn't know what to say. Unfortunately, she could no longer be sure of anything about her brother. He seemed to have changed very much in the past ten years, and it could be that this fellow understood Roger better than she.

"And I would not be keen to have my brother see me with a lone Welshman for my escort, if I were you," he said wryly. "Think of the scandal, my lady."

Madeline's eyes widened and she forgot to hide a smile of sudden excitement. Of all things, she had not considered what might happen if she returned to Roger and let it be known she had spent the night alone with a man. And worse, from Roger's point of view, at least, a Welshman who might very well be a rebel. A scandal might be the very thing to prevent a wedding.

Then she frowned. As much as she did not like the idea of marrying Chilcott, she was not certain she was willing to lose her reputation to prevent it. Then she realized the Welshman was smiling at her. "You must have been a very poor soldier, David, to let a woman sneak up on you," she remarked calmly.

"Give me the sword before you hurt yourself," he said, rising.

"No."

As she backed away, still keeping the weapon pointed at him, he suddenly dove for her, knocking the sword from her hand and sending it skittering across the packed earth of the floor. He landed on top of her and knocked the wind out of her.

"Why didn't you run when you saw I was asleep, Lady Madeline de Montmorency?" Dafydd asked. He drew back a little and looked at her, aware of her body beneath him and his proximity to her luscious lips.

"I need an escort and, unfortunately, you are the only one available."

"Not much cause to help you, maybe, if you put my sword at my throat," he noted dryly.

"I wanted to know who you are."

"I am your escort. That will have to do."

"I suppose," she said, pouting. She gave him a sidelong glance that was at once proud and impertinent, questioning and very enticing. "Will you please get off me? You are..."

"What?" he asked softly, leaning forward so that his lips were close to hers. "What am I, my lady?"

Gently he kissed her. At first, he simply enjoyed the long-denied sensation of a kiss. And then, miraculously, wonderfully, he realized she was returning his kiss, with a tentative innocence that bespoke passion awakening. The notion that he could inspire such a feeling within her increased his own ardor. His tongue tenderly yet insistently probed her lips, until they parted for him.

When his tongue thrust slowly inside her mouth, Madeline could scarcely comprehend the host of feelings struggling within her. The foremost was nearly overpowering surprise. Touch of any kind was forbidden in the convent, even to the touch of a hand when passing food. The kiss alone had been intoxicating; this was beyond that, sending her spinning into a realm so exciting that she could barely think beyond the pleasure as his lips moved over hers, delightfully slowly, firm and possessive.

And if a kiss could make her feel that way, what of the other things some of the other girls had spoken of, secret things, whispered about in the corner of the garden when the holy sisters were not near?

Heady with the excitement, Madeline clutched his muscular shoulders, his flesh hot beneath her hands, and instinctively began to undulate beneath him.

He had saved and protected her. He would help her still. He was strong, handsome, virile. A warrior.

And then she felt his hand upon her breast. Startled, she thrust him back. "Stop!" she cried, surprised and horrified not so much by his unexpected action as by her own lack of self-control. This was too much intimacy, too soon. What she felt must be lust, could only be lust. Blushing with shame, she shoved him away. "Stop that!"

Indeed, his grin could have been lust personified. "You like being kissed."

"No, I do not." She squirmed beneath him, trying to make him let her up.

In response, he moved his hips, the slight motion awakening a yearning so strong she could scarcely believe it.

She lay still, staring up at him, horrified. "I . . . I want to be a nun!"

"I thought you were getting married."

"Yes. No. Get off me!"

"Very well." Mercifully he rolled away. "You want to live among women for the rest of your days?"

"Yes."

"That would be a great waste," he murmured, smiling at her as he rose slowly and reached for the dalmatica.

"How dare you!" she cried as she scrambled to her feet. "I am betrothed!"

He pulled on his garment, then faced her, his expression unreadable. "How dare *you?*" he asked coolly.

"*Me?* It was you! You knocked me down, you—"

"If you do not wish to be kissed, do not look at a man that way. If you are indeed betrothed, you should act like it."

She drew herself up. "What 'way' did I look at you? And I am acting like a betrothed woman! I keep asking you to take me back to my brother." She had merely regarded him as she would any other man . . . hadn't she?

"Are you trying to say you did not enjoy the kiss?"

"No, I did not! I could not enjoy the embrace of a . . . of a peasant!"

"You do not know I am a peasant."

"You are not a nobleman."

His infuriating smile broadened.

"Do you intend to help me or not?"

"I said I would, so I will."

"Then you will please have the goodness to stay far away from me."

"As you wish, my lady."

"I'm hungry. What is there to eat?"

He pulled out yet another piece of stale bread from his pack and tossed it at her. She caught it just before it landed on the ground and then watched as he picked up his weapon and walked toward the horse. "We should go soon," he said.

She took a bite of the bread and marveled that her teeth did not remain behind. Chewing slowly and avoiding meeting his gaze, she nodded. "Aren't you going to eat?"

"No." He saddled the horse and tied on his pack. She kept silent as she ate and watched him. He was no nobleman, say what he would. He couldn't be.

And he should not have kissed her. It was all his impertinent doing. Indeed, she would do well to be rid of his company. Truly, she did not enjoy his lips upon hers. How could she? He had taken a great liberty.

Would he try to take another such liberty before he left her?

"We must go."

His blunt words roused her from her reverie. Brushing the crumbs from her garment, she joined him as he left the byre. Outside, the sky was cloudy, yet she did not think it would rain again soon. Puddles were plentiful, however, and the leaves of the trees still dripped. All in all, the scene before her was as dismal as her future if she returned to her brother.

But she had to find out what had happened to Roger—Roger, whom she had almost forgotten, just because this rascal claimed that her brother was probably uninjured.

The Welshman linked his hands together and waited, crouched beside the horse. Obviously the intention was that she should ride, so she placed her foot in his hands and let him lift her onto the saddle. Then she waited with bated breath for him to join her. She could almost feel his body behind hers, touching her, and told herself that she was dreading the contact.

He did not mount the horse. Instead, he took hold of the horse's bridle and began to walk toward the road.

"Where are we going?" she asked coldly.

"To a Norman's manor I know of."

"Whose manor is it?"

"Sir Guy."

"Sir Guy?" There was something vaguely familiar about the name, but Guy was common enough. "Is that all of his name you know?"

"Yes."

"How is it you are welcome at a Norman's manor?"

"Would you rather I left you to find another escort, my lady?"

There was nothing she could say to that, so she fell silent. After all, she needed to be safe and she needed to find Roger. She couldn't do that by her-

self. Surely a Norman nobleman would be better
able to help her accomplish those tasks than this
mysterious Welshman.

The shaded, narrow road to Sir Guy's manor
wound through the thick forest of oak and beech,
pine and hawthorn. The sky was gray and thick
clouds had blocked out even the midday sun. The
air was close, rank with the smell of damp underbrush and decaying foliage. All was still and quiet,
and not even a bird's song interrupted the silence.
No bright spring flowers pushed their way to the
sunlight here. It was as if they had stepped into a
bard's tale of a forest under the spell of a witch or
evil sorcerer.

As Dafydd plodded along beside the roan, he
told himself he was glad he would soon be far away
from Lady Madeline de Montmorency. Either she
could have taught Delilah a thing or two about se-
duction, or she was the innocent creature she
claimed to be. That look, as she lay beneath him,
that sultry, pouting glance at once dismissive and
challenging—was it art, or was it a natural response? Whatever it was, he would have been more
than mortal to resist kissing those full, red lips.

And no matter how much she tried to deny it, she
had responded. Oh, he might have startled her at

first, but soon enough she was eagerly kissing him back.

God's wounds and blessed blood, what kind of trouble had he gotten himself into this time? She was a Norman and the sister of a man hated by the Welsh.

Just as he despised all Normans. He could see good cause for his hatred, too, the few times there was a break in the trees. Ragged, bowed peasants worked narrow strips of farmland. They all looked old, thin and sickly, barely able to work. The buildings he spied were little better than the byre in which he and Lady Madeline had spent the night. And strangely, he saw not one young person, nor any child. All was back-bent, joyless silence and hard toil.

Dafydd desperately tried to recall what the holy men had said of Sir Guy. That they did not approve of him had been easy to guess, but he had put that down to the naïveté of men who lived a sheltered, chaste life. Was there more to it? Was Sir Guy a greedy, cruel master who kept men and women working past their prime, when they should have been resting and sleeping in the springtime sun? Had something occurred to drive all the younger people, who could travel with greater ease, away from this place?

He did not know, and there was no one he could ask. Lady Madeline was obviously ignorant of Sir Guy's existence, not surprising considering she had spent the past years of her life in cloistered seclusion.

Just as she was apparently ignorant of her effect upon him.

"Has there been famine?" Lady Madeline asked with pity when they passed another group of ancient peasants. "Mother Bertrilde often said the world was a harsh place of disease and lack of food. Sometimes I thought she said such things to keep us content within the walls of the convent."

"No famine."

"But these people..."

"Peasants, they are, my lady. Have you never seen peasants before?"

"Not like these." Clearly she was as puzzled as he.

It could be that he was making a mistake heading this way, Dafydd thought. What if Sir Guy recognized him for a Welshman and probably a rebel as easily as Lady Madeline? If the man's treatment of his peasants was anything to go by, he would get no mercy from Sir Guy.

Dafydd decided he would send Lady Madeline toward the manor alone once he could see it. That would be the least risky thing to do.

Suddenly he felt a sharp tug on the lead at the same time he heard Lady Madeline's startled gasp. His gaze followed her shaking finger pointing at something hanging from a tree some distance away, like a grotesque pennant. "What...what is it?" she asked in whisper.

"A body," he replied stonily. He had, unfortunately, seen such things before. "It is a corpse, probably some poor soul convicted of a crime, hung and left to rot as an example of Norman justice."

"There are so many!"

He turned his attention from her beautiful, horrified face and looked along the way. Yes, there were other such examples of Norman justice. The sight sickened him and he quickened his pace. He had no wish to be in the presence of such things any longer than need be.

"They must have done something terrible," his companion said quietly.

"Perhaps this one stole some food, or got caught poaching one too many times," he answered grimly, nodding at the first body they passed.

"But this is so terrible! Will they get a proper burial soon?" He could barely hear Lady Madeline's question, for she held her sleeve against her face because of the stench.

"I doubt it."

"Blessed Holy Mother! That is more than unjust."

He paused a moment to look back at her. "It is the Norman way, my lady. Ask your brother about it when you see him."

"Roger would not do such a terrible thing."

Dafydd commenced walking again. "Are you certain?"

"Absolutely. I have not seen him in ten years, but he cannot have changed *that* much," she replied, willing herself to believe it. "He would punish wrongdoing. It is his duty. But to leave the body— no, Roger would not do that."

"Ask him."

"I will. And I will tell Sir Guy to take these down at once."

Dafydd's step faltered. He could believe she would do that, which would surely be a mistake. Any lord whose peasants appeared so completely downtrodden and whose vengeance extended to the display of corpses would surely not take kindly to an order from anyone. Lady Madeline's offended sensibilities would give her request just such an unwelcome tone.

The trees thinned and Dafydd realized the road was leading down into a wide, rocky valley. The sun was low on the horizon, for a brief time finally visible as it traveled below the edge of the clouds and the earth. Its final rays colored the clouds with a fiery red, like bright blood on a gray tunic. In the valley, a mist was rising and ahead, shrouded by the damp swirling air, he could see a large, walled manor. The valley seemed oddly lifeless, the manor grim as a crypt.

Perhaps it would be wiser to turn back and go to the village, he thought as they came to the end of the trees. Although he stood a greater chance of getting caught with his stolen goods there, and although it meant an even longer journey in Lady Madeline's company, it might be the wiser course. Lady Madeline would protest, but that was of no consequence. He felt in his bones that they would both be safer in a village. Even if he was apprehended there, the holy brothers would surely have more mercy on him than this Sir Guy.

Then, through the trees behind him, he heard the sounds of hoofbeats and men shouting as they galloped along the road. For a moment, his Welsh blood conjured up images of ghostly riders, demons loosed from hell to wreak havoc on earth. That vision was swiftly replaced by a sudden urgent desire to get away from this place.

Before he could turn the horse, a group of about twenty men appeared, the noise they made nearly as dreadful as the silence had been before. The troop was not as large as he expected from the noise. Still, they easily outnumbered him. They all rode superb horses and wore expensive cloaks trimmed with fur against the chill evening air.

Dafydd knew they were trapped. They could not turn back now without being seen, or indeed without these fellows blocking their way.

Not daring to look at Lady Madeline, he waited for her to proclaim her identity. She would be safe enough, while these men would try to take him. Thank God he was near the wood. He had been chased many times, and never caught. Hopefully he could get away quickly and—

Lady Madeline was still silent, even as the man at the head of the group spied them and pulled his magnificent black stallion to a stop. He was of middle age, handsome in a narrow-eyed, sleek way, very finely dressed and well armed, as were his companions. He ran his gaze over them in a questioning, impertinent manner that instantly disgusted Dafydd, and he could guess that the fellow would meet with a rebuke from Lady Madeline, who was of at least an equal rank with this man, who had to be Sir Guy.

Dafydd glanced at Lady Madeline and had to suppress an exclamation of surprise. She looked so different! She slouched in the saddle, her posture a caricature of her former upright position. Somehow she had pulled a few strands of her hair loose, so that she looked unkempt. The most surprising thing, however, was her idiotic smile and the vacuous expression in her eyes.

What was she doing?

"How now?" the newcomer said with the languid drawl of a well-bred Norman. "What have we here?"

"I am Sister Mary of the Holy Wounds," Lady Madeline announced brightly, her tone high and rather shrill—and completely new to Dafydd. "I simply cannot tell you how happy I am to encounter gentlemen before the sun sets! And so many, and so well armed. Oh, yes, indeed, it is quite a relief. I was so afraid I would have to spend another night in the forest, on the ground, with bugs and animals and I don't know what all crawling around! It's terrible, I assure you. God has surely answered my prayers, and so well, too—"

"Greetings, Sister Mary," the leader said when she paused to take a breath. He was surveying her with a somewhat less enthusiastic air, which pleased Dafydd. Still, the manner of this man and his friends remained rude and impertinent, and there was something unsavory about them. He wondered if Lady Madeline had chosen this ruse because she thought so, too. "I am Sir Guy de Robespierre."

"Ah! I thought so! Charmed to meet you, Sir Guy, absolutely charmed! By the holy martyrs, who ever would have thought a pilgrimage would be so difficult! Such accommodations as we have had to endure, although all in the name of holiness, of course." Sir Guy and his men looked at Dafydd in a way that made him even more uncomfortable. "Oh, I almost forgot! Permit me to introduce Father David of Saint Stephen the Martyr." She emitted a high-pitched giggle. "I do believe we have taken the wrong road. I tried to tell the father here that we should not turn, but he just ignored me, and quite right he was, too, or we surely would never have arrived at your charming manor. That place in the valley is yours, is it not?"

"You are most welcome to dine with us, Sister, and stay the night. You and the father."

Dafydd looked at the men accompanying Sir Guy. Most of them looked rather bored, but not the man on Sir Guy's right. He was extremely well dressed, in a fine cloak of scarlet velvet trimmed with ermine, and he was staring at Dafydd in a way that filled the Welshman with anxiety. Did he guess that "Father David" was nothing of the kind?

"Farold, aren't we fortunate to be able to assist these people?" Sir Guy said to the man.

"Yes, Sir Guy," Farold replied with a slow smile that made Dafydd even more uneasy, especially when he turned his cold scrutiny onto Madeline. To be sure, she had transformed herself, but she was so lovely—no disguise could hide that.

"We will only trouble you for a night's lodging for us and for our horse," Madeline replied. "A simple meal of bread and water will be most appreciated. Nothing very fancy for pilgrims! I do hope you have twice-ground flour, though. If I never eat another coarse brown loaf, it will be too soon."

"Oh, we can offer you both considerably better fare. I promise you, you will not soon forget the hospitality of Sir Guy de Robespierre."

The men seemed to find this vastly amusing. Dafydd tried not to betray anything by his expression, for he was certain Farold was still watching him intently. Nonetheless, he moved closer to the roan.

Lady Madeline glanced down at him, then gave Sir Guy another vacuous smile. "Well, we really should refuse your invitation. Father David and I have sworn a pledge of poverty. However, you put it so charmingly, I would hate to refuse."

"And you, Father? Will you partake of our hospitality?"

Lady Madeline giggled again. "Father David has sworn a vow of silence, I'm afraid, so he cannot answer. He is very strict about it. He hasn't said a single word to me the whole journey!'' She leaned closer to Sir Guy. ''I cannot tell you how relieved I am to have some company, Sir Guy. What I was thinking of when I began this pilgrimage, I have no idea—well, I suppose forgiveness, eh?''

Sir Guy spoke again. ''Welcome to my estate. Allow me to escort you. Father, would you care to ride? I'm sure one of my men can be persuaded to share his mount with you.''

''Oh, how kind of you to offer, Sir Guy, but he really should walk. It's part of his vow, you understand. I realize this will slow us down terribly and I beg your indulgence. Now, tell me, how is it your manor is so far from the main road? It seems so very lonely to me! And this fog, surely the air is most unhealthy.''

Dafydd had little choice but to walk along behind Madeline's horse and listen as she continued to rattle on to Sir Guy. She was doing a very good imitation of a stupid woman, and he wondered where this ruse was going to lead them.

Chapter Five

Roger, his head still aching so much that each movement was new cause for agony, glared at Father Gabriel standing at the foot of the bed. The only person he wanted to see was Albert, who had gone to lead the search for Madeline at first light.

Father Gabriel shifted from foot to foot as if he had a bug down his dalmatica, and twisted his hemp belt as if it were rosary beads. The priest had been doing so ever since he had come into the room. Another holy man, a lean and silent fellow with a mournful face who had been introduced as Father Jerrald, stood beside the door. "I trust you are feeling better, my lord?" Father Gabriel inquired.

"Except for this damnable pounding in my head."

"Ah. I hope the draft I prepared will soon ease your discomfort."

Several more long moments of silence passed, while Roger continued to stare, Father Gabriel continued to fidget and Father Jerrald continued to look like a stone effigy.

"What do you want, man?" Roger finally bellowed. "Do you have something to tell me of my sister?"

"Unfortunately, no, my lord," Father Gabriel said with great humility and unmistakable sincerity. "We are all praying for her safe return."

"What is it, then?"

"Sir, please, I had no wish to trouble you at this time—"

"Then leave me alone. I will see Sir Albert when he returns, or my sister when she is found."

Father Gabriel cleared his throat, a barely perceptible expression of disdain on his face as he glanced at Father Jerrald hovering near the door like an angel of death. Father Gabriel rarely disliked anyone, as he genuinely tried to see every man as his brother; however, Father Jerrald was the abbot's eyes and ears in his absence. The abbot would hear of everything that happened in the monastery while he was gone, and most especially everything that had to do with such an important visitor. Unfortunately, he would also hear if Father Gabriel refused to tell Sir Roger of the recent occurrence at the monastery regarding their departed guest, whom all suspected was a Welshman and, not unlikely, a rebel.

Although events of the outside world touched theirs rarely and briefly, they were not completely ignorant of important events. Nor were they as certain as the noblemen they encountered seemed to be that what the Normans did was always right. Abbot Peter had shown an admirable ability to sympathize with the local people, including several Welsh, and that tolerance had cast a mantle of gentle forbearance over the monastery. As for Father Gabriel and most of the brothers, they would have kept silent about the departed guest. His wounds would put an end to his fighting days anyway, and Father Gabriel had seen enough to suspect that the man's activities might have had a very good cause. Not many outlaws interested in mere thievery had such a noble bearing, or such a grateful demeanor when they were brought wounded to the monastery.

Unfortunately, the sudden arrival of a man who seemed to embody the power of the Normans in one forbidding, imposing, merciless figure had filled Father Jerrald with a sense of duty and an obvious desire to impress their important visitor. He had been adamant that they tell Sir Roger about the Welshman, who Father Gabriel hoped with all his heart was far away by now. "It seems we have been robbed, Sir Roger," Father Gabriel said at last.

"Robbed? Of what? When?" Roger demanded with his usual blunt forcefulness.

"A horse. A robe."

Roger lay back and subdued a groan. The last thing he wanted to be troubled with now was a minor robbery in a monastery. "Who do you think took them?"

"Well, my lord, we do not know."

The man nearest the door took a step forward. Father Gabriel shot the fellow a defiant glance. "We do not," Father Gabriel said firmly. "We *suspect* a man who has been staying here while he healed."

Roger subdued a weary smile. Father Gabriel was usually meek and mild, but it seemed he had some backbone after all, although Roger had little doubt who was pulling the strings at this particular moment.

The man near the door frowned and emitted a cough.

"To be completely honest," Father Gabriel said reluctantly, "he did disappear the same night as the horse."

"Which was when?"

"Two nights ago."

"Tell Sir Albert what the man looked like and also the horse. He can look for them while he searches for my sister. Will that suit you, Father Gabriel?"

"Yes, my lord."

There was another cough from the vicinity of the door.

"We also have reason to believe the fellow was a Welshman," Father Gabriel added reluctantly.

"So?"

The other man was obviously surprised, and that pleased Roger. He had a marked dislike for men who slunk about in the shadows. "It is not a crime to be a Welshman," he said.

"*Some* people think all Welshman are thieves," replied Father Gabriel.

"I am not one of them," Roger said. He gave the priest the briefest of smiles, which the holy man could not know was a rare sign of goodwill. "Contrary to what you may have heard. I punish wrongdoers, whatever language they speak."

"I am glad to be set right, my lord."

"Very well. Tell Sir Albert the fellow may be a Welshman. Is that all, Father?"

At that moment Albert himself came hurrying into the room. He had obviously traveled far, and fast. Roger sat up abruptly. "What news?"

"We believe she is alive, my lord," his friend reported, breathing heavily as if he had run at full speed from the stables.

"Where is she?"

Albert's face fell somewhat. "We...we do not know exactly as of yet, my lord. The trail was difficult to follow because of the rain and—"

"Then how do you know she is alive?"

"We found evidence that someone spent the night in an old byre not far from where we fought the outlaws."

"Some*one?* Is she alone?"

Albert cleared his throat. "No, my lord. Bredon believes she is not alone."

Roger didn't doubt his huntsman. If Bredon believed more than one person had been in the byre, more than one person had been in the byre. "How many are with her?"

"He thinks two people spent the night there, my lord, and one horse. He...he found no sign of blood, so we trust neither one was injured. We also have reason to believe one of the people was Lady Madeline, because Bredon found some very long, dark hairs in a pile of straw."

Roger felt some measure of hope, but there were many Welshwomen with long, dark hair. It could be that the hair belonged to a complete stranger. "The two were gone when you found the byre?"

"Yes, my lord."

Roger stared at the bedclothes. If she was alive, she was hopefully well, but not alone. It might mean that the outlaws had taken her for ransom, or simply their pleasure? He forced his mind away from the last possibility to focus on the hunt, and that is what it would be. He would find Madeline and the men who had kidnapped her, and if *any* harm had come to her, those men would regret that they had ever left their mother's womb.

"Where is Bredon?"

"Tracking the horse, and the one who appears to be on foot. The horse seems to have a most peculiar gait. I returned to tell you of the news."

"My lord?" Father Gabriel interrupted quietly.

"What?"

"The horse we are missing... it has a most peculiar gait, from an injury."

"Are you suggesting my sister is in the hands of your thief?" Roger demanded.

"We do not know for certain he is a thief, my lord."

Father Jerrald snorted derisively, albeit quietly. Roger turned his glare onto the man, who stared at the floor.

"Albert, which way are they going?"

"Bredon thinks, my lord, that they took a road leading west, through the forest."

Father Gabriel's sudden audible gasp drew both men's attention.

"What do you know?" Roger asked sternly.

Father Gabriel's face was filled with sorrow and sympathy. "First, my lord," he said, "I will say that if your sister has met with our lately departed guest, I think you have little to fear."

"This fellow who may be a thief?"

"Well, be that as it may, my lord, I...um, I think she would be safer with him than many others."

"Explain yourself, Father!"

"The man—the man who stayed here for quite a long time recovering—he is at heart an honorable fellow." Father Jerrald moved, and this time it was Father Gabriel who turned to glare at him. "I believe myself to be a better judge of character than you, Jerrald. I have had more experience." He turned back to Roger. "And I do not think he would harm your sister."

Father Jerrald looked about to speak, until Roger held up his hand impatiently. "Go on, Father."

"And I am also fairly certain he has some knowledge of fighting, to judge from his wounds."

Roger's eyes narrowed suspiciously. "I take it you think he will need this knowledge, if he is going to the west through the woods? Wales lies to the west, Father."

"And so does the manor of Sir Guy de Robespierre."

"Sweet savior!" Roger gasped. He had never met Sir Guy, for the man and his pack of followers rarely ventured far from his remote manor. Nevertheless, Roger—and most of the nobility except perhaps a young woman raised in a secluded convent—had heard of the man's disgusting and base behavior with women. And with men.

"The man might have thought to simply take her to the nearest manor."

Roger started to rise.

"Sir Roger, please! I fear you will make yourself ill!" Father Gabriel protested.

Roger shook off the priest's detaining hand. "Albert, fetch my clothes. And my sword. Get my horse saddled. We will leave at once." Albert hurried from the room. Roger looked at Father Gabriel. "You will come, too, Father, to identify this thief."

"But my duties here—"

"I did not ask about your duties here. Father Jerrald will oversee the monastery in your absence, won't you?"

The man's eager response, and apparent disregard for what was happening beyond his own sudden elevation, was pathetic.

"How far is it to the manor?" Roger asked.

"It is quite a distance along that road. I understand Sir Guy likes his, um, privacy. It will take some time, my lord, and the day is more than half gone. You are not yet well enough—"

"That is not your concern, Father, but I will ask that you come with me." Roger's expression softened for an instant. "If Madeline has fallen into that man's hands, she may need such help as only a man of God can give."

Father Gabriel nodded in agreement.

"I must say, Sir Guy, I feel so much safer with you and your men to protect us!" Madeline said as they drew closer to the forbidding outer wall of the manor. Ever since they had turned down this lonely road, Madeline had struggled to recall what she knew of anyone named Sir Guy. For some reason, the name had a taint of scandal about it.

When she saw the manor in the fog-encased valley, she had recalled what it was she had heard, long ago when she had first arrived at the convent. A young noblewoman of great rank had been brought there. No one except the Mother Superior and the most senior nuns tended to her, but that did not stop the other sisters from telling what they guessed. Madeline did not hear much, for the whispers would cease when the youngest girls drew near. Nonetheless, she had heard enough to know that something terrible had happened to the woman at the hands of a man named Sir Guy de Robespierre, who had cared nothing for the woman's rank or family and who lived far from other people, in a valley that was as dank and unsavory as his appetites.

Madeline blessed her decision to play the ignorant fool when he had approached, hoping three things: that it was not Sir Guy de Robespierre, but another Sir Guy; that if it was the same Sir Guy, claiming to be a nun might afford her some protection; and that if she rendered herself as unattractive and stupid as possible, he would leave them alone. So far, only the final hope was not completely dashed by his behavior and manner toward her. Thank heavens she was not alone!

Sir Guy turned to her with an ingratiating smile. "I agree this is a most fortuitous meeting. There are countless thieves and brigands about who would not heed your holy calling, but see only two travelers, alone. I heard talk that some have even dared to attack Sir Roger de Montmorency."

"Sir Roger de Montmorency?" she asked with wide eyes as she tried to subdue both her excitement at news of Roger and dread for what she might learn. "Who is he?"

"A most powerful Norman knight. I heard they wounded Sir Roger and they've taken his lovely sister, who I understand is quite a beauty, perhaps even as lovely as you. Did you not hear of this?''

"Oh, you flatter me, Sir Guy! To tell you the truth, though, Father David and I have been rather lost of late. The only time we spoke to anyone was to ask directions. I knew nothing of this terrible business. Sir Roger was wounded, you said? Not mortally, I hope?''

"No. He's in the good hands of the brothers of St. Christopher, I hear. His death would have been quite a tragedy, eh, Farold?'' His companion's lips curled in what Madeline supposed was meant to be a smile. "He is a well-made man, I understand.''

"The poor young lady! Attacked! And taken by horrible outlaws. And beautiful, too, you say? What was the name?''

"Madeline. Lady Madeline de Montmorency.''

Madeline reined in her horse. "No! Madeline? I met a Lady Madeline in a convent once—what does she look like?''

"I have never had the pleasure of making the lady's acquaintance.''

"Yellow haired, is she not? Very ruddy complexion?''

"I do not know,'' Sir Guy replied somewhat wearily.

"Yes, that is it. Blond, and very tall. Thin. Some say she is surpassing elegant, but I thought she was rather gawky. And proud! Good heavens above! I never saw such a vain creature. You are quite certain you haven't met her?"

"I believe I would recall her if I had," Sir Guy replied.

"Yes, yes, of course you would. Well, well, well, I daresay she will not be so haughty now, in the hands of an outlaw."

"Farold and I are fairly certain it was a *band* of thieves who have been harassing my lands. Welsh rebels, in fact."

"Of course! How silly of me! It would take more than one man to defeat a Norman. As for these outlaws, I trust you will deal with them rigorously, as I see you have already dealt with other miscreants." Madeline's voice softened. "I saw the bodies . . ."

"That is by way of example. Tell me, Sister, where is Father David from?"

"Cornwall," she replied without a moment's hesitation.

Farold nudged his horse closer to Dafydd and the Welshman struggled to keep a scowl from his face. By now he had decided that whatever Madeline was up to, it would be best to go along, at least until they could both get away from this place. She could have identified herself and abandoned him to a cruel fate at the hands of these men, for surely they would not harm Sir Roger de Montmorency's sister. He was not certain either Sir Guy or Farold believed the web of lies Lady Madeline was spinning. Now, he didn't doubt that she was in danger of a different sort, and he would not leave her to face it alone.

"I am sure the good father here would have kept you safe," Farold remarked. "He seems a brawny enough fellow."

"Oh, I wish I could be so sure!" Madeline said with a twitter. "I confess Father David *looks* impressive, but he has never wielded a weapon. He has spent all his life in a monastery, you see."

By now they had reached the imposing gates of the manor. Dafydd's steps slowed, for he felt as if he were being led to his own execution.

After they entered, a thin, elderly man who offered no word or greeting swung the gate shut behind them. The clang echoed like the tolling of a funeral knell.

Dafydd surveyed the spacious yard. The stables were to the left, and other outbuildings crowded the walls. This place, too, was curiously silent, as if any sounds of talk or mirth or even orders were given with hushed voices, or else discouraged completely.

Sir Guy's men waited while stable boys appeared to take their mounts. The slender but seemingly well fed and well dressed boys said nothing, and never looked any of the men in the eye. They only grabbed the horses' bridles and hurried away. One came to take hold of the bridle of the roan, and for an instant, Dafydd caught a look in the lad's eyes. He was quite obviously terrified, and Dafydd's heart went out to him. Sir Guy must be a severe master, indeed.

The old gatekeeper suddenly appeared at Dafydd's elbow. *"Gochel!"* he whispered before moving off.

Welsh for beware. Dafydd watched the old man totter away, more dread filling him.

"You must allow one of my men to take your sword, Father," Sir Guy said, drawing his attention. "There is no need for such weapons here."

Dafydd kept his face inscrutable as he shook his head.

"Father David never removes his sword until he sleeps," Madeline said quickly. "I am always afraid he's going to injure himself with it."

"Well, I suppose a holy man should keep his weapon handy, even if it gets little use," Sir Guy replied with a sly grin. "Wouldn't you agree, Farold?"

"Yes, Guy," Farold replied.

"I do not understand you, Sir Guy," Madeline said with an air of befuddlement. "Is there some reason he might require his sword?"

"I was not referring to *that* weapon, Sister," Sir Guy answered. The other young men exchanged amused glances. "But of course he may keep his sword, if it makes him happy."

Dafydd could not believe any man would make such a coarse jest before a lady, and a supposed nun, at that. What kind of base, disrespectful men had he led Madeline to?

Sir Guy headed toward the large stone hall. It was strong, impressive, old but well maintained. Dafydd also managed a good look at the entourage that accompanied Sir Guy. It was composed of several young men, well dressed and well fed, although none had quite the appearance of plenty as Farold. How could one explain this, Dafydd thought, when his tenants looked to be starving and incapable of working hard enough to tend the fields and bring in the crop? It was a mystery, but the answers were not as important as finding a way out of this manor.

"Welcome to my hall," their host said as they entered. Once again, there was little choice but to follow, and once again Dafydd wanted nothing more than to take Madeline's hand and flee the place. "Although I am happy to be of assistance, Sister," Sir Guy continued as he led them forward toward the dais, "I would also have been happy to rescue Lady Madeline de Montmorency. I am sure her brother would be most generous with his thanks." He looked at her far too shrewdly, but the only response he got was that idiotic giggle and she began to chatter away like some kind of demented bird and exclaim about the fine furnishings.

Dafydd noted that while the hall was richly furnished with heavy oaken furniture, most of it looked old and scarred, as if Sir Guy's men had carved pieces from it for their amusement. There were several faded and smoke-stained tapestries, clearly made long ago. The rushes on the floor were clean, however, and the linen upon the tables pristine. Torches already burned in their sockets upon the walls, sending dark smoke curling upward. Huge dogs roved about, growling and snapping at each other, and fighting for any bit of food that lay on the floor.

Sir Guy's men scattered to the different tables as he led his guests to the dais, where a long table stood ready for the evening meal.

Dafydd realized with some surprise that there were no women in the hall, only several youths splendidly dressed as pages. They were all quite comely, with complexions as fine as any girl's and well-groomed shoulder-length hair, but there was something in their eyes, like those of the stable boy. They were terrified.

He glanced at Madeline and caught her unguarded expression, which was one of revulsion. Did she guess what kind of place this was, what kind of men Sir Guy and his followers might be?

"Perhaps you would care to wash, Sister? I will gladly allow you the use of my chamber."

"Oh, you are most thoughtful. Perhaps later, Sir Guy. Blessed saints, your hall is most sumptuous. And these squires—how very many and how well you dress them! I am most impressed, Sir Guy, truly. And the aroma from the kitchen! I have not had a good meal in such a very long time. Father David and I welcome your hospitality, I must say. I fear we might overindulge."

"There is nothing wrong with indulgence," Farold said quietly, taking a seat beside the one Sir Guy indicated as Madeline's.

Dafydd saw the way Farold looked at her, and he would gladly have slit the man's throat.

Madeline giggled as she took her place. "But Father David and I cannot overindulge! That would be a gross sin, I assure you. But it all looks so tempting," she remarked as the first of the food was placed before her.

"Yes, indeed it does," Farold agreed, smiling over her head at Sir Guy.

Dafydd could only stare with hopeless impotence.

"We shall be happy to spend the night in the stable, after the sinful luxury of this meal," Madeline said, apparently unaware of the undercurrents in the room.

"Sister, you wound me," Sir Guy replied, placing a bejeweled hand upon his breast. "Would you deny a sinner like myself the opportunity to converse with holy ones? Why, Farold, too, would be most upset, wouldn't you, Farold?" He went on without waiting for any reply from his friend. "Farold likes priests."

"Well, they are certainly a necessity," Madeline replied with a high-pitched giggle. "I fear I shall have to make a confession of gluttony soon." After a swift glance at Dafydd, she began to eat.

He, however, had no appetite. He was scanning the room, desperately seeking a way of escape. One door led to the courtyard, another, at the far end of the hall, apparently to the kitchen. The kitchen was farthest from the stables. The fastest way out would be the main door. But how to get there without attracting undue attention?

"That is a lovely thing," Madeline suddenly said. Dafydd saw that she was pointing at the dagger hanging from Sir Guy's belt. "Blessed Mary, are those emeralds in the hilt? They are! Indeed, I have never actually seen emeralds before. May I hold it?"

Sir Guy gave his guest an indulgent smile and held it out to her. "I would be only too happy to let you handle my dagger."

The men around him laughed openly. But only for a brief instant, because the moment after Sir Guy delivered his dagger to Madeline's hand, she was holding it at his throat.

"What—!" he exclaimed, pressing against the back of his chair.

"Everyone sit down!" she cried. After some hesitation, they wisely obeyed.

"Have your men throw down their weapons," Madeline ordered.

"I don't understand!" Sir Guy protested.

"I think that you do." Aware that the Welshman had jumped to his feet, Madeline glanced at him before pressing the dagger into Sir Guy's throat. "David, he does not think I will hurt him, but you will, won't you?"

"I would happily run him through right now," Dafydd replied hotly, his hand clenching his sword as if anxious to do it.

But however evil these men were, and Madeline could guess that they were very evil indeed, she could not abide the thought of murder. "Gather the weapons." She glanced at the youths standing anxiously nearby. "Will you help us?"

They looked at Sir Guy, then each other. One, older than the rest, stepped forward. "With pleasure," he said scornfully.

"I need something to bind them."

The lad said a few quick words and some of the boys scattered, to return in a few short moments with stout ropes. The rest joined Dafydd picking up the discarded weapons.

When Sir Guy, Farold and the others were tied, Madeline hurried to the door. "Come, David, let us leave this place at once."

"What about them?" He gestured at the squires.

She smiled at the youths and spoke to the one who seemed to be their leader. "Run away," she said kindly. "Take what you can from this vile man's manor and get as far away as you can. A year and a day from now, you will be free."

As David joined her, she gave Sir Guy a scornful smile and drew herself up proudly. "I am Lady Madeline de Montmorency, Sir Guy, and rest assured, I will tell my brother all about you and your men. I suggest you contemplate begging forgiveness for your sins, although I doubt even God himself will look kindly on you."

With that, she turned and left the hall—to encounter a strange sight. Pouring in through the gate of the courtyard was a horde of poorly dressed peasants, shouting and waving swords, axes, even pitchforks, their faces filled with anger and hate. As Madeline hesitated on the threshold, an arrow thudded into the door beside her.

"Run!" Dafydd shouted in her ear, grabbing her hand and pulling her forward. They sprinted across the courtyard to the stables.

"What is it? Who are they?" she panted.

"His tenants, probably." Dafydd hurried to the nearest horse and led it from the stall. "One of the boys must have told them what was happening. We'd best get away as fast as we can."

"But we have done nothing—" she began.

He grabbed her around the waist and set her on the horse. The shouting grew louder. "They won't care. We are strangers—you're a Norman. That's all that will matter to them!"

Without waiting for her to respond, he sheathed his sword and swung himself up behind her. He maneuvered the horse through the surging mob, beating off the one man who tried to stop them. When they were successfully through the gate, he kicked the horse into a gallop and rode as fast as he could from the accursed place.

Chapter Six

With Madeline safe in his arms, Dafydd would have ridden all night to get away from Sir Guy's manor. He was sickened, both in heart and mind, disturbed beyond anything he had ever imagined, desperate to escape Sir Guy and his men.

The horse he had taken had proven itself a superb animal, running hard and fast for a long time. Only after some time had passed did Dafydd realize he must have taken Sir Guy's stallion. It was lathered and panting, and the time well past midnight when he finally pulled the beast to a halt. Although he didn't know how far they had come, a quick glance at the sky told him they had ridden north and he knew they had gone past the place where the outlaws had attacked Madeline's party and even beyond the small village.

His first concern was Madeline. Without speaking, he reached up and grasped her waist, helping her dismount. She clutched his arms tightly and leaned against him when her feet touched the ground. "David, David!" she murmured.

"Dafydd," he whispered, wanting her to know his true name. Needing her to know. "My name is Dafydd."

"Those men, those terrible men! I am so sorry! I should have remembered sooner... I should have refused to go with them...."

"Hush," Dafydd whispered. "It is over. We are far away from them." He rocked her gently, listening as she wept softly, happy that she would let him hold her so. "We should get off the road. I don't think they will follow us, but we had best take no chances."

She raised her tearstained face. "What do you think happened after we got away?"

"I don't have any notion," he replied grimly. "I hope those lads are safe. We should be grateful for the attack. Sir Guy will be too busy to follow us, if he is still alive. Come, we should rest."

"Yes, you're right," she said, pulling away. She tried to walk, but she stumbled and he caught her. Deftly grabbing the horse's rein in one hand, he lifted her up and carried her toward a nearby stream in the woods, a wonderful feeling of tender protectiveness stealing over him as he did so. For years and years he had felt completely alone in the world. Until now. Together they had faced danger, and together they had escaped. It was almost worth the disastrous encounter to have this incredible feeling.

He set her gently to the ground and looped the rein on a nearby bush. "Staying here, we are. Until the dawn, anyway."

She nodded, looking up at him with misery. "Oh, Dafydd, if they had come upon me alone!"

"Or me," he said. He sat beside her on the damp ground. "You saved me, Madeline."

"I didn't like the way they looked at you." She smiled tentatively, and he was glad to see even that small sign of a return to normality.

"Thank you," he said sincerely. "Thank you for saving me. I confess I didn't think you guessed . . . about them."

"There was something not right about them, I saw that at once. And then I remembered where I had heard of Sir Guy before." Briefly she recounted the long-ago incident. "I decided the best thing to do was act ignorant until I could be sure. And then I saw how that fellow looked at you, Dafydd." She shivered with remembrance. "Those poor, unfortunate boys! I hope they will be all right."

"They will be better off free, at any rate. Surprised I am you would know about such things."

"I confess I never truly believed the rumors of men like that. And he was so greedy and cruel. He had so much, while his tenants starved. I can understand why they would attack him."

"Or why a Welshman would rebel?" he asked, looking intently into her eyes.

She nodded slowly, and with true understanding. "Or why a Welshman would rebel."

As she continued to gaze at him, her expression open and honest and companionable, his heart reminded him that she could never be his, not in any way. She was Norman, noble and betrothed, even if she did intrigue him more than any other woman ever had, or perhaps ever could. "That was a good ruse," he said lightly, moving away. "Did you learn to act that way at the convent?"

"In a manner of speaking. I was imitating Sister Elizabeth."

"Ah. A talent you have, then."

"I used to make the other sisters laugh, especially when I spoke like Mother Bertrilde."

"Was she like Sister Elizabeth?"

"Oh, no. She was very serious and very strict and spoke only to correct faults or issue orders."

Dafydd could tell from the tone of her voice that Madeline had not enjoyed her time under the tender ministrations of such a woman. Here was something new to consider. He had always supposed the

women who lived in Norman convents were leading lives of great luxury, beholden to no man. It
seemed, however, that Mother Bertrilde was as
strict as any father, brother...or husband. "You
will be glad to be wed, then, and away from the
place."

She drew off her wimple with a heavy sigh, and
he tried to ignore her as she shook out her hair. "I
will be honest with you, Dafydd, because now we
are equal."

"Equal?"

"You saved me, and I saved you. You could have
left me when we heard Sir Guy and his men approaching."

His heart seemed to miss a beat. Yes, equal. He
felt that way, too, and had never expected to feel
that way about a woman. Yet she was so different,
so special—and she apparently realized that something was happening between them. Something
wonderful that should not, must not happen. "I
wouldn't have left my worst enemy there," he answered, trying to sound matter-of-fact.

"I hope I am not your worst enemy," she said
with a small smile.

"You are not my enemy at all."

"I know that, too, and that is why I trust you. So
I will confess to you that now that I know Roger is
not dead and is in good hands, I have no wish to

return to him. He is trying to force me to marry against my will.''

Again, this was something Dafydd had not considered, that she would be reluctant to be returned to her family. This something struck him as welcome news, and he told himself it should not. ''Can he make you marry?''

She gave him a determined look he was beginning to know well. ''He will try.''

''Your betrothed, does he know of your feelings?''

''No. He knows absolutely nothing of me, as I know nothing of him.''

''What's his name?''

''Chilcott.''

Dafydd shook his head. He had never heard it before. ''Why don't you want to marry him?''

''I have never even met the man!''

''Isn't that the Norman way?''

''For some—but I thought better of Roger than that, although I have not been in the same household since we were children. I thought he cared for me, but it seems his ambitions are more important.'' She felt betrayed, from the sound of her voice.

He knew that feeling well, for he, too, had been betrayed. Not by family, but by a man he had admired, who had turned out not to be filled with patriotic plans for a return to native rule by the Welsh, but with a selfish desire to see his family—and only *his* family—restored to greatness in any way he could, at any cost.

"Would *you* force your sister to marry?" Madeline asked.

"My sister is dead," he answered flatly. Yes, he needed to say it. To remember Gwennyth and how she died, at the hands of the Normans.

"Oh, I'm so sorry!"

"And my parents, too. Killed by Normans after they were forced to watch while they took my sister. I only escaped because I hid from them."

"I am very glad you did."

He stood abruptly. "I am going to swim in the river. I need to wash."

He didn't wait for her to reply, but strode off toward the glistening water. Rushes grew along the bank, their whispering in the slight breeze like ghosts chastising him for betraying his people. He yanked off the dalmatica, stripped off his chausses and boots, and waded into the cold, cleansing water.

He rose and took in a deep, shuddering breath before he became aware of a figure standing on the bank. "I am not your enemy, Dafydd," Madeline said softly. "I am sorry for what the Normans did to your family, and I wish with all my heart I could restore them to you."

"I know you are not responsible," he replied, wishing she would go so that he could dress.

"Is the water very cold?"

"Yes."

To his astonishment, she began to remove her clothing.

"What...what are you doing?" he demanded huskily.

"I am going to wash, too."

When her garments fell onto the ground and she stepped forth naked, he could only stare as she took a deep breath and walked into the river.

Ever since her parents had died and Madeline had been separated from Roger, she had felt completely alone in the world. Until today. Until here and now. She wanted him, needed him, desired him. He had reminded her of her fate, a marriage to a man she did not want. True, she might be able to refuse Roger's first choice, and perhaps a second, but he was a strong-willed man. Eventually he would see that she married someone to further his own ends. He was a man; he would never understand what she wanted in a husband.

So here, now, she would choose a man for herself. This man, this warrior, protector and comforting companion whose family had suffered so much at the hands of her countrymen. She stood upon the smooth, uneven rocks and watched him make his way through the water, droplets glistening on his chest in the moonlight, and when he took her in his arms, she leaned into him gladly.

Filled with powerful desire, she pulled him close and kissed him, not trying to rein in her passion, but letting it loose. She wanted to feel his arms around her, wanted to feel his lips upon hers, wanted him to take her in his strong arms and carry her to the grassy banks where he laid her down.

She welcomed the warmth and weight of his body upon hers. Her hands explored him, marveling at the tautness of the muscles beneath his damp flesh, her fingertips lightly touching the mottled skin of his scars. His hands, too, ventured over her, followed by his soft lips. She arched her back, giving herself to him and giving in to the myriad wonderful sensations he aroused.

He whispered soft words in her ear as he took hold of her hand and guided it below his waist. She touched him, for an instant pulling back. He let go of her hand. Then, half shy, half eager, she grasped him unaided. His gasp and the look of desire smoldering in his brown eyes as he looked at her was her reward as she parted her legs more from instinct than knowledge.

"Annwyl," he whispered as he caressed her and gently pushed inside. *"Annwyl..."* Beloved.

A fleeting, momentary pain was soon forgotten as he began to thrust. With cries of almost anguished delight, she responded eagerly with her mouth, her hands, her body. Flames of passion licked along every limb. She was like metal in the heat of a furnace, molten, pliable, ready to be made new in his care. Everything he did increased her fervor. Intensified it, until the moment of exquisite, intense release. He buried his hands in her hair and groaned as he stiffened, then relaxed against her.

They lay thus, entwined in each other's arms, panting and sated, for a long time.

For that long time, Madeline was happy. Delightfully happy, until she thought of something that she had not before.

What if she got with child?

What if she bore this Welsh rebel's child? She would be shamed, cast out, denigrated. She shoved Dafydd away and scrambled to her feet.

"What is it?" he muttered, standing, too. Naked in the moonlight. Still magnificent. She could not speak, for the shame was hers alone. *She* had been the one to go naked into the river with deliberate design. He would have stopped at any time, she knew without doubt, as he had when she pulled away for that brief moment. No, the blame, and the shame, were hers alone to bear, and alone she would bear them. "I . . . I'm cold."

He picked up her gown and approached her, a smile of such warmth on his handsome face that she was reminded of why she had done what she had. Nevertheless, she took the garment and turned away to put it on. "We should hide. There may be other outlaws."

"Yes." He pulled on his chausses and boots, picked up his sword, then paused and looked at her intently.

She could not bear his scrutiny. "Perhaps in those bushes."

Dafydd watched her crawl under the shelter of the broad-leafed undergrowth, there to lie down as calmly and silently as if nothing at all of import had happened between them. He led the horse into the underbrush and tied its reins to a branch, then he joined her, moving close to her, but she shifted away and turned her back to him.

What was the matter with her? Was it him? Or regret for what they had done together? He felt anything but regret, and he knew he had not been wrong about the willing desire in her eyes. "Tomorrow I will take you back to the convent," he said at last. It would be dangerous for him to go south again, back toward the monastery, but he would not risk her safety.

"No." She did not even bother to face him.

"Then to the monastery. The holy brothers will help you."

"Roger has many powerful friends, but my parents did, too. I know of one who will surely listen to me, and assist me to convince Roger that I will not marry Chilcott. He lives not too far off."

What was wrong? She was suddenly so cold, so distant . . . but she had been the eager one! She had followed him into the river, compelled him to continue. . . . His heart suddenly plummeted to the pit of his stomach, to be replaced by the burning heat of shame at the discovery that he could have been so stupid. "Why the urgency, my lady?" he said coldly. "Since you are no longer a virgin, Chilcott will surely refuse to marry *you.*"

Finally she turned and looked at him. "There is no need for anyone to know what we've done."

"But then what good has your sacrifice been, this giving of your virginity to an uncouth peasant of a Welshman?"

"You do not understand!"

"Oh, yes, I do!" Oh, God, that he had been so stupid, so blind, so desperate for her love! "If your brother tries to force your hand, then you will be only too quick to tell him, or the potential groom, that you are no longer a virgin. It is a lovely plan, my lady. Wedding called off, high-handed brother outmaneuvered. Or perhaps you intend to wait until the wedding night and let the poor fool of a bridegroom find out for himself how he has been duped. Surely then he and your brother will be happy with a quiet annulment, so no one will know how you tricked them. Except for the uncouth Welshman, of course, but he is of no consequence."

"You are wrong!"

"You were not a virgin?" he said with mock admiration. "You are indeed a clever mimic, although there are some ways you could improve the performance. A few tears to show the pain of penetration, perhaps. A touch of fear to show your innocence."

"That was not a performance!"

"No matter. You got what you wanted, and so did I."

"You have no idea what I want," she said. "You have no understanding of my life at all, and I doubt you ever will."

"As long as I risk my own to save it?"

"For which I am grateful, as I have—"

"Shown? Demonstrated in a particularly pleasant manner? Delighted I am that you chose such a manner to thank me."

She frowned darkly.

"Intending to 'reward' me again, are you?"

"I will see that you are well rewarded, with money or a horse."

He smiled sardonically at her haughty words. "Not a servant, my lady, and not a whore, either."

"Neither am I," she said forcefully. "Nor will I beg for your assistance. If you will not help me, I will find someone in the nearest village who will."

"That is too dangerous. Are you already forgetting Sir Guy? There may be others like him about who will consider a lone woman fine prey."

Her frown disappeared, replaced by the lingering terror of their flight. As hurt and angry as he was, he was sorry he had reminded her of Sir Guy. He was almost sorry he had reminded himself, for he was forced to recall the fate from which she had saved him. Nor could he leave her to fend for herself, perhaps to face such a fate again. She was his responsibility now, whether he liked it or not. "I will take you wherever you want to go."

"I will see that you are rewarded."

"Not wanting a reward, me. I want your word that if I am endangered by aiding you, you will see that I am freed to go back to Wales."

"You have it, David."

"Dafydd! My name is Dafydd," he said curtly. So she had forgotten that, too. How little he meant to her, after all.

"Very well, then, Dafydd. You have the word of Lady Madeline de Montmorency."

He sat down a few feet away. "I will keep watch tonight."

She didn't reply, but turned away to go to sleep. Well, Dafydd thought, he could ignore her, too. An owl hooted nearby and he heard the small scurrying of a mouse in the grass. The horse munched the grass placidly, as if nothing had changed.

Yet it had. Very much. At least for him.

"By the blessed Virgin!" Roger exclaimed softly as he surveyed the pile of burned corpses in the ruined shell of the hall as the dawn illuminated the scene. Blackened timbers lay on the floor of what had once been a large stone hall. The stones, cracked by tremendous heat, lay scattered as if a giant had trampled them. Curls of smoke and the smell of burned flesh filled the early morning air.

Beside Roger, a sickened Father Gabriel muttered a brief prayer. His men, more used to slaughter, were nonetheless disturbed by what they had found.

"Save your breath, Father," Roger said coldly. "If there is any justice in the world, these men will roast in hell for all eternity."

"God's mercy—"

"Should be for those deserving of it. If even a portion of what I have heard of Sir Guy and his followers is true—"

"You are not God, Sir Roger," Father Gabriel interrupted with a surprising measure of strength in his usually quiet voice. "It is not for you, or me, or any man to judge them now."

Roger was not convinced, for he had heard many things about Sir Guy, and Father Gabriel had probably never even heard of half the sinful practices Sir Guy was said to indulge in. But there was no point in enlightening the priest.

Albert came beside him, a cloth over his nose. "Any sign of Madeline?" Roger asked anxiously. There were no women among the dead, but that did not diminish his anxiety.

"No, my lord," he replied. He gestured at an old man who followed him. "We did find this fellow, my lord, the gatekeeper, or so he claims."

"What happened here?"

The ancient retainer touched his forelock, a small smile on his lips as he surveyed the corpses. "A fight, there was."

This Welsh peasant was obviously delighted with his master's death despite his efforts to appear meek and shocked. Indeed, he was almost gloating, which might explain why he had stayed behind. Perhaps he would even be eager to describe the terrible death of Sir Guy and his followers. "Who fought?"

"I don't know, exactly. Many enemies had Sir Guy," the gatekeeper said. He nodded at the dead. "But they lost, eh?"

"Did you see a woman here recently?"

"Sir Guy often brought women here, whether they wanted to come or not."

Roger did his best to remain calm, despite his anxiety. "The woman I seek was dressed as a nun."

"Ah!"

"You've seen her?"

"Sometimes Sir Guy liked 'em dressed as nuns."

Roger's dread increased. Sir Guy sounded worse than he had heard.

"Pretty woman, was she, my lord?"

"Yes, very."

"Maybe I seen her, and maybe not."

Determined to know the truth, Roger grabbed the old man by the throat and thrust his face inches from his. "Listen to me and listen carefully. I am Sir Roger de Montmorency and I am looking for my sister, Lady Madeline de Montmorency. If I find out you knew *anything* of her whereabouts and that you did not tell me, I will send my men back here to find you. And then you will be very, very sorry indeed."

"There was a nun and a priest, together, came with Sir Guy before the attack," the old man spluttered, his eyes wide with fear.

"A nun and a priest?"

"Aye, my lord, truly!"

Roger let go. The old man gasped for breath as Father Gabriel stepped forward. "This priest, what did he look like?"

"He was short, skinny, rotten teeth, red hair," the old man said with conviction. "But the lady was a beauty."

Roger and Father Gabriel exchanged glances. It was not unlikely that one Welshman would protect another. "Were they on foot?" Father Gabriel inquired.

"Yes."

Father Gabriel said, "If you will please excuse me, Sir Roger, I find this place nearly unbearable."

Roger nodded his agreement. He watched the priest head for the stable before facing the old man again. "Where are they now?"

"They run off when the fightin' started."

"Both of them?"

"Together they was. On foot."

Roger drew in a deep breath. All this was not the good news he hoped for, but it seemed that if the nun was indeed Madeline, she was not hurt and had escaped Sir Guy before the fight. "Albert!"

"Yes, my lord?"

"Have Bredon and the dogs search the road and the lands nearby."

"Aye, my lord." Albert departed quickly.

"Old man, who did this?" Roger's gesture encompassed the ruined hall.

The old man wet his lips nervously. Roger drew him aside and said, "Neither I, nor my overlord Baron DeGuerre, had any liking for Sir Guy and his men," he said quietly, "and few will mourn his death. But there are questions that must be answered, and it would be better to find out here, now, easily, before others are made to suffer. Was it outlaws?"

The old man nodded.

"And his tenants, too, perhaps?"

The old man made no response.

"And what of the squires?"

"The what?"

"The youths. I have heard tales."

"He used 'em somethin' terrible, him and those others!" the old man said, fixing his eye fearlessly on Roger. "You won't find 'em now, though. They all run off after they took what they could, and small enough recompense it would be, my lord,'' he finished defiantly.

Roger caught himself before he nodded in agreement, but he would not send his men to pursue the youths. He would tell the baron what he knew and suggest they make some show of seeking retribution, then quietly give this manor and lands to someone more deserving, which would be almost anyone. Roger realized Father Gabriel had returned and was hovering behind his men. "You may go, for now," he said to the gatekeeper.

Father Gabriel hurried up to him, a small bundle in his hands. "The roan, Sir Roger—it is in the stable."

"And that?" Roger nodded at the bundle.

"Still tied to it."

"Open it," the nobleman ordered.

Father Gabriel sighed, but he obeyed. Inside there was a remnant of bread, a flint and a bag of coins. Father Gabriel's eyes widened when he saw the money.

Roger's expression became sardonic. "If this fellow is the man you seek, it seems he stole more than a horse and some clothes."

Father Gabriel nodded. "So it appears."

"And you still believe my sister is safe with him?"

"I do," Father Gabriel answered with conviction.

"Despite your faith in him, he may yet demand money for her safe return."

"He brought her here, did he not? If he intended ransom, he would not bring her to any Norman."

"He almost got her killed, or worse."

"If I understand the circumstances, Sir Roger, it seems he saved her, rather." Father Gabriel smiled slightly. "Believe me, my lord, that a man who spends his whole life in the company of other men soon learns many small signs of trustworthiness, or duplicity. Had I a sister, I would have no fear for her."

"I suppose that should comfort me," Roger said with a scowl.

"No, my lord. Your faith in God should comfort you."

Roger turned his attention to the bundle. "Little enough, and now they have not even that. The old man said they were on foot. They cannot have gotten far, if the gatekeeper is not lying about the fellow taking a horse."

"Why should he do that?" Father Gabriel asked.

"Because the gatekeeper is a Welshman, and this thief is a Welshman who can be hanged for steal-

ing a horse. Perhaps he thinks to help his country-
man, or merely to spite me. Who knows?"

"You seem eager to distrust the old man."

"I know more of the world, Father. The real
world, of Welsh and Norman, than you could learn
in a monastery."

"What do you intend to do?"

"Why, continue the search, of course."

Father Gabriel frowned. "I think it would be
wise to rest, Sir Roger. You have ridden all night
and you may overtax your strength."

"My strength is my concern."

"You will not help your sister if you fall ill."

Roger sighed. "Oh, very well. But only because
the horses require it. We shall rest here and resume
the search at noon. Will that suit you, Father?"

"That, and one other thing."

Roger raised his eyebrow quizzically.

"We will stay until we have given these men a
proper burial, along with the other unfortunates we
will cut down from the trees."

Chapter Seven

At first light, Dafydd roused Madeline, ignoring the beauty of her half-parted lips and the fanning of her dusky eyelashes upon her pale cheeks. Still angry, he bluntly ordered her to get on the horse. He expected her to protest, but for once she did not question him.

She commanded him to continue north along the main road, claiming that was the way to her friends. He, not wishing to appear more than slightly interested in her life, did not talk to her except to ask the distance to these friends. She was not sure of that, and was only certain that their home lay to the north and west.

So they proceeded in silence, until they took a short pause to refresh themselves at a small brook. "We'll have to sell the horse," Madeline said as she mounted, preparing to start their journey again.

As before, Dafydd walked at the front of the stallion, where he would not be able to see her.

"No. It's too much of a risk," he replied decisively, trying very hard to keep his tone civil despite his chaotic feelings. He would sell his soul before he would let her see how she affected him when she was apparently unmoved either by his anger or his passion, now that she had achieved her own ends.

"It does not matter how dangerous you think it," Madeline said just as resolutely and continuing to act as if nothing very special had happened between them the previous night, whereas he was constantly distracted by memories of her in his arms. "We simply must sell this horse. We need food and other clothing."

She had obviously gotten what she wanted of him last night; he would not acquiesce to this scheme so easily. If she could think of anything beyond her own comfort, she would see that it would be too dangerous for them—for *him,* at any rate—to try to sell the horse stolen from Sir Guy. It had been his intention to get new clothing when he had the coins stolen from the abbot. That would have been a simple transaction. Selling a horse, though—that was something else again, especially for a Welshman, since many Normans and Saxons considered Welshmen thieves and would look askance at one trying to sell so fine a mount.

"We should get off the road," he said, changing the subject and reiterating a point he had tried to make earlier with little success. "Too many people have already seen us."

"My brother has Bredon, his huntsman, in his train, with his best hounds. If we stay on the road, our scent will be harder to follow mixed in with other travelers, and we will leave no sign of broken branches or crushed grass for trackers. And if we have other clothing, all they will see is two people journeying along the road—not some man imperfectly disguised as a priest."

He twisted and gave her a disgruntled look. "You don't look much like a nun, either." He let his gaze move slowly over her torn and stained habit, and then realized that was something of a mistake, because he was too aware of the delectable body beneath it. "You thought I was a priest," he said, getting back to the topic of the discussion, "when I saved you from that outlaw."

"I was in no state to believe anything but your garment, and that outlaw was only a boy," she said peevishly.

"You were worried enough about that boy to want me to bind him," he reminded her.

"I was not myself."

And are you now? Or were you last night? This train of thought was pointless. "It is dangerous for us to sell the horse, and without it, how do you intend to get to these friends of yours?"

"We shall walk."

He snorted derisively and scratched where the hot wool made his arms itch.

"I can walk that far, and if you think you do not need other garments, suffer then. But we need food and we have nothing to sell except the horse," she said as if he were a simpleton. "We should do so at the next village we come to. Tomorrow must be market day, for we have already passed many people on the road. Besides, we have surely come far enough from Sir Guy's that this horse will not be recognized."

Dafydd didn't answer. She was right that Sir Guy lived far away and in relative isolation, too, so it might not be quite as risky as he feared. But he was not going to give her the satisfaction of agreeing with her. She was not in command.

"We shall rest now," he announced when he spied a likely spot with a thick growth of rowan trees, hawthorn and prickly dewberry bushes, as well as blackthorn. He led the horse off the road, carefully holding back the shrubs so that the beast would not get scratched.

"It will be a long while yet before the sun sets," Madeline said as she held back a low rowan branch to keep it from striking her in the face.

"I know."

He tied the horse to a blackthorn limb and looked around with satisfaction. "You should be safe enough here."

"Are you planning to go somewhere without me?" Madeline demanded suspiciously.

"We need to eat. Remember?" He broke off some long, slender branches whose ends he sharpened with the edge of his sword while she dismounted. "I can probably get a fish or a rabbit."

"How do you intend to cook it? We have no flint to start a fire."

He never paused in his movements. "Then not cooking it, are we?"

"I will not eat raw meat."

"Aren't you hungry?"

"Not *that* much."

"Enjoy your fast then, my lady."

She wondered what kind of barbarian she was traveling with. Raw meat was disgusting. As for his sarcastic comment about fasting, well, she had fasted many times. It was certainly true that she was hungry, but she could go some hours yet before she felt seriously weakened.

What truly rankled her was his brusque, abrasive manner, even though she knew it was her fault. Her sudden awareness of the possible consequences of what they had done together had made her curt and rude when she was really frightened.

He would suffer no serious repercussions for last night, nor perhaps did he understand what she might face. She had heard enough, from living not far from the border of Wales, that the Welsh did not view illegitimacy as the stain the Normans did. Nor did he, as a rebel and outcast, have so far to fall. She, however, was a Norman noblewoman and her life would be irrevocably destroyed by the stigma of bearing a child outside of holy wedlock.

Even his lack of understanding, though, did not alleviate his accusation that she had used him for a dishonorable, selfish purpose. It was unforgivable.

Dafydd sheathed his sword, then pulled off his dalmatica. The sight of his nearly naked body recalled last night, and she turned away, determined not to be reminded. Not to weaken. "Stay here and don't move," he ordered, and before she could protest, he disappeared into the trees.

Feeling abandoned and what she considered to be reasonable resentment at his treatment, Madeline sat down and cupped her chin in her hand. Who did he think he was, to order her about like that? He was acting no better than Roger. Was this the way all men treated women, like unthinking, unfeeling animals? No matter how harsh and strict the conditions at the convent had been—and indeed, both Roger and Dafydd would have been surprised to discover just how harsh and strict Mother Bertrilde could be—her life seemed infinitely better there. Of course, had she stayed at the convent, she would never have met Dafydd and never experienced—

Well, that was not going to happen again. She had erred once and would not repeat the mistake, despite her appreciation of his efforts to help her and despite her vivid memories of his kisses and caresses, as well as her even more vivid recollection of the feelings his voice, his eyes and his body aroused within her. Such thoughts would do her no good.

She surveyed the bushes. It was nearly May, and too early yet for any berries to be ripe. There might be eggs in the nests of birds, but raw eggs sounded little better than raw meat.

Then she heard the sound of voices. Not men, she thought with some relief. Children. Happy voices, a most pleasant change from the peasants on Sir Guy's land. She shivered as she thought of Sir Guy and his men, then rose and cautiously made her way through the underbrush.

Two boys walked along a narrow path, talking and laughing gaily. They were clearly brothers, sharing the same tow-colored hair and stocky build.

One was elder by perhaps a year; the other, not as tall but slightly heavier. He had to hurry to keep up with the older one, who seemed to be engaged in a race. He did not run, but his pace was quick and he kept glancing at his younger brother to see if he was keeping up or perhaps ready to pass him.

She smiled to herself. Roger used to do that to her, too, back in those happy days when their parents were alive. Those days he had forgotten.

She glanced at her dirty, stained woolen gown and took off her wimple. Although filthy, the fabric was very good. Maybe these two lads had a mother who would trade for some fabric, or even a change of clothes, Madeline thought as she watched them. Maybe she could even get some food in addition to more suitable garments. But Dafydd had told her to stay here....

At that moment, her stomach growled. With sudden resolve, Madeline began to stealthily follow the boys.

They went a fair distance before they reached a brook and an open glade, in which she could see a simple farmhouse. It was not large, but the wattle-and-daub walls were in good repair. Smoke curled out of a hole in the thatched roof. Some hens scratched in the yard and there was a pig in a small pen. As Madeline crept closer, the smell of fresh-baked bread wafted to her, making her mouth water. She could also see, spread out upon the banks of the brook to dry, a woman's much-mended gown, a linen shift, a man's tunic, some aprons and what she took to be children's clothing.

A slender young woman, also towheaded, came out of the farmhouse and called to the boys, who ran to her, their competition forgotten. Madeline waited as they all went toward what looked like a small barn. She heard a cow moo. Milking time.

Swiftly Madeline stood up and removed her gown so that she was wearing only her linen shift, which was in better condition than her outer garments. She folded the gown carefully and wrapped it in the wimple. If she left everything, surely that would compensate for an old gown, a tunic and a loaf of bread.

She dashed toward the farmhouse, staying under cover of the trees as long as she could. She entered the house, spotted the bread, laid the bundle on a stool, snatched up the still-warm loaf, ran back outside, grabbed the gown and the tunic and sprinted across the brook. Once back in the covering undergrowth, she sat panting a moment until she could catch her breath. Then she began to hurry toward where she thought she had left the horse.

Before she had gone very far, however, Madeline halted in confusion. She had left no markings to guide her and had paid more attention to the children than to the trees or bushes.

She was quite lost.

Father Gabriel sighed softly as he rode behind Sir Roger and Sir Albert. Up ahead he could hear the huntsman, who moved as silently as a cat, leading his huge and various hounds along the side of the road.

If Father Gabriel understood matters correctly, the hounds had picked up a trail heading northward, confirmed by the muddy hoofprints of a horse traveling fast but weighed down. The huntsman had been most emphatic that the horse must have borne more than one rider, to account for such tracks. Unfortunately, the hounds had lost the scent not many miles from Sir Guy's ravaged manor, and the road had joined with another ancient track that was made of stone, leaving no clear marks.

Nevertheless, after they had seen to the disposal of the bodies of Sir Guy and his men, Sir Roger had insisted on searching as far northward as they could until dark, then they had camped in the forest close to the road.

Now they were riding through a large beech wood and the road wound away under the heavy canopy. There was little underbrush here and Father Gabriel could see Bredon, the huntsman, and his dogs some distance ahead. Sir Albert and Sir Roger rode at the head of the cortege, and a line of several soldiers fanned out from the road, by their bowed heads obviously searching for any signs of tracks. Other men had spread even farther afield in the search.

Father Gabriel watched as Sir Roger dropped back beside him.

"Are you weary? Do you wish to rest?" Sir Roger asked with the merest hint of courtesy in his tone, and with his eyes still alertly scanning the trees and bushes.

"Not at all," Father Gabriel answered. "But what of yourself? That was quite a blow you took and—"

"And I have had worse, I assure you, Father." He gave the priest a shrewd, measuring look. "How did you sleep?"

"I confess that although I have slept on plain boards and spent countless vigils kneeling on bare stones, nothing quite compares to the torture of sleeping on the damp, cold ground with a small rock lodged against my back."

Sir Roger gave a deep bark of a laugh. "I know that pain myself, Father, and trust me, it shall pass. At least it does not look to rain again. This day promises to be one of the finest we have had all spring."

"And you, Sir Roger? How did you sleep?"

"I've had better nights." A moment passed. "Is there some religious house to the north?" Roger demanded.

"Not that I am aware of," Father Gabriel answered honestly. Apparently the time for polite pleasantries was past, brief as it was. "The nearest is some miles farther north."

"This outlaw you think Madeline may be with, what kind of man is he?"

"Kind, my lord?"

"Yes. He is a Welshman, you said?"

"I believe so, my lord."

"Believe? It was my understanding he had been in your care for over a year. How can you not be sure? Did he speak French? Or Saxon?"

"He did not speak at all, my lord," Father Gabriel admitted.

Roger turned an aloof, dark eye on the holy man.

Sir Roger was a marvel, really, Father Gabriel reflected. The epitome of the Norman nobleman. He was bold, fierce, determined, handsome, and his smile not without a certain charm, perhaps because of its rarity.

"Yet you are convinced he is a Welshman, and an honest one, at that," the nobleman noted dryly.

"Whatever race he belongs to, Sir Roger, I believe he is an unusual man."

"Sir Guy de Robespierre was an 'unusual' man.''

"Oh, the Welshman is nothing like that!" Father Gabriel protested. "He is quite honorable, I am sure. He also has an amazing will to live, or he would have been dead long before he reached us. He is clever, for it would take a clever man to realize that his speech might betray him as an outsider, possibly an enemy."

"Or a rebel. And need I remind you that he has now stolen two horses, as well as the abbot's money?"

"Out of necessity, I firmly believe. He did help your sister, Sir Roger."

"But if he is so good and honorable, why has he not brought Madeline back to me? Or left her in safe hands?"

"Perhaps that is what he was trying to do. As I said before, he may not have understood the few things he might have heard about Sir Guy, and even then, Sir Guy was seldom spoken of at the monastery. Would Lady Madeline have heard about Sir Guy?"

"I doubt it. Sir Guy's manor was farther from the convent than the monastery, and most people were loath to talk of his disgusting way of life."

"Then you see, Sir Roger, it could very well be that he was taking her to what he thought was a safe place, the manor of a Norman lord, especially if they were not certain of your whereabouts.''

Sir Roger nodded. ''It is not impossible, Father.''

Father Gabriel's perceptions did not just pertain to wounded, silent men in the monastery, so he said, ''Pardon me, Sir Roger, but I have been wondering why Lady Madeline might not have gone back toward the convent or the monastery? She certainly knew she could find safe haven at either place, yet she is apparently going in the opposite direction.''

''Despite what you think, perhaps she is not free to do as she pleases,'' Sir Roger replied sternly. ''If this fellow is, or was, a rebel or an outlaw, she may not be able to go where she chooses.''

''I must say again, Sir Roger, that if she has met with the young man who has lodged with us at the monastery, you have little to fear for your sister's safety. Is there no other reason she might not seek you out?''

''Explain yourself, Father,'' Sir Roger demanded.

''I meant no criticism. It is my understanding, from Sir Albert and some of the others that she is on her way to be married. Sometimes, when a young woman does not wish to be married or dislikes the intended bridegroom, she runs away.''

The Norman raised his eyebrow skeptically. "It is *my* understanding, Father Gabriel, that you have lived all your life within monastery walls. What can you know of marriages and brides?"

"Because I have lived a secluded life does not mean I am completely ignorant of the ways of the world," Father Gabriel replied placidly. "I am merely trying to think of reasons as to why we are having such a difficult time finding her. If she does not *want* to be found, that would explain many things."

"That's nonsense."

Father Gabriel eyed his companion shrewdly. "Is your sister's nature like your own, Sir Roger?"

"Why do you ask?"

"Because, my son, if she is like you, I think you should consider where *she* might lead the Welshman."

"Are you saying you think my sister would willingly travel through the countryside with a man she does not know?" The young man looked as if Father Gabriel had suggested Madeline might deliberately infect herself with leprosy.

"If the alternative is unwelcome to her, it is not impossible."

"Madeline would do no such shameful thing."

"You sound certain, my lord."

"I am."

"I beg your pardon, my lord. Sir Albert gave me to understand that you had not seen your sister in some time."

"Be that as it may," Sir Roger said tersely, "I am quite certain Madeline has more pride and sense than that."

"Is there no other place Lady Madeline might have gone to seek help?"

"What do you mean?"

"I mean, my lord, that perhaps she believes you have come to harm. Might she not seek out some friend?"

"There is a friend of the family, Lord Trevelyan, whose castle is some miles away," Sir Roger said after a moment's thought. "And it lies to the north."

"Perhaps she is going there, where she is sure to find succor," Father Gabriel suggested hopefully.

"A wise idea, Father," Sir Roger said with a fleeting smile. "I will send Albert on ahead to inquire." Sir Roger nudged his horse forward, then glanced back. "Wherever she has gone, we *will* find her, and soon."

Chapter Eight

Dafydd stood in the middle of the small clearing in the bramble bushes and wiped his sweating brow with the back of his hand. Where was Madeline? The black stallion was still tethered and placidly munching on grass. The ground did not look disturbed as if a struggle had taken place. Nor were there signs of other people, such as a brother discovering his missing sister. Of course, had *that* been the case, the horse would surely be gone, too.

And he would probably have been captured and condemned to death, despite Madeline's naive assumption that she could sway her brother. More likely she had merely gone a short way to tend to some natural needs. Nevertheless, dread flooded through him.

He tossed the sharpened sticks, which had proven useless as weapons, onto the ground. ''Lady Madeline?'' he called out softly.

There was no answer. Could it be that she was keeping silent out of spite? He did not think her vindictive, but he did not know her well. And he *had* been harsh toward her, justifiably, of course, but still... "Lady Madeline?" He searched the ground for any clue as to where she might have gone, but he could see no signs in the decaying vegetation and dead twigs.

She would not have decided to go ahead on the journey by herself, would she? It was too dangerous. She was too intelligent not to understand that.

Or had she felt that she could acquire another escort in the village? If she revealed herself as Lady Madeline de Montmorency, she would surely be able to find an escort. That would mean a return to her brother, but perhaps that was of little consequence now.

Maybe she had indeed abandoned him here. He would not be disturbed or dismayed, he told himself. He would not worry about her. He was happy to be rid of her, and now he had a much finer horse, too.

There! He spotted a recently broken branch lying on the ground, likely caused by the passage of a person, and going away from the village. Would Madeline go that way voluntarily?

"Madeline?" he called again, his tone more intense, and he paused to wait for an answer.

"Madeline!" He followed the narrow trail. *"Madeline!"*

"Dafydd?" came a quiet whisper.

"Yes!" *I should not be so pleased,* he thought, willing his face to reveal nothing.

The bushes rustled as a woman stepped out onto the path. Something was different, but it was Madeline, thank God. *She had not left him.*

It took considerable effort for Dafydd to survey her rather than run toward her. Her wimple was missing—what marvelous hair she had!—she was not wearing her habit and she was holding something in her hands. He kept his eyes on the bundle, although he was very aware of the gown that was clinging to her body. It was of a dark-dyed linen, with lacings straining to hold the bodice together at the front. It looked as if the bodice would tear asunder at any moment, revealing her perfectly shaped breasts encased in the very thin white shift. Because the dress was obviously too small for her, her shift showed at the neck and also at the bottom.

He swallowed hard. "Where were you?" he demanded, marching up to her. "What is that you are wearing?"

"It's a dress," she answered matter-of-factly.

"I can see that."

"Then why did you ask?" She started to walk past him, as if he did not deserve an explanation.

He fell into step beside her. "Where did you get it?"

"I traded my habit for it."

"With who?"

"Some peasants. I've got a tunic for you and some bread, too." Triumphantly she held out the bundle and unwrapped it, revealing a round brown loaf and a garment. "Were you worried about me?"

"No," he lied. "If you want to find more outlaws, it is no concern of mine. What peasants did you meet?"

Her dark, shapely eyebrows knit together with annoyance. Obviously Madeline expected him to congratulate her for taking a foolish risk. "They live back that way." She gestured behind herself vaguely. "If I had seen outlaws, I would have hidden. You did not see me, did you? And you were searching, weren't you?"

"Did you tell these peasants who you were?" he asked, not deigning to answer her last question.

She gave him a withering look. "Do you think I am such a fool? What if my brother should come seeking me? I assure you, the peasants never even saw me."

Even though she had just confirmed that she truly wanted to avoid her brother, he kept his thoughts on this unwise act. "What do you mean, they didn't see you? You said you traded."

"I mean that I left my habit in payment," she explained in a rush. "There was no one in the house and my habit is made of much finer fabric than these clothes and the bread is very coarse although naturally that does not matter since we are both so hungry and I do think they got the best of the bargain—"

"You *stole* those things!" It was worse than he thought!

"In a manner of speaking, I suppose one could say that," she replied haughtily. "What is the matter with you? You act as if I murdered the whole family while they slept! But we are both hungry, and we needed the clothing. Besides," she said archly, "you are not an innocent when it comes to thievery, are you?"

"In a manner of speaking," he said, his voice hot with anger, "you are quite right. About everything, including my past. But you have stopped short, my lady, in your considerations. You have not reckoned on what *my* fate would be if we are caught with stolen goods. I could get *hung!*"

"But it was *I* who stole the things," she countered.

"*You,* my *lady,* are not an outlaw. A rebel. A Welshman. You are a highborn Norman noblewoman, the sister of Sir Roger de Montmorency. Who do you think the justice of the peace will accuse and convict? And if *I* am convicted, I assure you, I will be hung."

"I would not permit it."

He gave her a look that was both dismissive and scornful. "*You* would not permit it. Oh, my lady, I cannot tell you how safe I feel now."

"I will explain—"

"When you next see your brother, I suggest you inquire about Norman justice. It is swift and, I assure you, my lady, does not permit lengthy explanations, especially from Welshmen, or women. Have you already forgotten those corpses along the road? *That* could be my fate."

She reddened, feeling very ignorant and ashamed and angry at being made to feel that way. She had tried to help, and he was acting as if she had betrayed him completely. Her lips started to tremble and her eyes to fill with tears, but she managed to control herself. "Very well, Dafydd. I humbly ask your pardon for getting us food and clothing. I should have sat under a bush like a rock and starved. In future, I suppose I should let you assume all the risks."

"Madeline, I—"

"*Lady* Madeline," she interrupted. If he was going to treat her like a simpleton, at least she would remind him she was from a higher class.

"How far away were these peasants you traded with, *Lady* Madeline?"

"A fair distance," she mumbled, disgruntled, and picked at a hole in the tunic.

"That was why you were gone so long?"

"It...it took me some time to find the path again."

"Dear God in heaven, you got *lost?*" He put his hands under her chin and forced her to look at him. "Don't you *ever* leave me again!"

Her gaze searched Dafydd's angry face and her heart started to beat wildly as she stared into his dark eyes. He was truly angry, yes, but beneath that, she knew it was because he had been worried about her. He really cared about her, and she *had* been a fool not to consider the danger she was putting him in—the danger she might keep him in, as long as he was with her.

But she needed him. And he cared about her, far more than anyone else in her life. She would see that nothing, *nothing,* happened to him because of her. He doubted that she was capable of protecting him, but he had yet to discover that what Lady Madeline de Montmorency willed, she would ensure came to pass. "It doesn't matter, does it?" she said, no longer near tears. Indeed, she was hard-pressed not to smile as she slowly drew away. "I got back safe and sound. Here." She held up the garment. "Put it on. And then we can eat."

"Let us hope this fits me better than that gown does you," he growled, stepping away and once again running his gaze over her body.

She felt warm again, and not from shame this time. "I regret I did not take measurements." She surveyed him in retaliation, starting at his toes and proceding slowly to his face. "It should fit." It was exciting, the way he looked at her. Not nearly so exciting as his kisses, though—but she should fight such thoughts. She had forgotten that she had placed herself at far greater risk by making love with him than by trading her clothes for these goods.

"This is not the place to talk about it," he snarled, turning to lead the way back to the horse.

"This dress is cooler than my other clothes, which is important, since I cannot go about half-naked as you do."

"I couldn't wear that robe while I was hunting."

"Of course not."

He pulled on the tunic. It did not fit very well, being rather too loose. She much preferred him half-naked, and blushed at her lustful observation. "How many rabbits did you catch?"

"None."

"It would seem, then, that I am the better hunter."

He merely scowled in response.

She sat down near the biggest bramble bush and broke the bread in half. She held out part to him. "I will confess I acted impulsively. Mother Bertrilde always said I should think first and act later, but that is not always easy to do."

He took the bread, then sat several paces away.

"You must agree that it will be better for us to be in different clothing. Roger and his men will be looking for a woman in nun's clothes, and they will think I am alone, perhaps. This way, we can pretend to be a couple."

He took another bite of the bread.

"It will be easier when I sell the horse, too, if I am in peasant garb," she said.

"You?" He looked at her with a suspiciously puzzled expression.

"Of course me. As you have just pointed out, you are a Welshman. The horse traders might think you stole that stallion."

He shifted uncomfortably, then said, "You don't sound like a peasant. They might wonder what a highborn Norman woman is doing dressed in rags and trying to sell a horse."

"Oh, sir, 'tis true, sir, aye," she replied with a thick country accent and a twinkle in her eyes when she caught him off guard. "Not every woman in the convent was a highborn Norman noblewoman," she explained in her usual voice.

"Better it would be if I could keep the horse and sell you," her companion muttered in Welsh, which he obviously did not think she understood.

But she did, at least enough to get the gist of his comment, which stung her more than she cared to consider, just as his word last night had delighted her, when he had called her "beloved."

Still, this was not the time to allow her personal feelings to interfere. They needed to have a plan for the rest of their journey. "Shall we say you are my husband, if anyone sees us and asks?"

"No!"

She tried not to look disappointed at his swift, blunt rejoinder. "My brother, then. My strong, silent, bully of a brother. Yes, that could work."

"I have no intention of letting *you* try to sell that horse," Dafydd growled.

The florid young farmer, whose straggling blond hair stuck out from his head like a shaft of thatch, scratched his stubbled chin and ran his appraising gaze over Madeline, then the stallion, then her again.

Madeline tried not to squirm with discomfort as she stood in the small enclosure outside the village alehouse. Nearby, peasant women carrying baskets of produce, and farmers driving chickens, geese and the occasional sheep or cow, moved past, all clearly headed for the marketplace on the green of this middle-sized, prosperous town. An ancient wagon bearing bags of grain lumbered along the road, probably heading to the large mill on the river. As she waited for the young man to say something—*anything!*—she could hear the tradesmen calling to potential customers, and the cheerful banter of the haggling shoppers.

Madeline shifted her weight to her other foot, and wondered if she should have waited for a different prospective buyer. However, his clothes looked clean and well mended, his body well fed and his purse full. She also thought he would have less experience at driving bargains than an older man.

If only he would make up his mind and quit staring at her bosom as if he had never seen breasts before! Well, in a way, she had brought his impertinent scrutiny upon herself, for she had insisted upon doing the trading. Maybe it had been wrong to tuck her shift so low. Her breasts were rather shockingly displayed, but she had thought she might as well use every and any means to help her

bargain. She had long ago realized that the pretti-
est nuns at the convent inevitably made the best
bargains with the local merchants.

What would he say if he knew who she truly was?
As amusing as the notion was, she quickly forgot it
to concentrate on the business at hand, which was
to sell the horse.

"How much did he say you was to get?" the
young farmer asked.

Acting her role, Madeline bit her lip worriedly
and clutched the rope attached to the horse's bridle a little tighter as she repeated the sum. Dafydd
had told her what he thought the horse was worth,
and she was currently suggesting twice that amount.
That had not been his idea, but her own, and she
wondered if she had erred.

"God's oath, girl, seems a bit much," the farmer
finally said. "I'll give you half that, and that's too
much. Always had a weakness for a beauty," he
finished with a leer and a wink.

Madeline gave him her most distressed expression. "Oh, sir, my brother has a *terrible* temper,
that he does! He will beat me if I don't get what he
said!"

"Then he ought to be a better judge of horse-
flesh," the farmer retorted. "That beast ain't worth
near what you're askin', girl."

"What will I do?" Madeline pleaded, opening her eyes as wide as she could in what she hoped looked like stupidity and desperation.

He eyed her speculatively. "Maybe we could strike a bargain."

"Oh?" She smiled hopefully. "What kind of bargain?"

"Come here where it's quieter," he said, moving toward the alley between the alehouse and what she believed was a storehouse.

"I don't know... my brother said to wait here. Maybe if I knew you were going to give me what I want for the horse he wouldn't be angry if I wasn't right here...."

The farmer puzzled over this for a few moments. "I can't give you that much silver unless you... um... make it worth my while."

"How?" she asked innocently.

He came close to her and whispered in her ear.

Madeline swallowed hard. If Roger heard this man's proposition, the poor fellow would be thrown into the nearest dungeon. On the other hand, Dafydd would probably scowl and tell her such remarks were nothing more than she deserved. As it was, she decided next time—if there was a next time—she would dress more modestly. For the present, she saw no help for it but to proceed as she had planned, so she smiled slyly at the farmer. "What will your wife say?"

"I ain't got a wife."

"Well...you *are* a good-looking fellow and I don't want my brother to beat me...." She glanced over her shoulder at the door of the alehouse. "Perhaps if you give me the silver first..."

The farmer quickly pulled out a fat purse of coins. She dropped the horse's rope, snatched the purse and hurried to the door of the alehouse. "Oh, thank you!" she cried over her shoulder at the stunned would-be lover.

"Hey!" he bellowed, grabbing hold of the rope. "Hey!"

She paused in the door of the alehouse. "Yes?"

The farmer, scowling, marched toward her. "We made a bargain—"

A figure came to stand behind Madeline and the young farmer turned rather pale. "He has given me what you wanted for the horse," Madeline said nervously, pushing herself back closer to Dafydd so that her buttocks came into mind-numbing contact with his body and she inadvertently gave him a fine view of her cleavage, as well.

He nodded wordlessly and glared at the fair-haired farmer. He had grudgingly agreed to Madeline's plan because he grew tired of arguing with her and because it *was* a risk for a Welshman to try to sell such a magnificent horse. On the other hand, it might have been better if he had pretended to be a Norman. After nearly a year in the monastery, with plenty of opportunity to observe the Norman brothers, he could manage it, at least long enough to sell the horse.

Madeline had told him to say nothing but to look very angry when she came to fetch him at the alehouse, so here he was, acting the angry, silent brother when he felt anything but brotherly. All in all, he suddenly realized, it was a good thing he wasn't supposed to talk much. He could scarcely think with her in such tantalizing proximity.

"He's not married," Madeline said to Dafydd sweetly, and the farmer suddenly looked less terrified.

"Do you . . . do you live nearby?" the young fellow stammered hopefully.

"No," Dafydd growled. He grabbed Madeline's arm and pulled her toward the main road.

"Here, you!" the farmer protested. "You shouldn't be so rough!"

Dafydd turned and stared at the farmer, who gulped audibly, then scurried into the alehouse.

Still clutching Madeline's arm, Dafydd marched toward the crowded marketplace.

"You can let go now," she said quietly when they were out of sight of the alehouse. His hand dropped to his side. "I got twice what you said," she continued triumphantly.

"How?"

She halted abruptly. "What do you mean by that?"

"I meant," he said grimly, facing her, "how did you manage to get twice as much?"

"Clever bargaining," she said slowly and deliberately.

"You've never bargained in your life."

"How do you know?"

"You *said* you've lived in a convent for the past ten years."

"The sisters have to eat, and make their clothing."

"So you were a clever trader for the convent?" he asked skeptically.

"No. But I watched Sister Ursula."

"And she was a clever trader?"

"Yes, she was. She learned from her father, who started out a penniless peasant and died exceedingly wealthy. Unlike *some* peasants, he had ambition."

Dafydd ignored her gibe and started to head toward the market again. "Pull up your shift. No doubt the sight of all your...wares...addled that fellow's wits."

"What do you care? I got the money," she said as she marched angrily beside him. "You're not really my brother, you know."

"For which I thank God." Anger was good, he told himself. If she was angry, then he could be angry. And if he was angry, then he wouldn't feel anything else.

"I will buy some food."

"And another dress."

"Very well."

"Not here. You have already attracted too much attention."

"I spoke to only a few."

He paused and ran his gaze over her body. She pulled her shift higher over her breasts. "Exactly," he muttered. "Every man you passed noticed you."

"But we need another horse."

"We'll get one at the next village."

"You've led us so far from the main road, Roger will not seek us here."

"I am taking every precaution," Dafydd replied.

"Then we can get food there, too?"

Dafydd reached into his tunic and produced a loaf of fine bread.

"Where did you get that?" Madeline demanded.

"The alehouse."

"With no money?" she asked skeptically.

This time, it was Dafydd who looked discomfited as his pace quickened.

"So, the serving wench took a liking to you."

He shrugged.

"She will certainly remember you at least as much as the farmer will remember me," she noted dryly. "But of course, I am forgetting that you can do no wrong. It will be a relief to poor, stupid me when you leave me at Lord Trevelyan's."

Dafydd halted abruptly, the blood draining from his face. "Who?"

"Lord Trevelyan's. Dafydd, what is it? What's the matter?"

"We will speak of this later," he said. "When we are alone."

Chapter Nine

Madeline followed Dafydd as he sauntered toward the bank of the river at the north end of the village. He seemed in no great hurry, and although she was extremely curious to know what had caused his unforeseen reaction to the mention of Lord Trevelyan's name, she would not quicken her pace like the little boy struggling to keep up with his brother. As far as she was concerned, she was as equal to this Welshman as she could be to any man.

Not that she considered him any common man. Even strolling, Dafydd's erect bearing made him seem more noble than many of the noblemen she recalled from her childhood. He was so handsome, too, in his dark Welsh way, and strong and good. So completely tempting. Now, here, in the deepening dusk, it did not seem so wrong that she had made love with him.

You only think so because you know you are not with child, she reminded herself. She had made that

fortunate discovery this morning, while they had
waited outside the village. The relief she felt had
been even more overwhelming than when Dafydd
had first come to her rescue, for if she had been
with child, she would have been in a morass of her
own making.

A mossy stone bridge of great antiquity crossed
the river, leading to a fork in the road. One way led
north and west, toward Lord Trevelyan's estate, the
other north and east. With twilight rapidly falling,
the air was cool and the scent of wildflowers drifted
about them. Behind Dafydd she could see the
slowly moving wheel of the mill. Birds sang in the
trees and she could hear, far-off in the village,
mothers calling errant children home.

Madeline drew in a deep breath. She enjoyed not
just the fragrance, but the freedom to do so. In the
convent, they were supposed to ignore even such
simple sensual delights as the scent of flowers or
fruit.

But she allowed herself only a moment's pleasure, for there were other more important things to
consider. "What is the matter? I realize Lord
Trevelyan is a Norman, but surely you surmised any
friends of mine would likely be Normans," Madeline said as soon as they were alone and far from
anyone's hearing. "Naturally I do not expect you
to ride into the central courtyard of the castle and

proclaim your identity. And we did have an agreement.''

He didn't reply at once.

''Well?'' she asked, halting, determined to find out what his reasons could be for wanting to break his bargain.

Dafydd pulled a branch from the nearest willow.

''Nor do I think it would be such a sin to spend the night in the comfort of an inn.''

''I will not spend the night with you in any inn.''

He made it sound as if she were proposing sharing his bed! She also noticed that he chose the less significant thing to speak of first. ''I am not suggesting we sleep together. I am simply tired of sleeping on the ground. What difference would a good night's lodging make?''

''You should have taken a feather bed from those peasants, too,'' he suggested sardonically.

''And run *more* risks?'' she answered sarcastically.

''People would ask too many questions if we lingered in the village,'' he said, his tone matter-of-fact.

''All right, so I will concede that we cannot stay in the village. Why won't you go with me to the border of Lord Trevelyan's demesne?''

"I cannot go onto Lord Trevelyan's lands," Dafydd said in a tone of such condescending finality that she ground her teeth in frustration.

"But why?"

"I might have guessed you would argue," he said with at least a matching frustration, for which she had no sympathy. If he would explain himself, then she might agree, but if he was simply expecting her to accept this change of plan with no opinion, as Roger expected her to marry without asking her consent, he was very wrong.

"I said I would take you someplace safe," he said. "Lord Trevelyan's estate will not be safe for me."

"Because you are a Welshman? I assure you, Dafydd, Lord Trevelyan is not such a narrow-minded man. Why, he married his own daughter to a Welshman. And he knighted him, too, and gave him land. So you see—"

"I cannot go there."

"I will see that no harm comes to you."

"I do not need to be protected by a woman."

"You didn't mind my 'protection' before, at Sir Guy's manor."

He fell back into the sullen silence she was getting rather used to.

"Very well," she said at last, "do not take me. But how will I get there? I cannot go alone."

"I will take you back to the village and find you an escort."

Madeline turned away and went closer to the running waters of the river. "Someone like that farmer, perhaps? He will be anxious to help, although I will not reward him in the way he would most expect. Can you tell me what he meant, Dafydd, by this?" She repeated the farmer's earthy proposition.

She hadn't quite been sure what reaction she expected from him, but she had expected *something*. Instead, he simply looked at her as if she were talking about the weather. Then he said, "I believe you know what he meant, my lady. You are no innocent."

"Not anymore," she retorted.

His face twisted into a scowl and he shrugged. "You and I both know the truth of what happened. I will take no blame."

"Take no credit, either."

"Indeed, I do not. I think I was a fool to even touch you. Tell me, my lady, did you make love with me to punish your brother? Or to prevent the marriage? Or did you think if I made love to you I must take you wherever you wish to go?"

"I will not explain my reasons to you. However, I *did* think you would keep your word and take me to safety. Is it that you are afraid of Lord Trevelyan?"

"No, I do not fear Trevelyan," he replied, "although I do not think he is the saint you believe him to be. He did his daughter a service marrying her to a Welshman."

Madeline pressed her lips together for a moment, then spoke firmly and deliberately. "I thought you wanted to get to Wales. Trevelyan's lands are on the border. He is sympathetic to the Welsh. Why, then, will you not take me there?"

"Because it is too dangerous for me."

"You could take me back to the convent."

"It would not be safe for me to go back that way, either."

"God's blood, leave me here then! I will find someone to escort me myself. I will ask nothing more of you."

"Your brother will find you if you go back toward the convent," he reminded her.

"What is that to you? *You* will still be safe, and when you are safe, you can brag how you had a nobleman's sister on the banks of a river one dark night!"

He stared at her as if she had run him through with a sword, shocked and horrified, and yes, in pain. At that moment, she would have given much to recall her hasty words.

Before she could say anything, Dafydd spoke, his voice coldly deliberate. "If you think me capable of such behavior, perhaps I should leave you here. You are finished with me anyway, are you not?"

"Dafydd, forgive me!" she cried, her pride forgotten when she saw the look in his eyes. "I should not have said such a thing!"

His only response was a scornfully raised eyebrow.

Apparently she had humbled herself for nothing. She, Lady Madeline de Montmorency, had asked forgiveness of a Welsh peasant only to be rewarded with such a look.

"Is there no other place you could go?" he said after a long moment where she was conscious only of her blushing embarrassment. "No other person, or convent, where you could find sanctuary?"

"Mother Bertrilde is a powerful woman and my brother a powerful and respected lord," she replied, trying to regain her self-control. "No one would wish to offend either of them by giving me sanctuary, of that I am sure. However, there is one other place, the castle of Lord Gervais. My parents knew him well, and Roger was sent there to be trained after they died."

"And is it your intention to seek another escort, my lady?"

Her first impulse was to answer affirmatively. She didn't want him, didn't need him...but she did. And more, she trusted him. She suddenly realized there was no one else in the whole world she trusted nearly so much. Yet to humble herself again!

"I have said I would help you and I am a man of my word. Where does this castle lie?"

"To the north," she replied.

He nodded.

"And the east. Well inside England and away from Wales." She waited for him to refuse, but to her surprise, he did not.

Instead, he cautiously asked, "How far to the east?"

"I don't know. We did not study maps in the convent."

"Surely there was one of the holy sisters that spoke of such things—Sister Elizabeth or Sister Ursula or perhaps Sister Mary Francis the Mapmaker?"

"Make sport of me and my teachers all you like. They have already proven beneficial and you cannot deny that."

He did not deign to answer her directly. "Have you *no* idea of the distance?"

"The town is called Bridgeford Wells."

"Bridgeford Wells?"

"Bridgeford Wells," she repeated slowly and deliberately.

"I have heard of it. It is nearly sixty miles away, and we will have to walk."

"I can do it—if you can," she challenged.

"I will take you there."

"There will be one certain advantage. Roger would not be looking for us that way," she said, growing more enthusiastic about the plan—and not happy because Dafydd was going with her. "He will guess I have gone to Lord Trevelyan's. And if anyone is looking for you, will they not think you will go to Wales?"

"Since what time has a novice learned strategies?"

"You must agree that I am right."

"They cannot know for certain I am a Welshman."

She gave him a skeptical look. "Did you tell the holy brothers you were from Cornwall?"

"I never said a word the whole time I was with them."

"You cannot disguise your coloring."

"Are there no dark-haired Normans?"

"None like you." It was the truth, yet the moment the words were out of her mouth, she wanted to call them back, because they were true. There was no other man quite like him in all of England, but he did not need to know that she thought so. "Well, Dafydd, are you willing to take me there, or not?"

"I will go with you to Bridgeford Wells, where you will see that I am paid enough to get me to Wales and that I am guaranteed safe passage. That is all I want from you."

"That is all you will get."

Much later that night, when the ground in the forest was damp with dew, and Dafydd was still awake and keeping watch while Madeline slept a few feet away, he realized that she was shivering in her sleep.

His first impulse was to lie beside her to give her the warmth of his body. The second was to let her continue to shiver as a punishment for her behavior toward him during the day. She still acted as if she were the one in charge, as if she wanted to forget they had ever made love, and worst of all, as if he were a dishonorable coward. If she had been a man, he would have left her standing there, and probably bloodied.

But she was a woman, and a woman who aroused both passion and tenderness within him beyond anything he had even suspected he was capable of feeling. Then to have her say such things!

It would have been better if he *was* a dishonorable coward, because then he could leave her with no guilt.

He would take a route that was circuitous and hopefully difficult to follow, surmising that Roger de Montmorency was as single-minded and determined as his sister, and he would not rest until he found her.

She moaned softly and shifted in her sleep. It would not do for her to become ill, he reflected. Indeed, if she was sick when she reached safety, her friends might blame him. If she became so sick she died—although he could not truly believe anyone so vitally alive as Madeline de Montmorency *could* die—they might come hunting for him with vigor.

Yet they had no means to kindle a fire. With great caution lest he wake her, he lay beside her, his broad back against her slender one, with his arms crossed against his chest. She nestled against him with a sigh.

Dafydd muttered an eloquent curse and wished that he could hurry the dawn.

Just after the noon meal, Lord Trevelyan rose with a pleasant smile on his face when he saw who approached him in his large, well-appointed hall. "Roger!" he called jovially as the Norman knight marched toward the high table without pausing to acknowledge any of the luxuriously attired lesser nobility seated in the crowded room. They all stopped talking and waited with obvious curiosity, the women especially, and more than one had a lustful gleam in her demurely downcast eyes.

"This is a most unexpected pleasure!" Lord Trevelyan continued. "Have you then decided to accept my offer of accommodation while taking your sister home for her wedding? I hope so, and tomorrow we can all set out together."

Lord Trevelyan paused, his countenance altering to one of concern. "Is something amiss? Where is Madeline?" He glanced at his son-in-law, Hu Morgan, who had been sitting beside him until Roger de Montmorency entered, when he had risen to greet their visitor. Lord Trevelyan's gaze returned to Roger, who halted before the dais. Roger looked sick and exhausted, as if he were at the end of his considerable strength.

"What has happened?" Lord Trevelyan demanded, seeing an urgency that dismissed any courtesies.

"May I speak with you in private? At once?" Roger asked, and Lord Trevelyan couldn't help noticing that whatever was amiss, it had not subdued Roger de Montmorency's imperious manner. However, that was not important now.

"Of course," the older man replied. "Come with me to the solar. You, too, Hu."

The two men trailed behind Lord Trevelyan and Roger surreptitiously surveyed Morgan. He had heard of this Welshman, for his parents had been good friends of Lord Trevelyan. Roger had not been at the wedding of Liliana Trevelyan, being in the north on business for Baron DeGuerre, and like many, had wondered at Lord Trevelyan's choice for his only child.

Now it did not seem such a bizarre match. Morgan was a fine-looking fellow, whose movements bore the mark of a natural warrior and whose eyes glowed with unmistakable intelligence. And of course, Lord Trevelyan was so rich and had so many influential relatives, few would dare to question his decisions.

When they reached the solar, Roger forgot Morgan and got at once to the matter of primary concern. "Madeline is missing," he announced.

"*What?*" Trevelyan asked incredulously.

Briefly, and passing over such unimportant matters as Madeline's reluctance to abide by the plans her brother had made, he explained what had happened in the past few days.

"This is indeed unfortunate news," Lord Trevelyan said, shaking his gray-haired head. "I wish with all my heart your sister had made her way here, Roger, but unfortunately, she has not."

Roger did not take a proffered seat but began to pace with agitation, noticing nothing about the small stone chamber, although it was furnished with a simple elegance lacking in most Normans' private rooms. "I had thought she would come here with all speed."

"We would have been only too glad to welcome her," Lord Trevelyan said. "But now my men will be at your disposal to help in the search for her. Hu will organize them."

"How long has she been missing?" Morgan asked, going to the door. "If she is alone and on foot, she may very well be traveling slowly and with caution."

Roger sighed, and finally sat down in an elaborately carved oaken chair, his gaze coming to rest on Lord Trevelyan's Welsh son-in-law. "We think she is not alone, and whether on foot or not, I do not know."

"Not alone?" Lord Trevelyan asked, puzzled.

"She may be with a Welshman who came to the monastery of St. Christopher's badly injured. He left there and Father Gabriel thinks that he may have met with her."

Lord Trevelyan and Morgan exchanged glances. "There has been no request for ransom?" Morgan inquired.

"None." Roger's lips twisted into a smile. "Father Gabriel thinks he may be trying to help her. I am not convinced."

"You said the Welshman was injured," Morgan observed.

"Apparently," Roger muttered. "What does it matter? He stole some clothing, coins and a horse when he left, but they abandoned them at Sir Guy's manor. He may have another horse, though, stolen from that reprobate."

"What does he look like, this Welshman?" Morgan asked.

"You'll have to ask Father Gabriel," an obviously confused Roger replied impatiently. "He's with my men."

Lord Trevelyan went to the door and called for a servant, whom he dispatched to the hall with orders to fetch the priest.

While they waited, Lord Trevelyan poured wine for Roger and his son-in-law. "Liliana will be most distressed at this news," he said quietly. When he saw Morgan's questioning look, he said, "She played with Madeline when they were children."

The sound of hurrying feet clattering along the stone corridor announced the arrival of Father

Gabriel. The priest was ushered into the room by the servant, who went out and closed the door softly behind him.

"This Welshman," Morgan began at once, "describe him for me. And the nature of his wounds."

"My sister is more important—" Roger interrupted.

"Quiet!" Morgan barked, and Roger scowled at the impudent young Welshman. "Tell me," he ordered the clergyman.

Father Gabriel complied, his expression somewhat wary. When he finished, Morgan nodded and looked at his father-in-law. "It could be him, the one I thought was dead."

"Dead? What are you talking about? Do you know this fellow?" Roger demanded.

"If it is the same man, I know something of him. I thought perhaps he had bled to death, but now I know I could be wrong."

"What about him?"

"He was with a band of rebels who attacked my manor and killed my friend."

"*What?*" Roger's glare darted from Morgan to Father Gabriel.

"Him it was killed the leader of this band, who in turn tried to kill him. That's how he was wounded. I let him go. To die, I thought."

"Well, apparently he did not." Roger flashed another angry frown at Father Gabriel. "Thanks to the holy brothers of St. Christopher. And do you also think my sister will be safe in his company?"

Morgan nodded. "I believe so, yes. Indeed, I have no fears for her, if she is with him."

Lord Trevelyan, who had listened thoughtfully all the while, spoke. "Let us assume, for the present, that Madeline is with this fellow. Where else might they go, if not to me? Has your sister other friends where she might seek help?"

"Unless she has met them in the convent, no."

"Could that not be possible? Have you asked the Mother Superior?"

Roger had not, and he realized at once that he might have made a grave error. He went to the door and sent the servant to fetch Albert. When his friend came, he said, "Go back to the convent and tell Mother Bertrilde what has happened. Then ask about her friends there. It could be she has gone somewhere we have never even considered. And try to keep this business as quiet as possible."

"At once, my lord," Albert said before he hurried from the hall.

Hu Morgan made a brief obeisance. "In the meantime, my lord, Sir Roger, I will summon my men to search," he said. He gave them the briefest of smiles. "I would like to see that man again."

"God's wounds, is this fellow some kind of saint?" Roger muttered. As he watched Morgan leave, he reflected that he would never understand the Welsh, and he didn't really want to.

"I will go, too," he announced. His voice dropped. "In case he decides to set him free again."

Fortunately, Morgan did not hear that last remark, or Roger's sarcastic tone.

Both Lord Trevelyan and Father Gabriel laid a detaining hand on Roger's arm, one on each side. "What is the meaning of this?" Roger growled.

"You look terrible," Lord Trevelyan said.

"He was wounded in the skirmish with the outlaws, my lord," Father Gabriel explained. "I fear he is overtaxing himself."

"Yes," Lord Trevelyan agreed. "Stay and rest awhile here, Roger," he offered. "You won't do Madeline any good if you're sick."

As much as Roger would have liked to disagree, he felt sick and dizzy, weak and exhausted. "Very well," he mumbled, turning back to sit down. "For one night only." He glanced at the holy man, who wisely did not protest.

"Perhaps Madeline has deemed it best to go home to your castle, fearing other dangers," Lord Trevelyan said pensively.

Father Gabriel cleared his throat audibly, and the two men looked at him. "There is, perhaps, another reason Lady Madeline might not come here," the priest said.

"Oh?"

"Yes. But Sir Roger would know best about that."

"She didn't approve of my plans," Roger admitted grudgingly. "She wanted to choose her own husband."

Lord Trevelyan sighed, and there was sympathy and understanding in his eyes. "Well I know how it is to deal with such a female. My own daughter had exactly the same notion."

"And you let her choose. You set a dangerous precedent there, Trevelyan," Roger said bitterly. "I would lay a good wager that she heard about Liliana and her Welshman."

"It was the best decision I ever made, Roger," the lord replied firmly. "I remember Madeline very well. I would have asked to be foster father to her when your parents died, if my own wife had been alive. And if she had not fought so much with Liliana—two stubborn girls would have been a nightmare. I take it she is stubborn still?"

"Yes." Roger finally sampled Lord Trevelyan's wine. "I was only doing what I thought best."

"What *you* thought best, or DeGuerre?"

"He is my overlord. I had no objections to the match."

"Have you met Chilcott?"

Roger eyed Lord Trevelyan warily. "No. Why do you ask? Have you?"

Lord Trevelyan sighed. "No, but I remember his father. A lascivious, brutal man. An uncle took Reginald away to Sicily, and I think that was a good thing. I know a few men who have met him there. Fortunately, I understand Chilcott is not at all like his father. Indeed, rather the opposite, being a harmless and simple fellow."

"So I was given to understand."

"Yesss..."

"But?"

"But do you think Madeline would be happy with him? How did this arrangement come about, if you don't mind my asking?"

"DeGuerre contrived it."

"You are untroubled by that?"

Roger's eyes narrowed. "Should I be? I trust my lord with my life."

"Your sister's, too, apparently," Lord Trevelyan said mildly.

"The contract has been made, signed and delivered. She should not have run off!"

"I am not saying you did wrong and she did right. And I am not forgetting she could be being held against her will by this man, who may not be the same fellow Hu met before. Even if he is, I know less of him than Hu, although I respect Hu's judgment. What I am trying to say is, I don't know that Chilcott would be the most suitable match for Madeline, unless she has changed greatly."

"She hasn't," Roger muttered.

"Might it not be wise, when she is found, to at least allow some flexibility?"

"DeGuerre wants our families united."

"Do you know why?"

Roger's lips curled into a knowing smile. "Indeed, I do. Although you are too diplomatic to say so, I already know Chilcott is a fool. DeGuerre thought to have him allied to a better commander."

"To you?"

"To me."

Lord Trevelyan nodded. "That has the ring of truth to it. DeGuerre is a clever man who appreciates the value of a good commander and has the wisdom not to offend a wealthy man, even if he is a fool. But you have no objections to the alliance, then?"

"None whatsoever." Roger thought a moment, regarding this old friend of his parents and deciding to tell him the truth, although he had some difficulty forming the words. His mind was foggy, because he was tired. "I thought Madeline would be safe with a fellow like Chilcott. Another, stronger man might look askance at her stubborn whims. I thought he would let her have a freer hand."

"Well," Lord Trevelyan said, giving Roger a fatherly smile, "now we come to it. Did you tell her this?"

"No."

Lord Trevelyan sighed for the stubborn arrogance of this older brother, then smiled. "I would suggest you not be reticent when she is found."

"Then you think we will find her?" For the first time since Madeline had disappeared, Roger permitted some of his doubt and anxiety to show.

"If she is anywhere within thirty miles of here, Hu will find her," Roger heard Lord Trevelyan say as the room seemed to swirl about him and he fell into a swoon.

Chapter Ten

"Look! There's a badger!" Madeline cried softly, pointing at the chubby creature ambling across the path. The day was warm and sunny, the sky free of clouds, the air fresh with the scent of blossoms and growing things.

Dafydd's only response was a frown. She seemed curiously excited by the sight, just as she had seemed rather jovial lately, no doubt because she felt she was in command of the situation.

Let her think what she liked, he told himself. It made no difference to him. At least she had purchased a less revealing gown, just as he had wasted no time purchasing a flint. There would be no more nights beside her, he had vowed when he had awakened two days ago to find her snuggled contentedly in his arms. Since then, he had been careful to stay as far from her as he could.

Unfortunately, that was not proving very easy. Although the new garment she wore was not nearly so tight as the other, he was well aware of her shapely, exciting body beneath it. He also caught himself simply enjoying watching her: her smile, her eyes, her hair, her gestures.

God's blood, he should have gone with that serving wench at the alehouse. He didn't doubt she would have been only too willing, and then perhaps he would find it easier to ignore Madeline.

"I need to rest," Madeline said a few moments later, not waiting for an answer as she sat down under a large and ancient oak tree.

Dafydd frowned and set down their pack. To speak the truth, the shade was cool and so welcome, but he would not admit that he could use the rest, too. Nor would he tell her that his shoulder ached a little from too many nights sleeping on the cold, hard ground. "We have not come very far this morning," he said, furtively examining her as he sat beside her. "You told me you could make the journey."

"I can," she replied. "I am just tired and need a brief rest."

She did look pale, and there were dark circles under her eyes. Why, she looked not just tired, but sick, which worried him. Despite her assurances, this trek was too much for a highborn woman surely used to walking no farther than from the sleeping quarters of the convent to its chapel. He should take better care to see that she rested. They still had several miles to go.

"Would you care for some water?" he asked not unkindly.

She shook her head, her hand on her stomach.

Which made him think of something else. Perhaps the night they had made love, they had made something else, too. "Do you feel . . ." He paused, not certain of the Norman word for nauseous.

"It is nothing serious," she assured him with a weak smile. "It is my women's time."

So, not with child. He told himself that naturally he was pleased by this.

"Quiet!" she whispered suddenly. "Listen!"

From the distance came the far-off muffled jingle of a harness, a low baying of hounds, the hoof-beats of horses and the sound of men's voices. Madeline thought she recognized one of the voices, but before she could be sure, Dafydd grabbed hold of her arm and pulled her into the nearby bracken. Her cramps forgotten, she paid no heed to the thorns scratching her arms, either.

"Dogs!" Dafydd swore softly. Quickly he led her farther until they splashed through a narrow, muddy stream. "Up there!" he ordered, taking hold of her and shoving her up to the lowest branch of an oak tree. "Go as high as you can and keep still!"

"Where are you—?"

He didn't answer, for he was already shinnying up another nearby oak tree with the bundle's rope between his teeth. Through the branches of her tree, Madeline could make out a group of riders, five in number, on the road, with kindly Lord Trevelyan at their head and another knight at his side. They had dogs with them, but the beasts seemed confused and unsure of the trail.

She had but to climb down from this tree and show herself to Lord Trevelyan to be finished with this adventure comprised of dread and discomfort. Lord Trevelyan would take her to his fine castle, where she could bathe and have a hot meal and a decent bed. Nor would Lord Trevelyan, who had a daughter near in age to her and who had known her from infancy, let Roger bully her into marriage.

Yes, all she had to do was climb down from this tree... and leave Dafydd behind forever.

She stayed in the tree.

"I think we've come too far," Lord Trevelyan said, pulling his horse to a stop not far from her tree. "They wouldn't be this far east, Hu."

"They might, if he's trying to lead us a merry chase," replied the man Madeline realized must be Lord Trevelyan's son-in-law. Hu Morgan was a Welshman, too, and she glanced at Dafydd—and was startled by the grim look of recognition on

Dafydd's face as he watched Morgan. How did Dafydd know Lord Trevelyan's son-in-law?

"He's clever, so it's not going to be easy catching him," Morgan observed.

Madeline was glad she had hesitated. As much as she wanted to enjoy the creature comforts she had done without of late, she might have endangered Dafydd. That would be a poor recompense for his help.

"But what of Madeline? Surely she would find a way to help us locate her?"

Morgan nodded. "I have to think Father Gabriel might have hit on something there. Perhaps the lady doesn't want to be found."

Who was this Father Gabriel, and how did he know so much about her? She glanced again at Dafydd but could detect nothing in his still, expressionless face. He blended into the foliage like an animal used to hiding from a formidable predator.

"I don't know what I'm going to tell Roger," Lord Trevelyan said, shaking his head. "Is he any better this morning? I thought I would faint myself, to see a man like Roger swoon!"

Madeline suppressed a gasp. She had assumed Roger was well. Or at least she had told herself so, selfishly focusing on her own problems. She leaned forward to hear better.

"It is not serious. Father Gabriel is quite convinced he simply needs to rest. Liliana says he's looking much better this morning."

"Thank heaven for that," Lord Trevelyan replied, and Madeline echoed his sentiment. "This looks hopeless, Hu. I suggest we turn back to the main road."

Morgan nodded and the mounted men turned their beasts back the way they had come. Madeline began to breathe easier, until Morgan paused and glanced back over his shoulder, directly at her tree. She held her breath.

But just as quickly, Morgan turned and rejoined the others, and they disappeared from view.

Madeline looked toward Dafydd, but he made no move to get down, and neither did she. She would wait until he thought it safe.

She eyed him from her perch, noting the thoughtful expression on his face, the still-grim set of his lips and his watchful eyes.

After what seemed an interminable time, Dafydd climbed down and went to the bottom of her tree. He caught her deftly as she slowly made her way down and set her lightly on her feet. "Do you think they saw us?" she asked anxiously.

He shook his head. "No, or not going away."

"How do you know Hu Morgan?"

"Who's that?"

"You know as well as I. The man with Lord Trevelyan."

"That was Lord Trevelyan?"

"Yes," she answered, puzzled because she believed that he truly didn't know the older man, yet she was just as certain he knew Morgan.

"Why did you hide, then?" he asked, his gaze shrewd and all too penetrating.

"I wasn't sure who it was at first," she said, taking refuge in a lie.

"They were in plain sight."

"It was so unexpected. I was confused and uncertain..."

"*You* uncertain?" He gave her a skeptical look. "Your brother is in Trevelyan's castle, too, I gather. You could be riding there now, safe and sound."

"I...I know. I didn't want them to take you prisoner."

"You it was assured me I'd have nothing to fear from Trevelyan."

"And I still think so. I just can't be sure, and I owe it to you to see that no harm comes to you."

"Ever the gracious lady," he replied sarcastically. "I don't need your protection."

"Maybe I *should* have gone with Lord Trevelyan."

"Go after him, then," Dafydd challenged, crossing his arms defiantly.

Did he want her to go? she wondered, suddenly afraid to look into his eyes and see confirmation there. Then she realized she was behaving like a coward. If he wanted her gone, she should face the truth and leave. She took a deep breath and raised her eyes to his. "Is that what you want?" she demanded.

"Yes," he said, but she saw a deeper truth in his eyes.

"Truly?" she asked, wanting him to say what she saw in the dark depths, wanting him to admit to the emotion there that set her heart on fire and filled her with wild elation.

He could not continue to meet her steadfast gaze. "What does it matter what I want?" he muttered at last. "I am a Welsh peasant and you are a Norman noblewoman."

"Tell me, right here and now, that you wish I would go away and that you would be happy never to see me again," she insisted. "Or let me go with you to Wales."

"This is foolishness!" he cried, turning and striding away.

He could not bring himself to lie to her. He knew now he was no better than a boy besotted by his first love. He had realized it the moment he understood that she could have left him there, to go with

Lord Trevelyan. At that instant, the idea of being without her had filled his heart with pain.

So this was love, he thought bitterly. A wondrous, desperate emotion. Despite her words, he knew that they could not be together. Too much existed to separate them. Oh, perhaps not now, when they were both filled with the heat and joy of their passion, but later, when the days passed, and she began to think upon the things she had given up. No, there was no future for them.

"Dafydd, answer me!"

"Madeline," he said forcefully, "I have nothing to offer you. No castle, no money, no home of any kind."

"I don't care."

"You should. You will, in time."

"Listen to me, Dafydd. Life under Mother Bertrilde's rule was as harsh as anything you have experienced. I would gladly trade everything my brother or any other Norman could give me to stay with you for the rest of my life."

A fleeting feeling of hope and joy crossed his face, only to disappear nearly as quickly when he twisted away. "No matter what we feel, it is impossible."

"*Why?* You love me. I know you do."

"Madeline, say no more," he warned. "You are who you are, and I am who I am. There is no changing things." He started to walk again, and she fell into step beside him.

"Where are we going?"

"To take you to Lord Trevelyan."

She halted abruptly. He thought things could not change. But they had for her the moment she had set eyes upon him, and she would make him see that she was not the woman he seemed to think she was.

She was a woman passionately in love with him, and try as he might to deny it, she knew he loved her, too. He simply saw the obstacles, but she was not one to let an obstacle stand in her way. She only needed more time to let him see that they could have a life together, that she was indeed willing to cast aside wealth to be with him. "You said you would take me to Lord Gervais."

"Trevelyan's is closer."

"What about Morgan?"

"Yes, I was forgetting Morgan." He sighed wearily. "Very well, to Bridgeford Wells, then."

They reached the stream, and he started to walk through it, following its course.

"Must we do this?" she asked, lifting her skirts. "It's so muddy."

"Do you want to go to Bridgeford Wells or not?" he demanded without a backward glance.

"Yes."

"Then we don't want to leave any trail for dogs. Now be quiet and follow me."

She felt a stab of doubt. He was being so rude—maybe she had overestimated what he felt for her. Still, there was no doubt in her heart that she wanted to stay with him, safe and free. Nevertheless, his cautions had lodged a nagging doubt in her heart. Was it possible that she was being naive? Was he right to think that the way she felt about him could change, that she might come to regret her life with him?

After they had walked north some distance, thankfully leaving the stream and continuing through the woods, she realized that he was holding his shoulder. "Are you in pain?" she asked softly.

"That was an uncomfortable place to wait, in that tree." He sounded tired, but not so cantankerous as before, which she took to be a good sign.

"How do you know Morgan?" She came up beside him, noting his drawn face. He had been so worried about her and yet he did not look as if this journey were so easy for him, either.

"Him it was left me to die in the mountains."

"*He* wounded you?" She nodded toward his shoulder.

"No. That was Ivor, the leader of the rebels I was with. I didn't approve of his tactics, and he didn't approve of my opposition."

"So he fought you?"

"Yes."

"What happened? Did you kill him?"

"No. Morgan did that, when I was lying as good as dead in his hall."

"Then how did Hu Morgan come to leave you on the mountain to die?"

"I asked him to."

She halted, and waited for him to stop and turn toward her. "You asked him to, and he agreed? Why, if you were a rebel?"

"Because I tried to stop Ivor, I suppose. Or perhaps it was the eloquence of my request," he added sarcastically.

"Or perhaps he saw what I see, an honorable man."

"Madeline," Dafydd said with a sigh, "don't. I don't love you. I'll never love you. You're making a fool of yourself."

"I'm not the one lying, Dafydd. If you don't love me, why are you taking me to Lord Gervais?"

"Because I said I would."

"So you're an honorable man."

"But I don't love you."

"Dafydd," she said softly, approaching him and putting her hands on his shoulders. "Honorable men do not lie, so I want you to tell me you do not care for me, if that is the truth."

"Madeline," he warned. "Enough of this!"

"I'm sorry I was so discourteous to you, after that night. I was afraid."

"I don't want to talk about that. It was a mistake, for both of us."

"It was before I knew how you felt, before I knew you truly cared about me."

"I never said I do."

"Now who's being stubborn? You do care. I can see it in your eyes. But if I had a child out of wedlock, it would have been terrible. I would be shamed. No one would respect me."

"Probably no Normans," he agreed. He lifted her hands from his shoulders, then joined them together within his own, looking down at them. "Why didn't you tell me of your fears sooner?" he whispered. "Did you think so little of me, Madeline?"

"I thought it was not your concern. I was the one, Dafydd, who came to you that night."

"But it would be the child of us both, Madeline," he said quietly. "Do you think I would abandon my own flesh and blood? Do you think I would leave my child to be raised by Normans?"

"I am a Norman, Dafydd," she reminded him. "The baby would be mine, too. But it doesn't matter, anyway. I am not with child."

"Good," he said, letting go of her hands. "If you can believe I would leave you to fend for yourself and the child alone, then you know nothing of me, and it is better this way."

"I know *something* of you, Dafydd. I know that you are good and honorable. I would know more, if you would tell me."

"But don't you see, Madeline? We are from two different worlds."

"Then we can make our own," she said. "Don't you understand, Dafydd? We won't have to be alone ever again."

He stared at her. Of all the things she could have said, this was the one that pierced the armor of his practical assertions. He knew what it was to be alone, too well. And so did she. Could their love not mean an end to such loneliness forever? Perhaps, just perhaps, they could share a life together.

He took hold of her shoulders and pulled her toward him, staring into her eyes. She shifted closer, bringing her body close to his. "What is it you wish for, Dafydd? What do you seek?"

"Peace," he answered truthfully, aware of her, loving her. "A home. A wife. Children."

"As I want a husband who loves me. Children. A home. I want *you*, Dafydd."

"Madeline," he whispered, bending to kiss her. He found a promise there, of happiness and love and family long lost to his life.

This was like a tale told by a bard. A fairy story of a princess and a peasant. Only the princess always discovered the peasant was a prince in disguise, and Madeline would find no such ending to this story. He pushed her away. "Madeline, this is wrong. This is a dream."

"No, this is our world," she whispered fervently. "I love you, Dafydd, with all my heart." She sank onto the ground and drew him down beside her. "It is absolutely right. Make love with me, Dafydd."

He wanted her, now and always. He loved her, with his whole heart. With all his being. Her life was his life, her dreams were his dreams, her fears, his fears... "What if you get with child?" he asked, nearly insensible with desire for her, yet prepared to rein in his yearning if that was what she wanted.

"It doesn't matter. Nothing would make me happier than to bear your child."

"Nothing would make me happier than having you for my wife," he whispered.

With gentle passion, he lay beside her, taking his time to explore her willing flesh, to taste her lips, to bury his hands in her hair as he had envisioned so many times.

But Madeline's patience for such lingering, tantalizing loving did not last long. She drew him to her, tugging his tunic off to expose his muscular chest. With heated caresses and whimpers of need, she quickly drove him to a peak of arousal that matched her own.

"Yes!" she cried as he entered her, driving deep with one swift motion. Then, with excruciating deliberation, he slowed and lifted her, shifting until she leaned against his chest, her legs around his waist.

With an instinct born of desire and need, she began to move against him, each thrust of her hips rewarded with a moan from him, which grew to a growl and then, as she reached the limit of tension, his cry of release drowned in her own.

She rested against him, her face against his chest, the sound of his rapid heartbeat in her ear.

"Madeline," he whispered hoarsely, "I don't think I could bear to live without you."

"You won't have to," she said with a sigh.

"Can you be happy in Wales?"

"If you are there, I will be."

He chuckled. "Oh, that I could be as certain of things as you are! But I will take you at your word. We'll go to the west tomorrow."

She pulled back, her brow furrowed with concern. "I should go to Bridgeford Wells first, Dafydd. We're not very far from there now, are we?"

"Why?"

"I owe it to Roger to let him know what's happened, and to make sure he stops looking for me."

He had forgotten Sir Roger de Montmorency. Yes, it was her duty to find a way to let her brother know that she was well and safe, but would a man like Sir Roger listen to Madeline? Worse, would he permit her to marry a Welshman, even one whose family had once been Welsh nobility, and to thwart his plans?

"I can leave a message with Lord Gervais," Madeline said. "Fortunately, Roger is not able to chase us himself, although I thank God he is not seriously ill."

Dafydd sighed and embraced her, letting her nestle against him. He could not believe that Roger would give up the search that easily. Still, if their best hope was to inform her brother that she was no longer his concern, that would have to be the course they took.

Madeline moved away and reached for the pack. She took out a thick blanket. "Here. It's not a feather bed, but at least we will be warm," she said, lying beside him and pulling the blanket over them both. "Tell me about Wales, Dafydd."

He wrapped her in his arms. "If you will tell me about your life before I met you."

She smiled and nodded. Then, letting himself hope, he talked of the land of his fathers and listened to the stories of her childhood until the moon was high.

Chapter Eleven

Although her parents had enjoyed Lord Gervais'
hospitality many times and he had visited them,
Madeline had never been to Bridgeford Wells. The
prospect of finally seeing this large and prosperous
town added to the joy and excitement of the past
few days, and her first view of it did not disap-
point her. The town was scattered over a wide area,
reaching from the broad, meandering river dotted
with boats past what had once been a protective
wall and now seemed to be more of a location for
people to lean their buildings against, to the gently
sloping wooded hill where she and Dafydd paused.
Many of the houses outside the wall were of more
than one story, and bespoke a well-to-do merchant
class.

The steady movement of people within and
without the town reminded her of a colony of ants.
Except that it was not the town that was the ant-
hill, but the huge, impressive stone fortress on a rise

behind it. Madeline knew the site had once boasted only a motte-and-bailey stronghold built of wood and wattle and daub. For the past several years, however, Lord Gervais had been rebuilding on the site, until his castle was the equal to any other defensive edifice in all the land.

Madeline glanced at Dafydd and saw that his brow was furrowed with concern, which did not surprise her. Here was a prime example of the might of the Normans, surely not something any Welshman would wish to see. To her, though, Lord Gervais' castle meant her freedom. All she had to do was tell him to relay the news of her decision to Roger; then she could go with Dafydd.

It could be that Dafydd was also worried because they had had to hide more carefully last night. Although she was traveling with Dafydd of her own volition, they had decided it would be wise to be cautious until she was able to explain her decision to Lord Gervais, in case Roger had sent search parties ahead. There had been many people on the road yesterday, too, something she had ascribed to their proximity to a large town. She thought Dafydd was far too anxious, but had not questioned his decision. He was wiser than she in such matters, and was in more jeopardy, so far in Norman territory. Of course, as her betrothed, he would be safe, but better to take care and avoid trouble before it started.

"You don't have to come any farther," Madeline said. "I can go the rest of the way by myself. I can meet you here later, after I have seen Lord Gervais."

Dafydd turned away from his contemplation of Bridgeford Wells and Lord Gervais' well-built castle. "No. I'll go with you. This place is so crowded, you might be in danger."

Unlike Roger's arrogant treatment of her, she found Dafydd's protectiveness touching, because she knew he valued her for herself, not as an instrument to fulfill his plans. "I assure you, this town will be safe enough, although I wonder what is happening to make everyone come here. It seems to be a festival."

"It's May Day," Dafydd replied, nodding at a giggling group of young girls tripping through the wide gate, their arms loaded with flowers: pink campion, whinberry blossoms, apple blossoms, blue, pink and white milkwort, yellow speedwell, to name but a few that Madeline recognized.

"Yes! Look," she exclaimed. "They've got the pole and see how they've decorated the doors. I hadn't noticed before."

Dafydd started walking toward a large group of talking, laughing peasants. "Two strangers will be less likely to be noticed if everyone is busy celebrating," he remarked with satisfaction as they fell in behind them.

"I haven't been at a May Day for so long," she murmured, stopping for a moment to pick some yellow cowslip at the side of the road. Around them, birds chattered gaily, as if they, too, sensed it was a holiday. The sky was a brilliant blue, dotted with clouds that might turn to storm clouds later, but for now, were mere puffs that provided occasional shade. "Not since I was a little girl. Mother Bertrilde thought it was too pagan."

"Mother Bertrilde must have been a hardhearted creature."

"Oh, she was. But very devout. And I suppose she meant well enough," Madeline said merrily. She noticed how his gaze kept straying to the castle, which did seem rather like a great stone vulture looming over the river and the town.

"Dafydd?" She halted and put a detaining hand on his arm. Another company of hearty peasants, laughing and joking, passed them with a greeting and a wave. She waited until they had gone by before she continued. "Dafydd, would you mind if I waited a little before I went to see Lord Gervais? I would so dearly like to enjoy the May Day."

"I would rather be away from here."

"Yes," she replied with a nod. "I know. But look—they've set the pole on the green. Can't we stay just for a little? Please?"

Dafydd surveyed the crowd. The place was full of Normans. And Saxons. And some Welshmen, too, by the looks of them. What if somebody recognized him? What if a voice suddenly shouted, "That fellow there—wasn't he one of Ivor Rhodri's men?" And yet, Madeline wanted to stay and she was looking at him with such an adorable, delectable excitement in her shining eyes. "I suppose no one will pay much attention," he said, hoping it would be so.

She smiled gloriously, and his heart leapt in his breast. She was his, and he could scarcely believe it. He loved her, and wanted to make her happy. What harm could a little celebration do?

There was more than a touch of grim determination on Sir Roger de Montmorency's face as his cortege approached the final part of their journey to Bridgeford Wells. He could see, even from this distance, that Lord Gervais had finished the keep at last, and a fine-looking structure it was. Heaven help any fool that tried to take that castle! Or starve them out with a siege. It would take years, given the wells inside and the storehouses full of provision.

Thank God, the town was now only a mile or two away. It was nearly noon, but he knew Lord Gervais would not think their arrival inconvenient. If anything, he would bemoan the fact that they had not been able to partake of the first meal of the day. They might have, if the road hadn't been crowded with peasants, peddlers and other revelers apparently intent on celebrating the first day of May as loudly and inconveniently as possible.

Behind, Roger could hear Bredon and the hounds, and he wondered if it would have been better to leave them with Morgan and Trevelyan, who had given their promise to continue the search for Madeline when Roger left, after Father Gabriel had finally given his approval for his patient to ride.

Albert reined in beside him. "A fine day, my lord, and I must say you are looking very well."

"So I should. Two days abed! Treated like a helpless infant! I should have insisted that priest get back to his infirmary." He turned and scowled at Father Gabriel, riding placidly some ways behind.

"He wouldn't have gone," Albert said. "I think he's curious to see what happens."

"Him and everybody else who hears about this business," Roger growled. "Two days, and in that time, who knows where Madeline might have gone, or what might have happened to her?"

"Morgan seemed quite convinced that she was headed in this direction, and I must agree that if she did not go to Lord Trevelyan's, she would probably come here."

Roger only frowned even more. "And how does he know this? What evidence? Nothing but a hunch, he claims." Roger sighed skeptically. "Probably some kind of Welsh mysticism. Second sight. Saw it in the entrails of a sheep, perhaps. Maybe I am the greater fool for following the man's advice."

Albert cleared his throat awkwardly. "Well, Roger, if Madeline is not here, you can enlist more aid from Lord Gervais. Your foster father will surely be only too happy to help you look for your sister."

"Although that means more people finding out what has happened. And when she is found, more chance of scandal."

Albert was not fooled by Roger's manner. He knew his friend was more concerned for his sister's welfare than her reputation. Still, he could sympathize. Roger was an ambitious man, and Madeline was jeopardizing his plans.

"Well, there is no hope for it, I suppose," Roger concluded grimly. "If she isn't found this day or the next, I will have to inform Chilcott that the wedding will have to be postponed. And the baron, too.

Damn Madeline! I almost wish she *was* hurt, or being held by outlaws. It would be easier to explain.''

"Surely, Sir Roger, you are not serious?" said Father Gabriel in a softly condemning voice.

Roger twisted in his saddle, another frown on his darkly handsome face. "Of course I don't really mean it," he snapped. "She's my sister, after all."

"I feared you had forgotten that fact."

"I might have found her by now, if it wasn't for your insistence that I stay in bed."

Father Gabriel did not seem overly upset by Roger's angry words. "It would have done no good to your sister to have you deathly ill. Besides, Lord Trevelyan and his men were doing a fine job, and they have promised to continue searching."

Another group of May Day revelers surged past them, forcing Roger to rein in slightly. "God's teeth, I wish this rabble would get out of the way!"

"Peasants enjoying a simple holiday, Sir Roger. Surely not worthy of such venomous words," Father Gabriel said.

Roger gave Albert a disgruntled look, then spoke to the priest. "I am surprised you approve of this 'simple holiday.' "

"A little harmless fun is never amiss."

"Perhaps," Roger growled, "but I am here on business." He stood up in his stirrups to look ahead. "We will go to Lord Gervais at once, if we can ever get through this mob. Albert, while I see if Madeline has arrived there, detail some men to search the town."

The Norman knight in the service of Lord Gervais watched the dancers cavorting about the green with a wry, amused grin on his face, which changed to an appreciative one when his attention turned to one particularly lovely young woman, with lithesome grace and long, flowing dark hair. She was a beauty, and it was a pleasure to watch her dance.

There was something rather familiar about her, too, but Urien Fitzroy, whose duties included the training of young nobles sent to Castle Gervais for instruction in the arts of war, did not think he had ever seen her before. Happily married though he was, hers was a robust, ruddy beauty not easily forgotten.

With vague and amused interest he wondered what the devil she thought she was doing ignoring the young man who had first appeared on the green with her. The poor fellow had obviously refused her invitation to dance, and then had gotten the first of five pints of ale before finding a spot on a bench on the opposite side of the green, where he had a clear view of the Maypole, and the girl. Try as he might to look as if he were ignoring her, it was clear that he was somewhat anxious and even annoyed by her enjoyment of the festivities.

Fitzroy sighed for the follies of youth. The man should simply do what she so clearly wanted, and dance. What was wrong with him, that he did not? Still, he could recall very clearly trying to ignore a certain fiery young wench, to no avail. He smiled to himself and surreptitiously raised his mug to the young man. Maybe these two would wind up wed, too.

"Fitzroy!" the burly brewster called. With two large mugs of his ale in his fleshy fist, he moved through the crowded alehouse and out the door to join his friend. "Jupiter's bolt, what a crowd. The wife can hardly pour fast enough."

"Then you had better help her, or there'll be hell to pay."

"Aye," the brewster acknowledged. Nevertheless, he sat down on the rough bench beside the knight and proceeded to consume his ale in leisurely gulps. "Jove's rod, those fools'll dance all night."

"I would, too, if I stood a chance of getting near that wench," Fitzroy remarked with a grin and a nod toward the green.

The brewster gave him a dismayed frown.

"Married I may be, and to the best woman in the world, but I'm not in my grave yet, either. You must admit, she is a pretty thing."

"I do have eyes."

"Especially for a beautiful woman."

The brewster grinned with remembrance, then frowned. "But—" he nudged Fitzroy and nodded significantly toward the tall, dark-haired fellow "—she's not alone."

"Who are they? I think I would recall her, and that brawny fellow, too."

The brewster shrugged. "Don't know."

"He's a Welshman, or I'm a fool."

"Maybe." The brewster hauled himself to his feet. "Best get back to work, or the wife'll make me rue the day I married her! Give my best to Fritha."

"I will." Fitzroy raised his mug in farewell as his friend hurried back inside, then watched the dancers again, only this time, his gaze alternated between the girl and the man who stared at her, darkly brooding. She might be sorry she started this little game, he thought, for the young man had a stubborn look about his mouth that did not bode well for reconciliation. Still, surely it would be difficult for any man to remain angry with such a beauty.

He took another long gulp of ale, then found himself sitting in the shadow cast by the stranger's large body. "Greetings, friend," Fitzroy said jovially, using the few words of Welsh he had learned while in the service of a lord who had lived there.

"You're not a Welshman," the man said decisively, and with obvious disgust.

"No, I'm not," Fitzroy agreed amicably, responding in the Norman tongue.

"How dare you look at her like that!" Dafydd growled. He glared at this rogue who had the effrontery to stare at Madeline. At first, he had been afraid that this fellow, so arrogant and so obviously a nobleman, had recognized her, until the fellow smiled and kept watching her without rising from his seat.

"Who?" the fellow replied innocently.

"You know who! Stop it, or I'll beat your head in!"

"Your sweetheart, is she? Then you should dance with her."

"Shut your mouth, you impudent cur!" Maybe he wasn't a nobleman, and maybe he couldn't offer Madeline a castle . . . maybe he could only offer her his love and a little stone hovel in the middle of a valley or on the top of a mountain . . . maybe she was wasting herself caring for him when she could have any man—but by God, he wasn't going to let some Norman lout look at her like that!

The Norman's eyes narrowed and he rose slowly, displaying an impressive build. "Watch your tongue, Welshman," he warned. "I'll pass over your insults this time because you are drunk, but I will not brook more."

"I'm not drunk, and I tell you, quit staring at her, you Norman scum!" Dafydd cried, taking a swing at the fellow's head.

The man stepped back, and the blow narrowly missed him. His eyes widened, and with some pleasure Dafydd guessed the fellow finally realized he wasn't drunk, or at least not very much. He, too, went back a pace, and raised his hands, ready to pummel this Norman dog into the ground.

The brewster came bustling out of the alehouse. "Please, sirs!" he pleaded worriedly. "This is a day for celebration, not a fistfight!"

"I'll kill him," Dafydd muttered between clenched teeth, certain that this Norman's intentions were little removed from those of Sir Guy.

The brewster had the effrontery to smile. "You don't know who you're challenging, Taffy. I think you had best think again before offering to fight him."

"I'll knock his head off," Dafydd vowed angrily, "and yours too for calling me that name!" Which was condescending at best, insulting at worst and in his current humor, Dafydd saw only the insult. His hands balled into fists and itched to come into contact with the Norman's jaw.

Madeline herself pushed her way through the crowd that was gathering outside the alehouse. "Dafydd, what is the matter?" she asked, grabbing hold of his tense arms.

"This cur was looking at you."

"So what of that?"

Dafydd turned to her with dark, smoldering eyes. "It was an insult."

"If there was an insult, it was to me, not you. Please, there is no need to fight."

"I say there is! I am responsible for you, and I will not allow any man to look at you lustfully."

The man standing opposite Dafydd spoke. "Indeed, my dear, it was not my intent to insult you. I was enjoying the dance." He made a gentlemanly bow to Madeline. "I assure you, I meant no harm."

Who did this Norman think he was, some swain seeking her love? Or a bridegroom? "What's your name?" Dafydd demanded, fearing this man would turn out to be Chilcott.

"Fitzroy. What's yours?"

"None of your business," Dafydd retorted, his relief now usurped by another surge of anger. "Are you going to fight me? Or are you a coward?"

The man's face darkened into a frown. "I will take such an insult from no man, and for no reason," he said slowly.

"Good. Fight me, then, or be known as the coward I say you are."

Fitzroy glanced at the brewster. "Well, Bern, clear a space. This fellow and I must fight. Since he has no weapon, we shall wrestle to satisfy our honor."

"Sir!" Madeline cried, still holding onto Dafydd's arm. She knew full well who he was about to fight, and knew it would be wise to leave. And not just because the muscular knight's face contained a hint of lethal menace. "It would not be fair. He is injured and—"

"Be quiet, Madeline," Dafydd said firmly. "This is an affair of honor."

"I won't allow it!" she said imperiously.

"She won't allow it?" the Norman said with some surprise.

"Be quiet," Dafydd ordered.

His opponent gave Madeline a slight smile that did not relieve her anxiety, although she thought he was prepared to be merciful. "We are only going to wrestle. It won't be to the death. Bern, take my tunic."

The brewster obeyed, and with an excited murmur, the crowd moved back and formed a rough ring. Some started wagering on the combatants, increasing the air of excitement.

"Dafydd, please, don't do this," Madeline implored, but he ignored her and stripped off his tunic. Several more women joined the voluble gathering.

Everyone gasped with awe when they saw his massive scar, and the Norman's eyes widened. "Perhaps we should reconsider."

"Not needing your pity, Norman," Dafydd sneered. "Now, let's get at it."

Fitzroy shrugged, then crouched warily, his arms held out ready to grab his opponent. Dafydd did likewise and watched the Norman shrewdly, as long as his patience would allow. Then he lunged to the left, and when Fitzroy pivoted slightly to avoid him, moved in toward the man's exposed side, grabbed him around the waist and tried to throw him to the ground.

Unfortunately, it was like trying to move a granite post. Fitzroy twisted in response and despite Dafydd's efforts to guard himself, managed to get a hold on him. The two men struggled in this awkward embrace for a few minutes, until Dafydd shoved upward hard with his shoulder, dislodging Fitzroy, who stumbled backward but did not fall.

By now, both wrestlers were panting heavily and covered in sweat, which made getting a good grip even more difficult. Not that Dafydd cared about the difficulty. In his troubled mind and anxious heart, this man had become all of Normandy in one person, and he would defeat him, come what may.

With a shout, he lunged again, low and fast, and caught Fitzroy, who reached under his opponent and with both hands, pushed hard up and away. Dafydd's hands slipped and he had to let go. In that instant, Fitzroy moved in to seize Dafydd, one arm around his waist, the other over his shoulder, and he pulled down in one continuous motion.

As he took hold of Fitzroy in retaliation, Dafydd fell to his knees, but he brought Fitzroy down with him. Then, with a sudden burst of passionate strength, he pushed Fitzroy over and fell on him, his muscular arm across Fitzroy's throat. "Yield!"

"I yield," Fitzroy croaked, and the crowd gave a great collective sigh.

Dafydd drew back and smiled grimly as he looked around for Madeline, who was not there. Stunned and exhausted, he got to his feet as the plump brewster rushed to his fallen friend and extended a hand to help Fitzroy stand. "She's not here," he said to Dafydd. "She went that way." He jerked his head in the direction of the open fields, away from the castle, and watched as the Welshman grabbed his pack and strode off after the wench.

"My God," Fitzroy muttered as he rose slowly and rubbed his throat, which was purpling with a bruise. "I must be getting old."

"He had blood in his eyes, Urien," the brewster said consolingly, handing him his tunic.

"The wench means a lot to him, obviously. Ah, well," Fitzroy eyed the dispersing crowd. "I will probably rue the day I took the fellow's challenge. A worthy opponent, though." A sudden glint of sunlight on metal and the flutter of a pennant near the castle gates caught his attention. "Lord Gervais has visitors," he remarked. "Armed and anxious by the look and speed of them. I had best see if my lord has need of me and my men."

Chapter Twelve

Dafydd found Madeline far outside the town, past the first fields and houses of the tenants, in a glade on the edge of a newly harrowed field. Here, the sounds of merriment were less discernible, and the smell of the overturned earth strong. She was sitting beneath a tree and made no acknowledgment of him as he came closer and tossed their pack onto the ground. "Madeline?"

"Is your fight over?" she asked coldly, running her gaze over him. "I suppose I am relieved you are not badly hurt."

"What are you doing here?"

"Wondering why you did such a stupid thing."

"It wasn't stupid. That fellow was looking at you as if you were some kind of common...common..."

"Wench? Whore? Or pretty young woman? And I take it I should be pleased by your childish display of male pride?"

He sat beside her. "I don't understand you. I fought for your honor."

"That's a very flattering lie, but a lie it is. You fought for yourself. If you were thinking of me, you would have allowed me to enjoy the dancing. You acted no better than Roger, as if I were something you own!"

He scowled and stared at the ground. "You mean you were enjoying the lascivious stares of all those men! Laughing and smiling and jumping about. That fellow had no right to look at you that way!"

"He didn't mean any harm."

"How do you know that?" Dafydd demanded, angrily stripping the leaves off the nearest bush.

She sighed, but in truth, she wasn't really angry with him anymore. The fight had seemed a stupid thing to her, an example of a man's need to exert his ownership over a woman, yet here and now, his defense of her honor had a certain undeniable charm.

Her expression softened slightly. "I see Sister Mary was right. Jealousy can make a man half-mad. But you know I love you. There was no need for such a display."

"*I* thought there was. That fellow needed to learn some manners."

"From you?" she asked lightly.

"From me. Or perhaps you think no Norman can learn anything from a Welshman?"

She took hold of his shoulders and forced him to look at her. "What is the matter, Dafydd, really?"

He didn't meet her gaze, instead shredding the leaves in his hand into tiny pieces. "Are you sure about being my wife, Madeline?" he asked quietly. He glanced at her, and she saw the vulnerability in his eyes. "I have nothing to offer you. No home, no family, no wealth, no power."

"Just yourself, Dafydd, and that is all I want," she said, enclosing his hand in both of hers. "Why can't you see that? Why is it so difficult for men to see that women can know what they want? That we are quite capable of knowing our own mind? I want *you,* Dafydd, stubborn Welshman that you are. Not wealth, not power, or a chilly, drafty pile of stone for a home. And I will come to you with nothing, for my brother will disown me. We will make our own home, and our own family." She took his face in her hands. "Now, will you please believe me?"

With a low, delighted chuckle, Dafydd bounded to his feet, lifted her into his arms and spun her around. "Very well. I believe you."

She smiled slyly as he set her down. "Why did you fight him, Dafydd, really?"

"Because he's an arrogant Norman."

"You weren't jealous?"

"No!"

She leaned against him and toyed with the neck of his tunic. "Not even a little?"

He shrugged his shoulders.

"You're not going to admit you were jealous, are you?"

"No."

"Well, you shouldn't have picked that particular man to challenge, you with all your talk of being cautious, even if he made the most rude proposition imaginable. That was Urien Fitzroy."

"So what of that?"

"He's not only one of Lord Gervais' most trusted men, he teaches the squires the arts of war. He taught Roger."

"Not much of a wrestler, for all that."

"You are indeed a stubborn fellow! It's too bad Roger can't meet you. He would see that I am not the most stubborn person in the world, as he always says."

"Yes, you are," Dafydd replied, flopping onto the ground and pulling her down beside him.

She snuggled against him. Their laughter filled the glade, until desire took its place. They pressed closer, caressing each other as they lay on the soft grass.

Dafydd and Madeline were aware of nothing except each other while they made love under the sheltering trees, with only the gentle whisper of the wind through the blossoming branches and the soft sounds of their passion and endearments to break the silence.

Roger sat in the vast hall of Castle Gervais and reflected that there seemed at least one good thing to come out of all this business with Madeline, and that was the chance to see Fitzroy again. Not that they were friends, exactly. If asked, Roger would have said simply that he appreciated the chance to see an old teacher.

Without knowing it, Urien Fitzroy had helped to make Roger what he was. Despite what Dafydd thought, Fitzroy had not been born a Norman nobleman, but a peasant's son. He was a ruthless taskmaster, a determined teacher and a wise man. Fitzroy had set the pattern Roger attempted to follow when he came into his inheritance. It was not Roger's fault that he had yet to learn to temper justice with mercy, and to see that a truly strong man could afford to lose once in a while and still be respected.

Father Gabriel had gone to the chapel for vespers, and Albert was still in the barracks with the rest of the men to make sure they were all accommodated. The hearth held no fire, for the day was quite warm. On the upper levels, the coverings had been drawn back from the windows to allow in the fresh spring air.

Wondering what was keeping Lord Gervais from the hall, Roger watched the swarm of servants as they prepared for the evening meal in the vast room. They spoke little, which he appreciated, and moved swiftly about, setting up the trestle tables, spreading the linen and preparing the torches. There was an air of subdued excitement, and he could easily guess that these maidservants were anticipating more May Day festivities when the meal was over.

At last Lord Gervais, a vital man despite his age, limped into the hall. "Greetings, Roger!" he called out. "I am delighted to see you, my boy, and so pleased you took me up on my invitation to stop here on your way home for the wedding. Where is Madeline?"

Roger rose swiftly and made his obeisance, noting that his foster father had grown slimmer since he had last seen him. "I had hoped she was here already."

Lord Gervais halted, puzzled. "Here? Already? Without you?"

"She is missing, my lord."

"Missing! What! How?" Lord Gervais sat down in the chair next to Roger. "Sit, now, and explain this!"

With a sigh, Roger once again complied, wondering how long it would be before all of England knew of this scandal. A maidservant came to serve them wine, but Lord Gervais waved her away when she approached him, his face becoming more and more agitated. "A bad business this, very bad. Yet this Father Gabriel thinks you need not fear for her? And Trevelyan and Morgan continue to search?"

"Yes, my lord," Roger replied.

"Ah!" Lord Gervais exclaimed, looking toward the door. "Urien, here is Roger de Montmorency."

Fitzroy made his small smile that Roger knew could mean many things, from mocking displeasure to genuine joy. In this case, Fitzroy seemed truly happy to see his former pupil.

"He comes to us with grievous news."

"Indeed?" Fitzroy said, his eyes full of dismay.

"Listen and hear what has happened," Lord Gervais replied.

Fitzroy did, with a furrowed brow and frowning lips, while Lord Gervais related the important details of Roger's story, mercifully sparing him another repetition. "This Welshman, his shoulder was scarred?" Fitzroy asked when Lord Gervais was finished.

"Yes," Roger replied.

"And I daresay your sister looks something like you, Roger?"

"I suppose so. Her coloring is like mine."

Unexpectedly and uncharacteristically, Fitzroy grinned broadly. "Then I have seen her. Today. In Bridgeford Wells. Quite unharmed, and dancing."

"What!" Roger was on his feet in an instant. "Where?"

"On the green, and she was with the Welshman, who is the first man ever to beat me in wrestling." He rubbed his throat. "A most impressive fellow. She left before we finished, though."

"Show me where you saw them," Roger demanded, already heading for the door.

"Certainly," Fitzroy replied, following him.

Roger paused in front of the young maidservant who had served them wine. "Find Father Gabriel and tell him we've got his thief." He looked at Fitzroy. "If that Welshman's touched a hair of her head, I'll have him drawn and quartered."

Lying awake and smiling, her head on Dafydd's broad chest, which rose and fell with the even breathing of his sleep, Madeline heard the soldiers before she saw them. "Dafydd!" she cried, shaking him. He was awake instantly, alerted by the alarm in her voice. They both scrambled to their feet.

It wasn't Roger, Madeline realized at once. Urien Fitzroy strode across the glade, followed by what appeared to be a full troop of soldiers. "Lady Madeline de Montmorency?" he inquired politely.

"No."

"It is no use to lie to me, my lady. You look too much like your brother."

"Very well, suppose I am. You have no cause to arrest me, or take me into custody. Or Dafydd, either. We have done nothing wrong."

"You, maybe, but the Welshman is said to be a thief."

Madeline raised her eyebrow in unconscious imitation of her self-assured brother. "Is he? Well, there is his pack. Search it if you like. You will find nothing stolen in it."

"Nevertheless, my lady, your brother wants to talk to you, and him, too, I gather, so you had best come along with me to the castle."

"What, is Roger there?"

"He arrived this afternoon." Fitzroy's expression softened a little. "He's anxious to see you, my lady. It may seem hard to believe right now, but he does care about you. Even now, he's out combing the forest for you, since you left the town and no one was certain in what direction you had gone. We had to split up to search for you. One of my men has already been dispatched to tell him you have been found. You had better come."

"I will not. If I have caused Roger any trouble, he has only himself to blame for trying to force me to marry," she said. "I hope you will have the goodness to tell him so when you see him."

"I see. He left out that part of the tale."

"And please also tell him that I am no longer any of his concern, or his responsibility. I am going to Wales."

"With him?" Fitzroy nodded at Dafydd, who stood silent, although his defiant eyes said much.

"Yes."

Fitzroy frowned. "You've placed me in a very difficult position, my lady."

She glared at him majestically. "Roger cannot blame *you* for my message."

"No, but Roger can blame me for not following orders. Your brother outranks me, so I have to obey, no matter what I may think." Fitzroy stepped closer and nodded at one of the soldiers, who took hold of Dafydd's arms roughly. Another soldier began to tie his wrists together.

"There is no need for that!" Madeline cried indignantly. "He has done nothing to harm me. Indeed, he has saved me from a terrible fate at the hands of Sir Guy de Robespierre. I will not allow you to bind him!"

"As I've said, orders are orders."

"What are they going to do to Dafydd?"

"I don't know," Fitzroy said. He gazed at her for what seemed a long time, his face inscrutable. Then he took hold of her arm and drew her away from the soldiers and their prisoner. "You may not believe me, my lady, but I understand how you feel. And I know your brother. Roger is not in a forgiving frame of mind right at the moment. It might be better for all concerned if this Welshman were to slip out of my hands, if you understand me."

Madeline glanced at Dafydd, erect and glowering at the Normans all around him. "You will let him go?"

"I will turn my back. What happens then is up to you, and to him."

"Why?" she asked warily. "Why would do this?"

Fitzroy's smile was as enigmatic as his eyes. "Because Roger needs a bit of a comeuppance, perhaps. Or maybe I'm ashamed to have the fellow who beat me about. Does it matter?"

"You have my undying gratitude."

"Fine. Now hurry up. Here, go talk to him, and take my dagger. To protect yourself, mind, and not to cut the ropes around his wrists." He gestured for his men to move away from the prisoner, and ordered them to form ranks with their backs to the couple. It was obvious they were puzzled by the order, but it was Fitzroy, so they obeyed. Then Fitzroy, too, turned away.

Madeline hurried to Dafydd and slipped the knife between the ropes to cut them off. "You must run from here, and get as far away as you can," she whispered urgently. "Roger wants me more than he will want you. If I stay, the chances are good he will not continue to search for you, especially when I tell him all you have done for me. I will make him see that we belong together."

"What are you talking about? I won't leave without you. Why is Fitzroy letting you do this?"

"I'm not quite sure." The rope fell to the ground. "Now run."

"Not without you," he said firmly. "You must come with me."

"No," she said, her voice quavering despite her efforts to be strong.

"Madeline! Do you think I would willingly leave you?"

She gave him a tremulous smile and tried to look more confident than she felt. What would she do without the comfort and strength she drew from his presence? "No, but I hope you will do as I ask. If anything were to happen to you, and it was my fault, I could not bear it. Go, so that I know you are safe."

He grabbed hold of her shoulders. "But what of you? Your brother will try to make you marry—"

"After the time we have spent together, do you think he could force me to wed another man? No, Dafydd, never! When he sees that I am not to be persuaded, surely even Roger will give up, and then we can be together."

"How will I know when that is? How will we meet again?"

"My lady," Fitzroy called softly, "I think I hear more men approaching."

"I will come to you at the monastery of St. Christopher. It will be a risk for you to go back, I know, but—" Now they could both hear the soldiers coming and she could make out her brother's voice among them. "It's Roger."

"I will not leave you to face him alone," Dafydd said firmly.

"Please, Dafydd," she replied just as urgently, "please listen to me! Believe that I can deal with him by myself. Trust me!"

"But to leave you here—"

"Dafydd," she said, tears in her eyes, as well as a determined gleam, "are you never going to have faith that I know what I am doing?"

He nodded, the sound of more soldiers growing louder. "I will be waiting for you at the monastery, my love."

"I will come, Dafydd. Now go! Go with God!" One brief kiss, and he did, the brief rustle of the underbrush the only sound of his passage.

She waited a moment to gather her strength, knowing that she would need every ounce of it. Then Madeline de Montmorency turned to face her brother and his wrath.

Chapter Thirteen

Nearby, Dafydd stayed low, then with practiced ease swung into a tall tree and watched Madeline, much less afraid for himself than he was for her. After all, he had been hiding from the Normans for years upon years, and could sit as still as any stone. At this time of day, it would be movement that would be detected first, not a man hidden by the foliage and shadows. Whatever else Madeline might think, he would not leave her to face her brother completely alone.

A tall, dark-haired nobleman, his cloak swirling about him, strode into the clearing, making directly for Madeline, who waited motionless beside Fitzroy, her bearing erect and resolute. Dafydd could imagine the stubborn fire in her eye. Indeed, he could see a mirror image of stubbornness in her brother.

So this was Roger de Montmorency. His hawk-like features did not look capable of displaying either pity or a compassionate heart. There was a definite resemblance in the siblings' features, yet what was stubborn determination in Madeline appeared as unwavering arrogance in Sir Roger. He could detect none of Madeline's softness there, no doubt trained out by men like Fitzroy, who had a measure of humanity about him, or at least he did now, in his later years. Perhaps when he had had the care of young Roger, he had not been so kind.

With increasing dismay and despite what Fitzroy had said, Dafydd realized that Roger de Montmorency did not seem pleased to see his sister. He gave Madeline no greeting, but simply stood and looked at her for several moments. Likewise, she remained silent—two adversaries glaring at each other in unarmed challenge.

"Roger," Madeline finally began, taking a tentative step toward him. "Let me explain—"

"Not here," her brother barked. He gestured at the assembled men. "Explanations can wait until we are alone." He turned to Fitzroy. "Was anyone with her?"

"Yes," Madeline answered. Roger slowly turned toward her, his face full of contempt. She went on defiantly. "A man who—"

"Be quiet, woman!" her brother roared. "I have said I will speak with you later. Where is he, Fitzroy?"

It was not Fitzroy who responded. "He escaped," Madeline said, and Dafydd heard the attempt to be strong in her voice. Oh, God, he moaned inwardly, he never should have listened to her pleas and plans and left her to face her brother alone. He also marveled at her courage to stand up to this man, and loved her all the more.

"Is this true?" Roger demanded incredulously of Fitzroy, who had not moved from his place.

"Yes, my lord," he replied, and he did not seem particularly impressed by Roger's anger.

"How could that happen? Didn't you bind him?"

"Are you questioning my ability to follow orders?" How quietly the man seemed to speak, but Dafydd could hear him clearly. There was no mistaking the implication that to say more would be to personally insult Fitzroy.

Madeline's decision to come to Bridgeford Wells had been a wise one. Here Sir Roger de Montmorency obviously lacked some of the absolute power he would wield at home, if Fitzroy's reaction was anything to go by.

Madeline had been wise to tell him to get away, too. For now, he was free and safe, and if he interfered, he would be outnumbered, and so probably captured, tied and useless to help her. Roger would have them both.

"I cut the ropes and set him free," Madeline announced. "He is well away by now."

"You did what?" Roger demanded harshly, and Dafydd cursed his impotence.

Madeline swept past Roger toward the road leading back to Bridgeford Wells. "Does it matter now? He is out of your hands, and you have me. Explanations can wait until we are alone."

She was amazing. Oh, dear God, how he loved her!

With mingled regret, hope and pride, he watched as Roger turned on his heel, barked an order to Fitzroy and followed his sister from the glade. Fitzroy gave a barely perceptible shake of his head, then ordered the rest of the men to march back to Castle Gervais.

When they had all gone, Dafydd climbed down.

He would not take himself back toward the monastery as Madeline had suggested, not now that he had seen Sir Roger de Montmorency for himself. He would stay nearby, where he could find out exactly what was happening between Madeline and her brother.

With stealthy steps, he began to back away—until he felt a knife against his ribs.

"Don't move!" a Welsh voice whispered in his ear. "What have we here, then?"

"Another Welshman," Dafydd said calmly in his native tongue. He twisted to get a look at his assailant, but the knife pushed farther against his flesh.

"Hands behind the back, if you please," the fellow said, his voice deep and rather familiar.

Dafydd complied and winced as his hands were bound tightly. "Do I know you?" he asked, desperately trying to recall anyone who sounded as this man did, with a voice as raspy as the wind through the bare trees in winter.

The man took hold of the bindings and jerked him around so that he could see who had come upon him.

Dafydd found himself face-to-face with the youth he had left lying on the ground the day he had first saved Madeline. In one hand, he held a dagger of great antiquity, in the other a cudgel.

Which he raised and smashed into Dafydd's skull.

In the spacious chamber Lord Gervais had kindly provided for her, Madeline paced impatiently, barely noticing her accommodation, although it was very luxurious. Had she arrived here directly from the convent, she would have been delighted by the detailed, brightly colored tapestries and bed hangings, the clean, embroidered linens, the silver ewer of herb-scented water and the large basin for washing, the costly mirror, the finely wrought candle holders and plentiful beeswax candles, and the wondrously rare, thick carpet on the floor. Under the present circumstances, all she took note of was the carpet, because she was staring at it as she paced.

Maids arrived, to distract her with a tub and hot water for a bath, and fine new clothes. It was only a momentary distraction, soon overwhelmed by her need to see Roger, so that she could explain everything and then go back to Dafydd. Despite her brother's uncharitable greeting, she was still sure she could make him appreciate that she belonged with Dafydd.

After the maidservants, who had spoken with hushed voices and avoided meeting her eye, had cleared away the tub, helped her into the soft fresh shift and scarlet brocade overtunic they said Roger had bought for her, and arranged her hair in a silver-netted crispinette, she ordered them to go. When Roger arrived, she would speak with him alone.

If only Roger would come! She would soon assure him that she was well, that Dafydd had been her protector, and that it was impossible for her to marry Chilcott. When he understood that she wanted nothing more than to be Dafydd's wife, he would let her go. She pondered asking him for her dower goods but decided she would not press for them, although they were rightfully hers. They would be a small enough price to pay if she could marry the man she loved.

Where in the name of the saints was Roger? She went again to the narrow window and scanned the courtyard. It seemed very busy, with servants bustling about, soldiers coming and going, horses being saddled or unsaddled, grooms rushing by and several noblemen either entering the hall, or leaving it.

It had been a long time since she had been in so large a place. Perhaps this activity was no more than usual, especially for a festive time like the beginning of May.

She strained to listen, trying to catch whatever snatches of conversation or orders drifted up to the window. A woman laughed and said something about a man; an old groom snapped at a young one to move faster; a boy cursed when he dropped an armload of firewood; a man who looked to be of superior rank summoned his men and said something about the "search."

The search for what? Not Dafydd, she hoped, although she felt in her sinking heart that she had guessed rightly.

She turned away at once. She must find Roger and convince him that there was no point trying to find Dafydd. She also silently prayed that Dafydd had taken her advice and left Bridgeford Wells.

Suddenly the door banged open and Roger strode into the room. He kicked the door shut and faced her, his mouth a grim frown and his eyes angry.

"I need to talk to you," Madeline said, trying not to sound belligerent. "Where have you been?"

"Where have *you?*" he countered, with no attempt to sound anything but arrogant.

"I tried to find you, after the first attack," she answered, hoping he would hear the truth in her voice, "but I didn't know where you had gone. Are you quite recovered?"

"I am well enough. And you? You seem uninjured."

His tone made it sound as if he were hoping she would turn out to be severely disabled. He walked over to the window and stood looking outside, not at her.

"I am very well. I have never felt better in my life, and for that, you can thank Dafydd."

"The Welshman you were with?"

She heard the callousness in his voice, and drew herself up. "Yes, the Welshman who saved my life. Who helped me when you left me."

"I was knocked unconscious. It was Albert's decision to take me to St. Christopher's. We searched for you."

"You didn't find me—and what was I to do? Dafydd saved me from the outlaws and helped me."

"Why?" Roger demanded.

"Because he is an honorable man," she answered, affronted by her brother's manner.

"And yet he did not bring you to me, this honorable man."

"It was dangerous for him—as your current behavior makes abundantly clear, I might point out. At first, he simply tried to get me to a Norman manor, but—"

"I know about Sir Guy de Robespierre."

"Then you know that Dafydd was in equal danger there, and yet he did not abandon me. He acted as any true gentleman would."

"How did you repay this 'gentleman'?"

"What are you implying?" she demanded. "Why are you acting this way?"

Slowly Roger turned away from the window, one dark eyebrow raised questioningly. "What way?"

"As if we have committed a crime!" she cried, walking toward him. "We have done nothing wrong."

His brows furrowed ominously. "You have been traveling about the countryside dressed in a peasant's rags with some outlaw and you have done nothing wrong?"

"Dafydd is a good man, Roger—"

"He is a thief and a rebel. He even stole from the monastery of St. Christopher."

"Only out of need. And he no longer wants to be a rebel."

Roger did not reply. Nevertheless, his eloquently dismissive expression and skeptical frown spoke volumes.

"He does not." She took a deep breath. "And you might as well know everything at once. First, I absolutely refuse to marry Chilcott."

"*You* absolutely refuse? Who do *you* think you are, Madeline, to go against my wishes, and those of Baron DeGuerre?"

"I am the daughter of Sir Folke de Montmorency and the sister of Sir Roger de Montmorency," she said firmly. "I am going to marry Dafydd ap Iolo, whose forebears were royalty."

"What nonsense is this? Royalty?" Roger scoffed. "*Welsh* royalty? There is not, and never has been, royalty among those barbarians."

"Say what you will, he wants me to be his wife, and I have gladly agreed."

"Don't be an idiot, Madeline, and don't think you can trick me, either, by telling me such outrageous lies so that I overlook your transgression."

"I am as serious as I can possibly be, Roger. I love Dafydd, and he loves me."

"Love?" Roger snorted derisively. "That is a pleasant fantasy spun by minstrels and noblewomen with too much time on their hands! I should think the convent would have safeguarded you from such idle silliness."

She went toward him, shaking her head. "Roger, I pity you, because I see that you truly believe what you say. However, you are quite wrong about my life in the convent, as you might have discovered at any time in the past several years if you had taken the trouble. Mother Bertrilde allowed no idleness. No frivolity. No laughter, no joy of any kind. You cannot know how I longed for you to come and take me away from there, only to discover you had prepared another prison for me!"

He blinked, but he did not look away.

"Well, I have found a man who truly cares for me. Who respects me, who wants me as I want him. I will be free with Dafydd. Free at last."

"You are being very foolish, Madeline," Roger said evenly.

She could not believe that her heartfelt words had not moved him. "I will be free, Roger, and I will be Dafydd's wife."

Roger's lips twisted scornfully. "Free? None of us is *free*, Madeline. We all have our roles and duties and responsibilities. That's the price for the privileges of rank. It is your duty to obey me, as I obey Baron DeGuerre."

"I do not want the privileges of rank, Roger. I gladly spurn them all to be with Dafydd."

"If this man is such a prize that you would cast aside everything—and I do not believe you will, when you have recovered from this short-lived, perhaps glorious adventure and inhabit the real world again—where is he? He has left you to face me alone."

"I told him to."

Again his face plainly showed that he did not believe her. How different he was from Dafydd! When Dafydd disagreed, she understood that he was genuinely trying to make her see his point of view, to sway her into agreeing. Roger didn't care if she agreed or not, just as long as she obeyed. "He *listens* to me! He respects me, more than you or Chilcott or any other man ever would or will!"

"Respect will not fill your belly. If you think I'm going to give you any dowry, you are sadly mistaken."

"I don't want your money."

"Maybe he will not be so keen to have you when he finds that out."

With compressed lips, Madeline went to her brother and slapped his face with all her might. "How dare you! How dare you imply that he has any such motive!"

Roger ignored the red welt growing on his face. "Poor, foolish, naive Madeline. I agree those years in the convent, whatever it was like, were a mistake, for clearly you have no knowledge of men's ways. This Welsh peasant must be seeking to enrich himself, and he has talked his way, as only the Welsh can, dear sister, into your heart, or at least enough for you to delude yourself into believing that you love him. Time would readily cure this delusion, if only we had it. Unfortunately, we do not. Already wedding guests are arriving at my castle, being fed and housed at my expense. I will brook no further delays to my plans. You are going to marry Chilcott, Madeline, and I am going to find this Welsh fellow and make it very clear to him that it would be in his best interest to get as far away from you as humanly possible."

"He won't care about your threats."

"Won't he?"

"No!"

"You *will* be Chilcott's wife."

He was so sure, so completely certain that his will would be done, that Madeline shot her last bolt. "Perhaps Chilcott will not want *me*, when he learns I am no longer a virgin."

Roger's hands clenched into fists and his eyes filled with cold hostility.

"Yes, it's true," she answered his unspoken question. "I gave that gift to the man I love, who is Dafydd ap Iolo."

"Are you bearing this lout's bastard?" he snapped.

She recoiled from his blunt question, then straightened her shoulders. "No, I am not. But I wish I was! I would be proud to bear his child!"

"I will kill him."

The words were so cold, so ruthless, so unmistakably a vow! "No, Roger!" Madeline cried. "I went with him willingly! I love him and—"

"You are nothing but a foolish woman duped by a clever man with a gilded tongue! I will have his blood for even thinking of touching my sister! He has debased you, me, our whole family! I will never forgive such an insult." Roger strode toward the door.

"Roger!"

He stopped and glanced back at her, giving her a look of such scorn that it filled her with pain, and righteous indignation, too. "Let him go, Roger. It was my fault, if fault it is."

"I mean to have his blood, Madeline. Then I will hang his worthless body from my castle wall, so that I have the satisfaction of seeing him rot!"

She gasped. "You mean it! Oh, how right Dafydd was to accuse me of not knowing Norman ways! *Your* cruel, evil ways! I am *ashamed*—more ashamed than I could be to bear Dafydd's child."

Roger took a deep breath, and his eyes lost some of their frigid obdurateness. "So, I am evil for upholding your honor."

"Not *my* honor, Roger," she said. "You think only of yourself, what you perceive as an insult to *your* honor. I tell you, I am infinitely more honored to have Dafydd's love than I could ever feel as either your sister or a Norman."

For a brief moment, Madeline thought her words had touched him, until Roger shrugged his massive shoulders. "Then you will have to content yourself with those small honors, Madeline, for I will find the Welshman and then he will die."

Madeline heard the awful finality of his words, and saw the implacable will in her brother's eyes. She rushed to him and grabbed hold of his arm. "Roger, please! Would you kill me, too?"

"Don't make an even greater fool of yourself, Madeline, by pleading for him. Despite the little store you put in our family honor, it is unworthy of a de Montmorency."

Regardless of his scornful words, she knelt before him, her mind desperately seeking some way to save the man she loved more than her life. "Please, don't do this! Let him go! I beg of you!"

"Get up, Madeline. Begging does not become you."

A terrible, irrevocable, horrible means to save Dafydd leapt into her mind, and although every particle of her rebelled at the idea, she knew that she must do whatever was necessary to save her beloved's life. "Roger, let him go—and I will marry Chilcott."

Her brother looked down at her, harsh and obdurate still. "You will do that, to save his life?"

"Yes, Roger. I will."

"With whatever honor you still possess, will you give me your word as a de Montmorency?"

She ignored his insult. "I give you my word."

"Then get up and be pleased to think that your abasement and your promise have saved the Welshman."

She did not rise. She simply stared at him, sick at heart for what she had done but sure that she had indeed saved Dafydd's life. "I am sorry for you, Roger," she whispered, "more sorry for you than even myself. You don't know how to love, and you never will!'' There was a flicker of pain in his eyes, yet it was not nearly enough to compare to hers, and she was glad to think she had wounded him even a little. ''Now get out and leave me to grieve for the happiness you have stolen from me, *brother.*''

Roger did, closing the door behind him, leaving her kneeling on the floor, spent, distraught, destroyed.

Madeline covered her face with her hands and, sobbing, leaned forward until her head touched the floor. The tears crept out from between her fingers and dropped silently onto the lifeless stones.

Chapter Fourteen

"Dafydd, Dafydd, wake up, boy!"

Dafydd groaned as he was shaken to a state of consciousness. His eyes fluttered open, and he realized it was night. His back was against a tree, and branches crisscrossed against the moon, so he knew he was in the forest. He thought his captor was not alone, but he could only make out indistinct shapes in the dark. More significantly, he discovered his hands were unbound. In one motion, he sat up and grabbed for the throat of the man kneeling in front of him.

"Dafydd!" the fellow cried, shooting backward to avoid the strong hands reaching out toward him. "Don't you recognize me, Dafydd?"

"Alcwyn? Is it you?" Dafydd cried with happiness and considerable relief, his eyes widening at the sight of a friend not seen since the day he had fought Morgan's men. Yet there could be no mistaking the craggy features and thick black hair and beard, or the missing front tooth, either. Alcwyn claimed he had lost it when he bit into a Norman's arm. "What the devil are you doing here?" Dafydd asked. "And who, by God's blessed blood, is that lad?" He nodded toward the young man who had come upon him in the forest.

"Well, with you and Ivor both gone," Alcwyn replied, gesturing at the small band of Welshmen Dafydd could now make out around a glowing camp fire, "the fellows and I have been doing a little of this and that. I've even discovered I have a talent for being a tinker." He pointed at an old, decrepit wagon decorated with hanging pots of various sizes, shapes and ages.

Dafydd rubbed his sore wrists and settled into a more comfortable position against the tree. "What do you mean, this and that?" he asked. Dafydd liked the smaller man, who had fought beside him countless times, and he knew him to be a decent fellow. His zeal for rebellion had been justly patriotic.

"Oh, you know, a little tinkering, a little trading, a little robbery."

"A little rebellion?"

"No, not anymore. Not since that fool Ivor was killed," Alcwyn replied bitterly. "Too bloody dangerous."

"What about ransom?" Dafydd gave the youth a questioning look.

"Why not?" the lad, who seemed to be about sixteen, cried defiantly. "I wasn't going to hurt that Norman wench."

"Really?

"Owain's hotheaded and enthusiastic, if you catch my meaning," Alcwyn said, handing Dafydd a small cask of ale. "Gets a bit carried away. Trained to be a Norman's squire, he was, but when the time for knighthood came, the *gwirionyn* said he wasn't going to knight a Welshman after all."

"She was only a Norman," Owain complained. "And you shouldn't have been helping her when you saw I was as Welsh as you."

"She's a woman, and I don't hold with attacking women," Dafydd replied evenly.

"Just going to get some ransom. They could afford it, by the looks of them. What are you, a Norman disguised as a Welshman, or a traitor?"

"Enough," Alcwyn said, rising and glaring at Owain. "This is Dafydd ap Iolo, fool. His family have been princes of Wales for years upon years. Traitor, indeed! Many there are who would say that of you for letting such an accusation pass your lips. Besides, he can slit your gullet with a flick of his wrist if he wants to. So shut that flapping mouth of

yours and be glad he didn't. Respect, boy, respect!
Or you will go from here this very day."

Owain sat back on his heels. "Dafydd ap Iolo?"
he whispered incredulously.

"Aye, the same," Alcwyn said, nodding. "And
him it was showed us what scum Ivor was. More of
us would have been dead, but for him. Now do you
understand?"

Owain nodded wordlessly, then cleared his
throat. "Forgive me, Dafydd ap Iolo, I didn't
mean—"

"Yes, you did," Dafydd said with a wry grin. He
took a drink and fingered the bump on the back of
his head.

"Just returning measure for measure," Owain
said with a little more respect, and some fear, in his
eyes.

"Temper your anger with thought, and you'll do
better. And leaving the women alone, is it? They
have enough hardships, even the rich ones." He
sighed wearily, wondering what was happening with
Madeline, if she was safe and if she had been able
to persuade her brother to let her have her freedom. "Where the devil are we?" Dafydd asked,
looking about him at the rocks and trees. "How far
from Bridgeford Wells?"

"Not that far. We come for May Day."

Dafydd could guess why. The crowd would make petty thievery easier and the pickings more plentiful.

"Tell us, Dafydd ap Iolo," Owain said, a look in his eyes that made Dafydd doubt that he was quite so awestricken as he had been when he had first discovered who he had brought back to camp, "what it is you're doing *here?*"

"Aye, Dafydd, dead we all thought you was."

"I nearly was."

"How'd you get away from Morgan?"

"I didn't—he let me go."

Alcwyn and his men leaned a little closer to hear, even Owain.

"I thought I was as good as dead, and asked him to let me breathe my last up in the mountains. He took me there and left me. But I found I wasn't ready to lie down and die. I managed to crawl away, and then a priest found me and took me to the monastery of St. Christopher's. I've been there ever since."

"Until you attacked me," Owain noted.

"On my way back to Wales at last, until I saw you with Lady Madeline de Montmorency."

"So what are you doing *here?*" the young man asked pointedly. "Far from the border, you are."

"Since you drove away Roger de Montmorency, I couldn't leave his sister in the forest, could I? I was taking her someplace safe, and away from Trevelyan and Morgan's land, which was too risky a place for me to go to."

Alcwyn looked a little askance. "This is a fair ways north and east for that, Dafydd."

"It was where she wanted to go."

"And then what? We could use a good fighter like you."

Dafydd shook his head. "My fighting days are done, Alcwyn," he said quietly. "I just want to get Madeline and go home."

"Madeline, is it?" Alcwyn questioned. "Since when you been so familiar with nobility?"

"Since she agreed to be my wife."

"S'truth?"

"God's truth."

"What kind of tale is this?" Owain demanded disdainfully. "What Norman noblewoman would marry a poor Welshman, even if he is Dafydd ap Iolo?"

"Shut it, Owain," Alcwyn warned.

"Just because you don't believe it doesn't mean it is not true," Dafydd responded with as good grace as he could manage in the face of such blatant rudeness. "She has agreed to be my wife."

"Then where is she?"

Dafydd stood up, towering over the slimmer, younger man. "Where are your manners, boy?" he asked, his eyes blazing. "That is no way to speak to me!"

Owain was on his feet in an instant. "I am Owain ap Gwydyr ap Ilar ap Idris—!" he retorted.

"Please, please," Alcwyn cried placatingly, getting between them. "A couple of hotheads here, I think. Come now, cool your tempers with some ale. We have enough to do to stay alive and one pace ahead of the Normans. No need to battle among ourselves!"

Dafydd was the first to shrug, and Owain the first to resume his seat. "Your words require an apology, Owain," Alcwyn pleaded, "although surely everyone will agree odd it is to hear of such a thing. He has a point, Dafydd, you see."

"I am not telling a lie."

"We know, we know. Especially these others who remember the old days. It's strange, that's all. Owain?"

Owain looked as if he would rather lose his tongue than apologize. Nonetheless, he grudgingly said, "Sorry for the disrespect, Dafydd ap Iolo."

"Where is the bride, then?" Alcwyn asked after a moment. "Is she meeting you hereabouts?"

"I hope so."

"Hope?"

"I am not as certain as she that her brother will let her go."

"Ah, that would be Roger de Montmorency. A proud man, that. He will have a worse time than our Owain to believe his sister would want to marry a Welshman."

"I agree with you. Unfortunately, I was not in a position to stay and argue my point."

"Well, since you must be waiting, you are welcome to stay with us. Accommodations not the best, I'm afraid, but we've shared worse, eh?"

"Thank you, Alcwyn. I would be honored."

As Roger opened the door to his sister's chamber in Castle Gervais, he reminded himself that he was going to remain calm. He was right about this marriage, and he knew it, so he should not allow Madeline's responses to anger him. She had sinned greatly and demeaned the family name. Surely by now, after nearly two days alone in the tower room, she would have come to see the error of her ways and grown reconciled to her marriage.

His sister was sitting in a high-backed, heavy chair, still as an old woman on the verge of sleep, facing the window with her hands idle in her lap. At least now she was properly dressed in a fine and modest gown, which was one of several he had bought for her, partly as a reminder of what money could buy, and partly to cheer her spirits. She had looked at them all and said nothing.

People were beginning to talk. Not Lord Gervais: he was too polite, although he couldn't quite mask his concern and Roger suspected he was anxious to be asked for advice. Because ever since Madeline had finally agreed to marry Chilcott, she had refused to leave this room. Everyone kept an eye on the servants who took her nourishment and saw them return to the hall with the trays of food virtually untouched. Then the heads would turn toward him.

For a moment, his heart went out to her and he felt a wave of guilt. She looked very young and very vulnerable, there in that chair.

No, he was right. What could she really know of men and the world? What kind of life could she have with a Welsh peasant? It was his duty to protect her, even from herself, and that he meant to do.

Unfortunately, the moment he caught sight of Madeline's pale face and the dark circles beneath her eyes as she glanced up at him, he knew that his hope that she would finally see reason and accept what must be was a futile one. However, he did not allow that disappointment to show upon his face when he said, "So, Madeline, are you willing to join us for the evening meal? Lord Gervais is most upset by your continued absence."

"I have no wish to see anybody," she replied flatly.

"Madeline," he said, a pleading note creeping into his voice despite himself, "you must understand—"

Her eyes flashed with that stubborn fire he knew too well. "I understand very well, Roger. I understand that I am to be the sacrifice to your ambition. I understand that my happiness is of no importance to you, as long as *your* will is done!"

Unbeknownst to him, the stubborn fire in her eyes was an exact duplicate of that in his own when his attempt at gentleness was so strongly rebuffed. "I *am* thinking of your happiness, Madeline, as you will realize when you are reasonable! How happy will you be living in a hovel at the edge of some clearing in godforsaken Wales, you and this man and your few smelly sheep?"

"That is for me to think of."

"No, you are my responsibility and I have no intention of shirking my duty."

"I *want* you to shirk it! I *ask* you to shirk it!"

"Madeline," he said, still desperately trying to speak calmly, "you must understand. This marriage between an unknown Welshman and a woman of the house of de Montmorency simply cannot be. Chilcott is the best choice for you, I assure you. He will let you run his household, and probably his manor, as well. He is rich. He is young. What more do you want?"

"I am not like you, Roger. I don't want more. I just want Dafydd!" She stood up and circled her brother slowly, surveying him coolly. "Is it not enough that you have forced me to obey your orders? What more do *you* want? You have won. Do you expect me to alter so rapidly, to suddenly thank you? If you do, you must be mad."

"I want you to understand that my decisions are for your own good."

"Listen to yourself, Roger. *Your* decisions for *my* good. I can make my own decisions!"

"I perceive that you are never going to see reason over this, Madeline, and so I will simply remind you that you have given me your word that you will marry Chilcott."

Madeline sighed. She had no need to be reminded of the hopelessness of her future. The only thing that gave her strength was her certainty that she was helping Dafydd. Roger had sent out no more search parties seeking him. By now, Dafydd might even be close to St. Christopher's. She had to get word to him somehow, to let him know that she could not come to him. The maidservants had mentioned that there was a priest in Castle Gervais who had arrived with Roger, a kind man from St. Christopher's. If only she could think of a way to speak with him ... "Have no fear, I will not break my oath."

"I didn't think you would. We leave for my castle tomorrow."

His words sounded like a death knell. "I...I want to see a priest."

"I daresay you need to confess," he replied. "Very well. I shall send Lord Gervais' chaplain."

"I have heard there is another priest here, an infirmarer from St. Christopher's?"

"What of it?"

"I cannot sleep. Perhaps he could also prepare a sleeping draft for me."

Roger eyed her shrewdly. He didn't doubt that somehow Madeline had discovered who Father Gabriel was, or where he was from. Perhaps she wanted to see the holy man to have the pleasure of talking with someone who knew the Welshman, or perhaps there was more to it. "I meant what I said, sister," he warned. "I will kill your lover, if I find him, for the dishonor he has done my family, and me."

"I know, Roger. Besides, what could I say, except that he was right about you all along?"

Roger bit back a curse for the sly Welshman who had seduced her. "Explain yourself, Madeline."

"He warned me that I did not understand the Normans, that I didn't understand *you*. I thought I did. I have discovered how terribly wrong I was. Now leave me, Roger."

"Madeline, I—"

"There is nothing you can say to me that I wish to hear. Leave me."

Roger sighed wearily, knowing that there was little point to argue further. He paused on the threshold and glanced back at her, truly unhappy to be viewed as the cause of her pain. Someday, surely, she would understand.

Chapter Fifteen

It was an awkward leave-taking, Father Gabriel thought, as he approached Lady Madeline to say goodbye. She was dressed in a sumptuous gown of red and gold, her dark hair was brushed and perfumed, her quarters the most luxurious wealth could provide, and yet, when Father Gabriel looked into her lovely blue eyes, he knew he had never seen a more sorrowful and pitiful young woman in his life.

Did Sir Roger de Montmorency not see what he was doing to his sister?

Lady Madeline obviously cared a great deal for the Welshman. Father Gabriel did not doubt that a forced marriage would finally prove to be the death of her. She was frail enough now; another month in such a weakened condition, and she could become seriously ill. If she died, it would be natural causes, but her brother and the unfortunate groom might just as well have murdered her.

At the moment, Sir Roger sat as immovable as stone and seemingly as compassionate, too. He didn't know what Sir Roger had to fear from a priest, but it was quite evident that the Norman knight had no intention of leaving the chamber, just as he had stayed in the room the last time Lady Madeline had spoken to him.

"I came to say farewell and Godspeed," Father Gabriel said quietly to Madeline.

"Thank you, Father," she replied softly, coming closer. "I am grateful for all you have done for me. And for Dafydd, too."

Father Gabriel gave Sir Roger an apprehensive glance, but perhaps he did not hear, for he said nothing. Or more surprisingly, perhaps her brother was choosing to ignore her reference.

"I will pray for your health, my lady," Father Gabriel said, taking her thin hand in his. She was much too thin, and too pale. Indeed, he could see a change even from the previous day, and she was now quite different from the ruddy-cheeked young woman he had met on her arrival. His prayers would be needed if she continued to starve herself as he suspected she was doing, whether by accident or design. "I will pray for your happiness, too," he said, and so concerned was he for her health that he did not feel the small piece of sheepskin she put into his hand.

She smiled, a winsome, pathetic smile with more of sorrow than of mirth about it. "I will need your prayers, Father, although happiness, I fear, will be impossible. Nevertheless, it will be a help to me to know that you are thinking of me, and trying to help me." She withdrew her hand very slowly and it was then Father Gabriel noticed the parchment. Her glance flicked to it, then back to his face. A secret message?

For her sake, he clasped his two hands together, hiding it. "Farewell, my lady."

"Your horse and escort are waiting at the gate," Sir Roger said.

Startled, the priest replied, "I thank you kindly for the loan of a horse, but I have no need or wish for an escort."

"There are many dangers on the road," the Norman observed.

"Perhaps, but I am a man of peace and faith. God will see me safely home."

"And you have no desire to be any more beholden to the cold, cruel Sir Roger, eh?"

Father Gabriel was rather taken aback to hear his motive put in such a way, although he could not argue about the truth of it. "There is no need to take your men from other duties."

"Father, in this *one* thing, I must agree with Roger," Lady Madeline said sincerely. "Please accept an escort."

"I shall lose sleep worrying about you if you go alone," Sir Roger said sarcastically. "I must insist you take at least one soldier."

So that you can be certain I head straight for the monastery and do not speak to anyone, such as a stray Welshman who might be lingering in the vicinity, Father Gabriel thought as he looked at the two people, so alike and yet in some ways so dissimilar. "Very well. One man," he agreed reluctantly. "Goodbye, my lady."

"God go with you, Father Gabriel."

"Farewell, Sir Roger."

The Norman's final response was a curt nod.

Father Gabriel hurried out of the room and along the corridor until he came to a small alcove. Once there, he opened the folded piece of parchment. It was a note, written in the hand of a woman convent-reared, which said: *Father, D. will go to St. C. Please tell him I cannot come to him and I am doing what I must to save his life. But I shall love him, and only him, forever. M.*

Father Gabriel refolded the parchment and sighed deeply. If only there was some better way than being a messenger that he could help these two desperate young people!

* * *

Alcwyn hurried into the clearing, a blowsy, pleasant-faced, buxom young woman at his side. Dafydd, sitting among the other members of Alcwyn's band, watched with slight interest and wondered who she was. Alcwyn's sweetheart probably. Alcwyn had said he was going into the town that morning, ostensibly to find out any interesting news. Dafydd suspected there was another reason, and here she was.

But they were not acting like lovers enjoying a brief tryst. They came straight for Dafydd and he suddenly realized they both looked very concerned. He rose swiftly, observing them warily. "What's the matter?"

Alcwyn halted awkwardly. "Mildred works in the castle kitchen," he said by way of introduction. "She's heard something I think you ought to know."

"What? Is it Madeline?" Dafydd asked, slivers of dread snaking along his spine.

Mildred licked her lips nervously. "She's leaving today."

Perhaps his fears were all for naught, if she was heading south toward the monastery, he thought. "Where's she going?" he inquired casually.

"North, to her brother's castle. For her wedding."

Dafydd's mouth went dry in an instant. "Her wedding?"

Mildred nodded and reached for Alcwyn's beefy hand. "Yes. She's agreed to marry Lord Chilcott."

"It's a lie," Dafydd said at once. "Madeline would never acquiesce. It can't be true."

"Go easy, man. Mildred's speaking the truth," Alcwyn said softly. "She's telling you the talk about the castle, and I heard the same thing in the alehouse in the town."

"It could be that de Montmorency is trying to persuade her to give in, and still hopes to make it happen," Dafydd said slowly, persuading himself that he had guessed Sir Roger's scheme. His voice lowered. "How is she? How is Madeline?"

"Nobody's seen her, except for the servants been taking her food these past days," Mildred said.

"She hasn't been in the hall?"

"Never once. I would have heard, because we've all been curious. You know, her being such a beauty, so they say. Sir Roger told Lord Gervais that she was too ill to come to the hall."

"Ill?" He stared at them helplessly.

"A priest from the monastery of St. Christopher's, he's been looking after her," Mildred said with pity in her eyes.

"They've sent all that way?" Dafydd gasped. Part of him was glad Madeline would be under the care of one of the brothers who had helped him, but more, he was worried that her sickness was severe enough to warrant such trouble and expense.

"They didn't send for him. He came with Sir Roger. Sir Albert had Sir Roger taken to the monastery after Alcwyn's men wounded him."

"They weren't supposed to touch him," Alcwyn muttered.

"His name's Father Gabriel," Mildred offered.

"Father Gabriel," Dafydd said. "Then Madeline is having the best possible care. Why did he come here with Sir Roger? Was the fellow hurt that bad?" It didn't seem possible, not when Roger had arrived at Lord Gervais' on the same day they had. If he were seriously injured, he would still be in bed.

Alcwyn cleared his throat and gave Dafydd a shrewd look. "I heard they brought the priest to identify a man they seek. A thief, they say. The priest wasn't terribly pleased by the idea, I gather, but Sir Roger wouldn't take a refusal."

"No," Dafydd agreed. "A man's holy office wouldn't stop him from getting his own way, I daresay. I hope I haven't caused Father Gabriel too much trouble."

Alcwyn slapped his knee. "I knew it! I knew it was you! But you're no thief, Dafydd. A rebel and a patriot, but not a thief."

"I am now. I robbed the abbot's cell before I left."

"You robbed a monastery?" Alcwyn asked incredulously. "One as big as that?"

"I had no money, no horse, no clothes. Nothing but my sword, which was in the abbot's cell. I had little choice."

"Maybe this Father Gabriel's searching for the thief," Alcwyn suggested.

Dafydd nodded, but his expression was doubtful. "It could be, although I would never have thought Father Gabriel a vindictive man. Maybe someone else has forced him to seek me out. Maybe the abbot's returned...no. Jerrald. I would lay odds it has to be Father Jerrald."

"But nobody's looking for you," Mildred said. "Not Sir Roger, not Sir Albert, not the priest. No soldiers have been sent to search the forest or along the roads. I'd have heard about it if they had. Father Gabriel's already gone back to the monastery. He left Castle Gervais this morning, just after he broke the fast."

"What's going on, then?" Dafydd muttered more to himself than to his companions. Madeline not yet free—that would be Roger's doing, of course. She could easily have underestimated the amount of persuasion it would take to make her brother see how she felt. Was there any way, any way at all Roger could force her to agree to marry Chilcott? He didn't think so.

Father Gabriel had been brought all this way to identify him—but was no longer necessary. Apparently the thief was unimportant, too, and not worth the trouble of pursuing. Maybe Madeline had managed to convince Roger to let him go. But how? A man like her brother was not easy to sway, especially where thievery and rebellion figured into the equation. What had she told him or given him to make him agree?

The answer struck Dafydd with the same force as Owain's cudgel. Herself. She had agreed to the marriage in order to save *him*.

Dafydd straightened, the galvanizing force of conviction coursing through him as he reached for his sword. "I have to get her out of there. Who'll go with me?"

Owain started to his feet, a fierce and hungry gleam in his young eyes. Others, less certain, milled about, glancing at each other and Dafydd ap Iolo, the very vision of a warrior prince ready to lead his men to victory.

"What part of the castle is Madeline in?" he demanded.

"I'm not certain." Mildred looked worriedly at Alcwyn. "They're leaving, too, later today."

"Let's get them!" Owain cried excitedly. "Sir Roger will be worth a huge ransom! You also can rescue your lady," he added almost as an afterthought.

"Forgetting the first time?" Alcwyn said to him regretfully, avoiding Dafydd's eyes. "He'll be on his guard now, more than ever."

Much as Dafydd wanted to do as Owain suggested, he knew Alcwyn was right. It would be much too dangerous for them to attack Sir Roger de Montmorency.

Dafydd's gaze scanned the clearing and the men gathered there. "I agree it would be hazardous to go against Sir Roger. Maybe it would be better to find Father Gabriel and see if I'm right about why Madeline changed her mind. Does he have much of an escort?"

"Only Kynan is with him," Mildred answered with a broad grin.

"So?" Dafydd asked when he saw the pleased expression on Alcwyn's face.

"He's my cousin," Alcwyn said with a chuckle. "Not much trouble from him, although we'll have to make it look good, for his sake."

"We?"

"Not going to let you have all the fun, boy!" Alcwyn chided jovially. "Especially when it's nothing more than a priest and my cousin we're after."

"I will go, too!" Owain cried out.

"That will be plenty," Dafydd said. "First, I will speak with the good Father Gabriel before he travels too far and find out about Madeline." He became more serious. "Are you in the mood for more of a skirmish, Alcwyn, in a few days' time?" he asked, his tone still light but his gaze intense as he waited for his friend to respond. "Not with Sir Roger's men."

Owain nodded excitedly, and the other men looked more than curious.

"What have you in mind?" Alcwyn asked warily.

"How far away is Sir Roger's castle?"

"More north, more east. More Norman, if you understand me. It's risky, Dafydd, to go farther from the border."

"Getting cautious in your old age?"

Alcwyn looked about to reply in the affirmative, then grinned and shrugged his shoulders. "What the bloody hell. Like the old days, eh? But if not Sir Roger—"

"The bridegroom, boys, the bridegroom," Dafydd answered with a sly smile. "He won't know what's happened, because our dear Sir Roger will be too proud to tell him that he couldn't watch over his sister properly. And he will be worth a very pretty penny."

"Maybe a sister?"

"At the very least, I would say, and more into the bargain from DeGuerre, perhaps."

The men began to chuckle and Owain looked as if he had just been granted his heart's desire.

Father Gabriel was still puzzling over some way to be of assistance to the ill-fated lovers when his guard—he could not think of the heavily armed fellow beside him as anything else—suddenly pulled up short. From out of the trees surrounding the road a gang of ruffians appeared, armed with swords and bows. Strangely, there was something curiously unfrightening about this band of outlaws. Perhaps it was the smile on their faces and the laughter in their eyes.

"Greetings, Father!" said a voice he did not recognize. Another man stepped out of cover and walked onto the road.

"Is it you?" Father Gabriel asked, relieved when he recognized Dafydd. "I am delighted to see you again. God has answered my prayers, for it is necessary that I speak with you."

"I hope you will continue to be delighted when I tell you that I must delay your journey for a while. I want you to tell me about Madeline, and I fear the middle of the road is not the best place to talk."

"Quite right!" the priest exclaimed. "I will be only too pleased . . . oh, but what of this fellow?"

His escort was sitting morosely on his saddle, probably dismayed at being caught in this ignoble predicament.

"Oh, we'll see that he's well cared for," the Welshman said offhandedly. Two men came forward and took hold of the horses' bridles. "This way, please."

Chapter Sixteen

Father Gabriel was soon comfortably settled in the Welsh camp. His escort, apparently led away to spend his captivity languishing under guard, was, in actual fact, swapping stories and ale with Owain and some of the other men. Alcwyn had discreetly left Dafydd and Father Gabriel alone.

"I am indeed glad to see you again," the priest said.

"And I, you. My name is Dafydd ap Iolo," Dafydd replied. "Sorry I am I did not tell you before. I thought it would be wiser, for your sake and for mine, if you didn't know who and what I was. Sorry I am, too, for stealing from you. I took only what was necessary."

"We all thought so," Father Gabriel said kindly. "Or rather, most of us did. Unfortunately, Father Jerrald did not. I confess that I have been hoping to meet Abbot Absalom on the road and give him my own explanations."

Dafydd had no wish to appear rude, but the politics of life in the monastery were not his concern. Madeline was. "Lady Madeline, how is she? Is it true she's going to marry Chilcott after all?"

"She is well in body," the priest answered, "for the moment anyway, although greatly sick at heart. She is doing what she has to do to save your life."

"Sweet Jesus, I *knew* it! But it must not happen."

"She also said—" Father Gabriel's voice dropped and grew even more sorrowful "—that she will love you and only you, forever."

Dafydd smiled. "I know that, too, Father. I feel the same, and I will not let her marry another man, especially out of fear for my safety. What is my life if hers is to be the sacrifice?"

"A sacrifice is what I fear she will make of herself," Father Gabriel murmured. "She does not eat. She looks pale and tired. If only her brother could see what he is doing to her by forcing her into this marriage!"

The mournful way he spoke made Dafydd want to assault Castle Gervais single-handedly and at once. "Did he beat her? Is she hurt?" he demanded.

"I don't believe he has struck her, nor has he injured her physically, my son. But he has caused her great anguish and great fear, and that can be worse than any blow. I believe he threatened your life if she did not obey him.''

"He'd have to find me first.''

"I know the man, Dafydd, and you must believe me when I say that no matter where you went or how you hid, he would find you. Madeline understands that, too. Sir Roger de Montmorency is a very vengeful man, I think, and you have upset his plans greatly.'' The priest coughed delicately. "There is also the threat of scandal. I think Sir Roger fears his plans are not secure even now. If Lord Chilcott finds out about Lady Madeline's... adventure... alone, with a man, for days and *nights*...''

"Then the marriage contract will be broken,'' Dafydd said with some measure of satisfaction.

"I would not be so certain of that, my young friend. Sir Roger is also a powerful man, and from what I have heard of Chilcott, I believe Sir Roger might be able to persuade the fellow to marry Lady Madeline anyway. In fact, given the possible scandal, he may consider the marriage even more necessary.''

"If Chilcott knew everything—'' Dafydd began hotly, then stopped himself.

"Knew what, my son? That the lady doesn't want him? I think Sir Roger could convince him to overlook that.''

"Madeline's already my wife, if not in the eyes of the Church," Dafydd said after a moment's hesitation.

Father Gabriel frowned. "There would be some basis for a scandal, then?"

Dafydd nodded. "So you see, Father, she and I are already more than pledged to each other. I want only to have her back, and I mean to have her safe with me as soon as possible."

"It would be rash foolishness to attempt to attack Sir Roger or his men," the priest warned.

"We've thought of that. It's Chilcott we'll go for."

"To what end?"

"To convince him that it wouldn't be wise to marry Madeline," Dafydd said.

"Even if you were able to do that, do you think Sir Roger would set Madeline free to marry whomever she wishes?"

"What else can I do?" Dafydd demanded desperately. All he could see in his mind was Madeline, alone and vulnerable at the hands of her forceful brother. His expression grew grimly determined. "We must save her and soon."

"As much as I dislike conflict, in this instance, I quite agree. It is not right to force any young woman into a marriage she does not want.

"Of course, once she is returned to you, you must marry her with a proper blessing. It is not right to make love outside the bounds of holy matrimony, either, Dafydd. It *is* right that you should make your relationship a legal one, as well as a physical one."

"Of course." Dafydd eyed the priest. "I must confess I am surprised to find you so firmly on my side, Father," he remarked. He pulled up some grass and twisted it in his fingers. "What if we 'detain' Chilcott? Madeline can be very persuasive. It could be that if she had more time, she could convince Roger to stop the wedding."

"You have never met Sir Roger, have you?" Father Gabriel asked.

"We have to do *something*. I don't want to hurt Chilcott, but I suppose I will do what I must," Dafydd murmured.

"I do not wish to see harm done to any man, my son." The priest also pulled up some grass and stared at it pensively. "If only I had a better idea of what sort of man Chilcott is, I might be able to help you think of something to stop the marriage. Unfortunately, nobody knows him, not even Baron DeGuerre, or so I hear. Chilcott has spent most of his life in Sicily, on his estate there. The abbot has met him. He stayed in Sicily while on a pilgrimage, but he didn't say anything about him, really."

"Sicily?" So far away. Nobody here knew the man....

Suddenly an incredible, wonderful, probably impossible idea burst into Dafydd's head, a plan such as Madeline herself would devise. "*Nobody* knows him?"

"His father, brothers and half sister live on his English estates, but they are far to the southeast. I understand they are not expected at the wedding because of the father's illness."

"What of the other wedding guests?"

"None but the abbot have met him, I would venture to say. Or even seen him. He has come directly from Sicily."

"Do you know anything of his looks?"

"I believe he is dark haired. Nothing more."

"Height, build?"

The priest shook his head. "I don't see—"

Owain appeared from a shadowed place in the trees nearby, where he had obviously been eavesdropping. Dafydd forgave him when he heard the youth say, "I know what he looks like. My Norman master took me to Sicily once."

"Describe him," Dafydd ordered excitedly.

"Your height, skinny as a stick, dark hair like the priest says. An overdressed, pompous fop," he finished with disdain.

"Wonderful! The abbot—when was he due to arrive at de Montmorency's castle?"

"I was not privy to his exact plans, but I believe he was to get there the day before the wedding."

"Excellent! Better and better!" Dafydd cried, his eyes glowing with all the excitement he felt.

"I don't understand—" the priest and Owain said in unison.

Dafydd jumped to his feet. "Alcwyn!" he called out, then he knelt in front of the confused priest. "A wedding is planned. Let there be a wedding!"

"But my son—!"

"Nobody but the abbot knows what the bridegroom is supposed to look like. If the groom and the abbot are waylaid and replaced by the *right* man and a priest with Madeline's best interests in his heart, then let the wedding proceed!" he finished triumphantly.

"Dafydd!" The priest stood up and eyed the excited young man dubiously. "Let me understand you. You are proposing that you and I replace Chilcott and the abbot?"

"Yes! Alcwyn and some of his men—ones who can keep their mouth shut—can take the place of the soldiers. It need not be for long—I can say I was delayed getting to Sir Roger's! It could work!"

"But so much could go wrong. What if somebody recognizes *you?*"

"What Normans are going to know...?" He paused and frowned. "Morgan. Fitzroy. They would know me, if they are invited to the wedding. Your escort would know about Fitzroy."

"Hu Morgan will be overseeing Lord Trevelyan's lands while he is attending the wedding," Father Gabriel said slowly. "I heard Sir Roger and Sir Albert discussing the guests and the necessity of advising them of the slight delay in their return to his castle. Are they the only people who might identify you?"

Dafydd's eyes twinkled with more happiness than he had felt since leaving Madeline. "The only Normans. Not cultivated any others' acquaintance."

Father Gabriel cleared his throat nervously. "Forgive me for saying so, my son, but I must point out that you are *not* a Norman nobleman. Do you truly expect to pass for one?"

Dafydd grinned mischievously. "I had the best teachers for the language in the monastery and lots of practice since with Madeline," he said, "and Owain can teach me the manners and etiquette on the way to Sir Roger's castle."

"Your scheme still seems very risky," the priest said.

"I'll take the risk."

"What of Alcwyn, Owain and the rest? Will you risk their lives, too?

Dafydd suddenly felt as if his heart had plummeted back to the dull earth from the glories of heaven. "No. No, I suppose I can't."

"And let us miss the chance for some *real* wealth?" Alcwyn charged, stepping out the trees. "God's wounds, Dafydd, thought you'd been attacked, you sounded so excited. Now, what is this about *you* not risking *us?* Why, this is the chance of a lifetime, boy! Chilcott's baggage alone will be worth a fortune, if he's as rich as I hear. And think of all the portables waiting to be snatched at the wedding, too. One chalice would keep a family in food for months. We could all settle down for good. By God's holy blood, Dafydd, if you've got the guts to walk into Sir Roger's castle, you can wager we've got the guts to follow you! And if you can pass yourself off as a Norman, we can learn a little Sicilian."

Dafydd smiled his heartfelt gratitude and turned to Father Gabriel. "Will you help us, Father Gabriel?"

"Only if I have your word that no one will be harmed."

"Treat the abbot and Chilcott as gently as newborn babes, we will, won't we, Alcwyn?" he replied. "After the wedding, we'll all slip away into the mists of Wales. Then the abbot and Chilcott can go—for a fee, of course. That would be only fair to Alcwyn and his men."

"Not needing to bother with a ransom, Daf-ydd," Alcwyn said quickly. "The baggage and what we can lift from the castle will be plenty, without the danger of lingering about to bargain with Sir Roger. When we're ready, we can send a ransom note, then leave the abbot and Chilcott and their men. They'll be found soon enough, and in the meantime, we can be halfway to Snowdonia."

"The abbot will feel most humiliated," Father Gabriel noted, and for a moment, Dafydd doubted the priest, until Father Gabriel smiled with rather a lot of devilment for a holy man. "But then, hu-mility is good for the soul."

Much had changed at her old home, Madeline reflected listlessly as she rode a short distance be-hind her brother's horse and they approached the walls of her family's castle. It was not nearly as huge or imposing as the strongholds of Lord Ger-vais and Trevelyan. Her parents had seen no need to enlarge the circular wall of the old castle. In-stead, they had added to the size and comfort of the interior buildings, so that visitors often remarked that Montmorency Castle seemed more like a big manor house than a fortress. Unfortunately, it looked more like a prison to her now.

The village around the castle walls had grown, and she wondered how many people she might recognize if she cared to look about.

How happy she would have been to come back here under different circumstances! If Roger had come for her with no talk of an arranged marriage, it would have been cause for celebration to be home again. If she were coming to be married to Dafydd, she would have rejoiced.

Now, however, she felt more sadness than anything else. Here she would give herself to another man, and not even the knowledge that doing so would save Dafydd could make her anything less than miserable.

Where was Dafydd now, she wondered, as she had so often during the whole of the long, tedious journey from Bridgeford Wells. Was he safe? Was he already back at the monastery? Had Father Gabriel given him her message? Would he understand?

There was the portcullis and the gate. Long ago she had ridden beneath them, crying and begging Roger not to let them take her away. Did he remember, too, how he had run after her and had to be restrained by Lord Gervais, who kept telling him it was all for the best that she go to a convent?

He must not, for there was nothing of that boy in this nobleman in front of her, a man so determined to achieve his own ends at her expense.

And yet, when the entourage rode beneath the portcullis, Roger half turned in his saddle as if he would speak to her. She held her breath and waited, but he remained silent.

In the yard, servants hastened to take hold of the horses. An older man, finely dressed in a way that showed he was more than a servant, hurried up to her, a smile on his round face. "Little Lady Madeline!" he cried, and suddenly she knew who it was.

"Dudley!" she answered with true joy as she recognized her father's steward. A trusted and loyal Saxon, Dudley had taken care of the estate until Roger came of age. "How good to see you again."

"You've grown, my lady," Dudley remarked with a chuckle. "Me, too, but only in age, eh?"

She smiled back, but instead of returning the smile, his eyes scanned her face and he frowned. "What's the matter? Are you ill?"

"She is merely fatigued," Roger said brusquely, striding toward them and glaring at Madeline. "She needs to rest." With that, he firmly placed her hand on his arm and escorted her toward the hall.

Dudley watched them go, the girl he had dandled on his knee grown into a fine, beautiful young lady—the most unhappy young lady he had ever seen.

Although Sir Roger was not a man given to empty courtesies and meaningless pleasantries, he looked more aloof and harried than Dudley could ever recall, too.

Dudley remembered very well the old lord and lady of this castle. Fine people, kind and generous masters, who had been well and truly mourned when they died within days of each other. It had been an honor to oversee their estate until their son reached an age to take over the role.

When Sir Roger had returned from his training under Lord Gervais, he had not been the happy, carefree lad Dudley had known, but that was to be expected. He, and most of the other servants who had served Lord and Lady de Montmorency, had hoped that Sir Roger would become more his old self as time passed and he grew used to the duties and responsibilities of his life. They thought he had, to a small degree, although he seemed very concerned with pleasing his overlord, the Baron DeGuerre. No one questioned that, until the news of Lady Madeline's betrothal. They had all thought Lady Madeline would come back to live at the castle and that perhaps things could be as they were in the old days.

No chance of that now, and Dudley's hope that she would be happy in her marriage had dwindled to nothingness the moment he saw her face.

With weary steps and the sudden unhappy thought that perhaps he had lived too long, Dudley followed Sir Roger and his sorrowful sister into the hall.

Chapter Seventeen

With the stealth born of years of practice and training, Dafydd and the rest of the men moved through the wooded countryside that was a few miles to the south and east of Sir Roger's castle, beside the road Lord Chilcott would use. They had been traveling five days, going slowly to escape detection, and to allow Dafydd time for Owain's plentiful instructions. Only the knowledge that his future with Madeline depended on how well he learned gave him the patience to suffer through it.

Dafydd, Owain and ten others had come to intercept Lord Chilcott; another band of men, led by Alcwyn, were on the southern road, waiting for the abbot.

Dafydd reached a place that afforded a clear view of the way for nearly a mile. The area was heavily forested, and it was midmorning. Farmers and others who might be going to market in the village outside Montmorency Castle would most likely have passed by already, so they had nothing to do now but wait.

Dafydd crouched and silently signaled the men to deploy throughout the trees.

Mercifully, they had not long to linger before a nobleman and his entourage came into view. The nobleman and his servant were mounted; his armed soldiers followed on foot. A heavily laden baggage cart came at the rear.

Dafydd glanced at Owain, who knelt nearby. A slow smile spread on the youth's face and he nodded.

Dafydd's gaze returned to the man Sir Roger had wanted married to his sister, who was riding a splendid white horse bearing immaculate accoutrements. Chilcott himself was young, not unattractive and wearing the most extravagant of fashions. His ornately curled black hair was covered by an elaborately embroidered cap; his striped tunic of light blue and green had enormous oversleeves slashed to show a dark blue undertunic; his scarlet gauntlets were also embellished with intricate embroidery; and his long leather boots had been painted to match his tunic.

Chilcott was also obviously a fool, for his garments and equipment were so decorated and therefore costly, he would be a target for any thief within twenty miles. His body servant, riding a fine mare, was nearly as well attired.

Dafydd was disgusted to think Sir Roger or any man would hope to see his sister wed to such a coxcomb. That it was a woman of Madeline's beauty and spirit made such a scheme even worse. Yet there was some gladness, too, in his heart, for this fellow seemed nearly his height, which would make his ruse that much easier. However, he could now see the whole of Chilcott's troop, dressed in identical ensembles. They were stocky, fierce looking and well armed, so perhaps this fellow was not quite the fool he seemed at first.

Dafydd rose stealthily. "It's time," he whispered. "Make sure you follow the plan," he quietly admonished Owain, then he marched out of the shelter of the forest alone and shouted, "Hold!" Three chosen men, including Owain, joined him and they faced the nobleman, who reined in abruptly, a startled and frightened look on his face.

"What is the meaning of this?" Lord Chilcott cried, his voice shrill and his eyes reminiscent of those of a rabbit startled by torchlight.

"Sir Roger has sent us ahead to seek out Lord Chilcott."

The nobleman relaxed visibly, and his expression became one of annoyance rather than terror. "I am Lord Chilcott. Well, what does he want? It had better not be another delay, by God! I have already put up with enough postponements.''

"We've been sent to show you a shorter route,'' Dafydd said peaceably.

Chilcott ran his haughty gaze over Dafydd and his men. "You have? Who, may I ask, are you?"

"A guide. He has few men to spare, with the preparations for the wedding and the arrival of the guests.''

"Huh! What guests? It is my understanding that most of the important people won't be there. Not even Baron DeGuerre, and this was all his doing. Something is not right about this, mark my words. I would have done better to stay in Sicily. Well, fellow, what are you doing standing there? Lead the way!"

"Yes, my lord," Dafydd said with a bow. Then he proceeded to walk down the road toward a fork. One way led to Montmorency Castle, the other toward a village to the south.

"I never should have let DeGuerre talk me into this marriage," Lord Chilcott grumbled. "I could have stayed in Normandy. It's much more civilized, I assure you. Why, I couldn't find a decent tailor in the whole of godforsaken London. And who are the de Montmorencys anyway? Minor nobility! That sister of his had better be as beautiful as they say!"

Dafydd had always thought of the Normans, except for Madeline, as an enormous gang of villains. He had supposed they had all considered themselves united by their alleged superiority to those they conquered. It was quite new, and even amusing, to hear one Norman disparage another.

Dafydd led Lord Chilcott and his men to the southern road.

"Such a strange thing, this business," Chilcott complained. "I mean, you would think Sir Roger would have the courtesy to meet me. Or send a proper emissary, not... you. Such rudeness! I wouldn't stand for it, except that DeGuerre sets such store by him.

"Really, I feel as if I am living among barbarians. I felt safer in the Alps, and they're full of *banditti* these days."

Although the man's chatter was tiresome and impertinent and Dafydd wanted to knock the vain fellow from his steed, he hoped Chilcott would keep on talking, so that he would not realize he was losing his men pair by pair as Alcwyn's men silently slipped behind a rank of soldiers and dragged them into the woods. The baggage cart and its driver had long since ceased to be on the road.

Nothing would happen to Chilcott's men, except that they would be prevented from going anywhere until Dafydd and Madeline were safely away.

Then they would be released with Lord Chilcott and the abbot, minus the baggage cart.

"At least I shall have three days at de Montmorency's castle to recover from this taxing journey before the wedding. I shall need them, if I am to appear my best before the wedding guests. I wonder what Sir Roger has planned in the way of entertainment. And I do hope he's got some decent cooks. You can't always tell out here on the frontier."

When Dafydd was sure the remaining number of Chilcott's men were easily outnumbered by Alcwyn's, he halted.

Chilcott finally shut his mouth for more than a moment and looked myopically about him. "I say, there, fellow, have you forgotten the way?" Chilcott demanded scornfully. "This doesn't look like much of a road to me."

"You're absolutely right, my lord. We've gone the wrong way."

"Well, if this isn't a nuisance! I shall tell Sir Roger of your incompetence the moment I see him."

"Which won't be for some time, I'm afraid, Lord Chilcott."

"What the devil are you talking about?" Several more Welshmen appeared on the road and came to stand beside Dafydd. "What in the—

Men!'' Chilcott turned to look behind him, and Dafydd almost felt sorry for the nobleman when he turned back with a pale face and frightened eyes. "What's going on? Where are my men?"

"They're going to be enjoying Welsh hospitality, my lord, same as you," Dafydd said companionably, drawing his sword out in a leisurely manner. "While we wait for a ransom."

"Oh, my God," Lord Chilcott moaned. Then he fell from his saddle in a dead faint.

Father Gabriel hurried toward Dafydd and his men as they returned to the camp. With an anxious face he looked at the finely attired man slumped over the saddle. "Is he hurt?" the priest inquired uneasily. "You told me no one would be hurt."

"I have kept my word," Dafydd replied with a grin. "He fainted, nothing more."

"Fainted?"

"Fainted. And this is the man Sir Roger thinks would make a good husband for Madeline!" Dafydd grabbed Chilcott by the hair and lifted his head. "Still, he has dark hair like me, and he looks the same height, so Sir Roger could have chosen worse."

None too gently Dafydd pulled Lord Chilcott from the saddle. He set him on the ground with more care, however, because he didn't want to stain

Chilcott's clothing. He couldn't very well arrive at Montmorency Castle with his clothes in a stained, torn state.

"Where are the rest of his men?" Father Gabriel asked.

"They'll be here soon enough." Dafydd pulled off one of Chilcott's scarlet gauntlets and tried it on. He flexed his fingers. "Any sign of Alcwyn and the good abbot?"

"Not yet. The abbot would not faint," the priest remarked worriedly. "He may even put up a struggle." The priest's face furrowed with doubt. "Perhaps I should not involve myself in this business. I would never forgive myself if anyone came to harm."

Dafydd was now unlacing Chilcott's blue and green tunic. "What of Madeline?" he demanded unsympathetically. "You yourself it was told me how ill she looked. What about her?"

"Yes, you're quite right."

At that moment, there was the sound of men pushing their way through the trees. Dafydd reached for his sword, gesturing for the priest to get out of sight. Owain and the others drew their weapons, too.

Alcwyn appeared, unceremoniously prodding the burly abbot ahead of him with his sword. The abbot's gown was somewhat askew, and he had the remnants of leaves in his gray hair. His face was as red as Chilcott's gauntlet.

"Sit down!" Alcwyn barked, his own face flushed and sweaty. He sheathed his weapon. "God's truth!" he swore, wiping his brow as he approached Dafydd, glancing at the young nobleman at Dafydd's feet. "I wish I had that fellow to find," he commented, nudging Chilcott with his toe. "The abbot did not want to join us and put up quite a fight, for a clergyman."

The abbot stared with round, fishlike eyes at Dafydd. *"You!"*

"Me."

"I knew you were a varlet! I tried to warn the others, but that stubborn fool of a Gabriel—"

"Be quiet, or abbot or no, I'll make you keep quiet."

At Dafydd's harsh and quite obviously meant words, the abbot grew silent. Then, and only then, did he notice that he was not the only person in possible danger. "Sweet, merciful God!" he exclaimed, "what have you done to Chilcott?"

"Nothing. He's having a little nap, is all. Owain, take the abbot someplace where he can rest in comfort."

Owain did not look pleased with the request, but he complied and, following Alcwyn's example, prodded the abbot with his sword, directing the clergyman to Alcwyn's wagon a short ways through the trees. There was a third encampment, some distance in the other direction, where Father Gabriel and Dafydd spent their time. Alcwyn and Dafydd had decided it would be the best and wisest thing to keep their captives and Father Gabriel well away from each other.

Dafydd bent down and divested Chilcott of his tunic. It was surprisingly heavy, and at first Dafydd attributed it to the fabric, which was soft and fine and of a type totally unknown to him. It must have come from far away, he reasoned.

He pulled on the garment and realized something was very wrong. He tugged it off and turned it inside out. Then he saw what the trouble was. There were pads stuffed with sawdust on the shoulders and upper arms, and a quick squeeze of Chilcott's upper arm proved Dafydd's suspicions. Chuckling, Dafydd ripped out the pads and tried the tunic on again. It fit very well.

"Iffwrdd," Alcwyn said, stepping into the clearing and carrying other clothes for the nobleman. "I wouldn't have known you in that attire myself. Looking every inch the nobleman, you. Or a prince who's been in disguise."

"I do?" Dafydd smiled to himself. "Well, my grandmother *was* a princess," he remarked pensively.

"Of course." Alcwyn pointed to the padding. "What's that?"

"The poor popinjay has not the muscles for his height, it seems, and he's sought to correct the deficit with sawdust."

"Well, he won't like these, then, at all." Alcwyn laid the rough homespun garments on the ground. "I'll help you with the rest."

"The others—have they tried the soldiers' tunics?"

"Yes. I think they fit well enough."

"Strange, all identical, eh?"

"I've heard of this. It's supposed to show the men all belong to the same lord."

"Huh. Well, we'd better tie Chilcott up before he comes to. What do you think of the abbot?"

"He's not very polite," Alcwyn observed. "Or peaceable, either."

"Didn't think he would be."

"Father Gabriel seems a good sort."

"Yes. So are you. And your men. I won't ever forget this, Alcwyn," Dafydd said, smiling warmly at his friend.

"Good. Might need a favor myself someday, and you can be sure I'll come calling. Where will I look?"

"I've been thinking about that. Madeline and I can't stay anywhere near here. I thought I'd try my luck in the north. My grandmother's half sister married a Norman. They tell me the Welsh is strong in her son. Maybe Emryss DeLanyea will heed the tie of family and let me swear fealty to him. For Madeline's sake, it might be better in such a man's castle than a Welsh village.''

"Aye, I suppose." Alcwyn tugged off Chilcott's hose. "There. He's down to his breeches." They both surveyed the half-naked nobleman. "God's truth, looks like a plucked chicken, doesn't he?" Alcwyn observed.

Dafydd chuckled his agreement, then grew more serious. "Three days to the wedding, he said. We'll leave at first light."

"Tomorrow? Are you mad, Dafydd? You'll be in de Montmorency's fortress for two nights and a day before the wedding. That's taking even more of a chance."

"Owain's been teaching me everything I need to know. I don't want Madeline alone in there any longer than necessary."

"Still, that much time..."

"Don't worry. The castle will be busy with the wedding preparations. Nobody should take much notice of you and your men if they keep to themselves."

"But what about you, Dafydd? Taking notice of you, they'll be. Watching you like a hawk."

"Owain's thought of that. If I get into trouble with the manners or the customs, he said I should tell them it's something they do in Sicily."

"I don't like it, Dafydd. Wait another day."

"I won't leave Madeline to suffer a moment longer than she has to," Dafydd said firmly, and Alcwyn realized it would be pointless to argue any more.

Chapter Eighteen

Madeline stood in her chamber and silently submitted to the women fitting her for her wedding dress. They twitted and fussed about her like hens who have spied the shadow of a hawk, only instead of cackling and flapping their wings, they whispered and commented and tugged and pulled.

Madeline didn't pay much attention to their ministrations. She was thinking about her old dress, the one she had taken from the unknown peasant woman. The one Dafydd had hated, although it seemed he could hardly take his gaze off her when she wore it. For that reason, she had liked it immensely.

It was gone now. Roger, claiming it was surely lice infested, had ordered it burned. He had purchased several others for her, and she had wondered if it was out of gratitude for her compliance, or to assuage his own guilt. She had seen little of him since their arrival here, so she had no idea of his true purpose. Still, it had always been Roger's way to hide when he realized he was wrong, rather than face the consequences. Either way, the gowns were simply cloth to her. And the food for the feast, though very expensive, would all taste like sawdust.

Dafydd would scarcely recognize her in this fine garment, she thought as one of the seamstresses adjusted the hem. For her wedding, she was to wear an overgown of heavy and ornate brocade, white with gold threads worked through it, which would lace at the sides with threads of gold. Underneath would be a scarlet long-sleeved dress of a thin fabric Roger had called silk. It was very costly and came from far away in the East. Her hair would be bound in a crispinette of netted gold and scarlet. On her head would be a jeweled circlet that had been her mother's. On the outside, she would surely look very regal and very fine. Inside, she would be weeping bitter tears and only the knowledge that she was doing this for Dafydd's sake would keep them from spilling out.

Indeed, when she glanced at the reflection in the burnished metal the seamstresses held up, she scarcely recognized herself. She supposed that really wasn't to be wondered at. She felt like a different person. A miserable person.

Nevertheless, she was not sorry for loving Dafydd. She did not regret anything about her time with him, except for her foolish decision to go to Bridgeford Wells. They should have left England for Wales at once, and found another way to inform Roger of her decision. She had been wrong about that and very wrong about Roger himself.

"If you please, my lady," the short, plump seamstress said, "can you lift your right arm again? See," she whispered to another tall, skinny woman, "those lacings can most certainly be tightened. It's not the seam at all."

"But if you tighten the laces too much, none of the undergarment will be seen. Better if we take in this back," the thin one said, tugging abruptly and almost pulling Madeline over.

"Stop!" she said impatiently. "It fits well enough."

The two women looked startled, as if they had forgotten they were dealing with a living woman and not some straw facsimile.

"Help me out of this now, and then leave me," Madeline ordered.

"But my lady, there's two more gowns for you to try on and—"

Madeline reached under her arm to begin to untie the side lacing herself, which galvanized the plump woman into action. "Here, let me!"

"Is there something about the dress you don't care for?" the skinny woman asked, finally displaying some discernment.

"All the gowns are lovely," Madeline replied, with somewhat better grace. *It's not your fault I would rather you were making my shroud,* she thought.

Suddenly the door crashed open and Roger strode into the room. "Get out of that," he snapped abruptly.

"When you leave the room, these women will finish removing the gown," she said coldly, curious and suspicious about Roger's sudden appearance.

"Wear that purple gown. I've just been informed that Chilcott and his party are outside the village."

Madeline's throat constricted and she could only stare helplessly. She realized that without being aware of it, she had been hoping something would prevent Chilcott from coming.

"Help her," Roger commanded the women. "Come into the hall when you're ready," he said to Madeline, the tone no different from that he had used with the seamstresses. Then he left as abruptly as he had entered.

The seamstresses stood mutely still, until Madeline sighed. Then they sprang to life as if they had been shot from a bow. With agile fingers and a minimum of talk, they divested Madeline of her wedding finery and scurried about gathering her new gown of purple, with silver trim and matching crispinette.

Madeline made no effort to either help or hinder. She had been dreading this day ever since she had made her bargain with Roger, and knew she had no choice but to submit.

But it was difficult. So very difficult... Her mind would bring back pictures of Dafydd, walking in front of her, leading the horse. Dafydd sitting beside her, silent, strong, so handsome in his plain garments. Dafydd wrestling Fitzroy because he was jealous.

"My lady, please!" the plump seamstress chided gently, pulling her away from her memories. "You're going to tear the seam if you keep pulling on that thread."

"Oh, listen! That must be him!" the skinny one cried. She hurried to the narrow window and leaned out. Her plump fellow servant also rushed to the aperture and her companion made way, but she was not so successful in her attempt to lean out of the window. Nonetheless, when she drew back, she was smiling broadly. "Oh, my lady!" she murmured, clasping her hands together like the most fervent of the novices at the convent, "he's so handsome!"

"And tall!" the other cried.

"And well dressed!"

"Come see!"

With reluctant steps, Madeline moved toward the window. She was in no great hurry to see the man who might as well be her executioner, but these women expected some curiosity from her, so to avoid gossip, she would look.

Madeline leaned out the window toward the gathering of mounted men and horses in the court-yard below. Yes, that was obviously a nobleman's retinue, wearing similar tunics. And that man seated at the head of them, on a fine white stallion, that must be Reginald Chilcott.

But there was something...

Then the man dismounted, swinging easily from the back of the prancing horse, smiling at Roger—and she knew. Instantly, without a doubt. Dafydd! Come here to save her?

Pretending to be Reginald Chilcott—as she had feigned Sister Mary of the Holy Wounds and a peasant girl! Her fears and dread disintegrated, to be replaced by an urgent need to laugh with joy. She started to, and clapped her hand to her mouth when the two startled seamstresses looked at her.

She turned away and coughed, realizing she must be more circumspect. Any sudden change in her demeanor would attract suspicion.

Oh, but Dafydd was *here!* Dressed in someone else's clothes, riding someone else's horse. Here to rescue her!

She took a deep breath and turned back toward the seamstresses, who were puzzled and curious. "I...I was so happy because he has come after all," she explained. "I was so afraid he would change his mind. I have been worried that he would hear about my troubles and think me unworthy! I was even too upset to eat. Oh dear, how sickly I will seem to him!" she cried, with unmistakable and quite real sincerity.

Seeing that the seamstresses no longer looked doubtful, she hurried from the chamber, pinching her cheeks in an effort to restore their hue. To have Dafydd see her this way—oh, but what did it matter? He was here!

She dashed along the stone corridor, the soft leather soles of her shoes making little noise above the pounding of her pulse in her ears. She slowed when she reached the stairs and with a very great effort, managed to walk slowly down to the great hall.

"My sister will be here to greet you shortly," Roger said as he stood beside Lord Chilcott in the courtyard. "She was trying on her wedding garments and had to change."

"Indeed?" Reginald Chilcott replied, his voice a cultured but somewhat unusual drawl. "I look forward to meeting her. Guiseppe!" he shouted, and a young man, obviously his squire, stepped forward.

"Take my baggage to my chamber after the horses have been seen to."

"My steward, Dudley, will send a servant to the stable to show you the chamber," Roger said to the squire, who nodded. Roger turned his attention back to Lord Chilcott. "I have had some refreshments prepared for you in the hall."

"You are too kind. I hope our arrival so early in the day will not cause any difficulties. You must forgive an impatient bridegroom."

"Not at all." Roger headed for the hall, making his way through the crowd of men, servants and horses and waiting for Chilcott to fall into step beside him. As he did so, he surreptitiously studied his future brother-in-law, who was not at all what Roger had expected. DeGuerre had hinted that Chilcott was a rather vain, conceited fellow of no great distinction except for his family name. If *this* man was vain, Roger thought, he had some reason for being so. He was tall, very muscular, handsome, and carried himself with a bearing that was at once noble and natural. No conceited coxcomb, although he was somewhat overdressed. More surprising, his accent was rather strange and his manners a trifle forced. "Guiseppe? That's an odd sort of name for a squire, isn't it?" Roger asked when Chilcott joined him.

"Not if one's mother is Sicilian," Chilcott replied coolly, surveying the castle fortifications with a very shrewd expression.

Roger had nearly forgotten that Chilcott had spent most of his life in another land, although that undoubtedly explained the man's rather odd accent. Perhaps he would want to return there, with Madeline. The notion was far from pleasing. Of course, he had been living apart from his sister for years, but he had taken comfort in the fact that she was not that far away.

Chilcott did not seem quite the simpleton De-Guerre had led him to expect, either. Maybe Madeline would be more reconciled to this marriage once she had met the groom, and maybe her brother's choice for her was not so clever. Somehow he couldn't see this fellow giving in to anyone completely, let alone a woman. "Ah, yes, Sicily. It is quite lovely there, I hear."

"No better place in the world, if you don't mind the heat," Chilcott replied with conviction. "Charming country, delicious wine." He leaned closer to Roger and winked. "The women are all hot-blooded, too."

Roger barked a short laugh that caught the attention of his servants. Roger de Montmorency's laughter was so rare, it was some moments before they returned to their tasks.

"I trust your sister has recovered from this nasty business?" Chilcott asked.

Roger cleared his throat before replying. He had sent no word about Madeline's recent experiences. How had Chilcott heard? Probably gossip. Some nobles were worse than servants in that regard. "She is quite well. A trifle pale, perhaps, but nothing serious."

"Good. I would hate the ceremony to be delayed. Oh, and I should tell you, so that you can inform your servants, that my men are a rather quick tempered lot and had best be left alone."

"Really?"

"Quite. They're the best fighters money can buy."

"Indeed?"

They entered the hall, a large, impressive room hung with tapestries, lined with trestle tables laid with fine linens that had not been taken down after breaking the fast, and a raised dais at the far end. Because one wall was part of the castle's outer wall, the room had a curved shape such as Dafydd had never seen before. He had never seen a stone fireplace, either, such as had been built into the wall.

He realized he was staring, and turned his attention to the stone stairs beside the dais that led to a second floor.

And there he saw Madeline, gliding down the stairs at the far end of the hall with a beautiful smile on her lovely face.

Every particle of his body yearned to run to her and gather her into his arms. He even took a step, then halted. Roger was there at his elbow, so Dafydd had to content himself—and very poor contentment it was—with simply watching her progress.

As she drew near, she kept her eyes lowered, except for one brief instant when Roger turned to a servant to order him to bring wine. She looked up at Dafydd then, and he saw the delight in her eyes that matched the happiness in his heart.

But how pale she looked! How ill! Father Gabriel was indeed right to be worried about her health.

"This is my sister, Lady Madeline de Montmorency."

"I bid you welcome, Lord Chilcott," she said, her voice frigidly, wisely formal. He had known he could count on Madeline to be clever enough to guess what he was doing.

Dafydd made a deep bow that had taken him hours to master. "I am so completely charmed, my lady," he said, rising.

Roger's gaze went from one to the other, and Dafydd suddenly hoped he wasn't grinning like an idiot. If he stayed near Madeline, he might betray his feelings. Although it was difficult, he decided he had better leave her presence for the moment.

He recalled that Owain had said Chilcott had a liking for fine horses and said, "I daresay Lady Madeline has much to do before our wedding. I suggest we leave her to it. I hear you've got some excellent horses, Sir Roger. May I see them before the noon meal?"

"Of course," Roger replied. "We shall join you later, Madeline."

"Very well," she said flatly, turning to go. They watched her for a moment as she went back toward the chamber stairs.

"I say, Roger, is your sister quite all right?" Dafydd asked.

"Yes. She's not been sleeping very well. It's nothing more."

"Good. Shall we go to the stables, then?"

Something strange was going on, Roger thought later at the evening meal as he leaned back in his chair and sipped his wine.

Perhaps it was just that Chilcott was not at all as he had anticipated. In the stables, the man had asked several perceptive questions, although he didn't seem to know anything about the new breeds popular in Europe. In the weapons store after the noon meal, he had taken one of the finest swords in Roger's arsenal and hefted it with great admiration. He had made some practice swings that bespoke experience of battle, yet Roger understood that Chilcott had never fought in his life, not even in a tournament. Of course, it could be that the fellow had simply had fine teachers.

But Baron DeGuerre thought Chilcott would never make a good commander. That was truly puzzling. Chilcott's men watched his every move with expressions that bespoke concern and devotion. Only the most worthy of nobles were able to command such respect from their men.

And what was he to make of Madeline? She no longer seemed so adamantly opposed to the marriage, although she had not said otherwise. His opinion came more from a change in her manner. She was polite, of course, and had conversed with Reginald Chilcott several times during the meal, although she seemed tense and edgy still. But there was something...something *more* in Madeline's eyes when she looked at him. Maybe Chilcott had impressed her, too. Of course. That had to be the explanation. And maybe, too, she had finally come to realize that her brother was right about the impropriety and problems of marrying beneath her.

His gaze roved over the high table, passing over Madeline and Chilcott and taking note of who had arrived later that day for the wedding—Lord Gervais, older and not looking very well, and Trevelyan, happy to be a grandfather. The two noblemen were having yet another argument about training squires. Albert was sitting farther down the hall, trying to engage one of Chilcott's men in a conversation without much luck.

The musicians arrived and the servants began to push the tables back for dancing. Roger thought it undignified to dance, but the others might enjoy it, so he had arranged for music. He noted sourly that a minstrel, a slender fellow with a girlish face, was among them. If the man tried to sing a ballad about lost love or regained love or any kind of love at all, he would put a stop to it at once!

Lord Gervais and Lord Trevelyan rose, still arguing, and moved to seats closer to the enormous hearth. Others, their voices raised in excitement, conferred about the type of dance they wanted. "Lady Madeline!" Albert called out, "you must decide, and lead the first dance."

Madeline smiled at Albert and glanced at Chilcott. "Lord Chilcott is too fatigued for dancing tonight," she said, "and me, too."

"Yes, I must beg to be excused," Chilcott said with a bow in Roger's direction. "The excitement of the day has exhausted me. With your leave, I should like to retire."

"As you wish," Roger replied, nodding his head in acknowledgment. "Good night, Lord Chilcott."

"You must call me Reginald," the groom replied. He turned to Madeline. "Adieu, sweet lady. Until the morrow."

Roger watched him go as Madeline resumed her chair and the dancing began. Chilcott moved with a supple poise that was very impressive, although as he walked, he kneaded his shoulder slightly, as if it hurt. Perhaps he had strained it in the armory. It must not be anything serious, or he would have said something, surely.

Roger faced his sister with a rare, wry smile on his face. "You seem reconciled to this match," he noted quietly.

"He is not what I expected," she replied, and he heard her sincerity.

"Your musicians are very good."

"I'm glad you think so."

"Lord Chilcott is not the only one fatigued, Roger. If you'll excuse me, I believe I'll retire for the night."

"A wise idea, Madeline. You will have even more to do tomorrow, I daresay."

"Yes, I will," she said, rising and heading for the stairs.

Roger lifted his chalice to his lips, a self-satisfied smile on his face as he watched Albert and some of the others dancing in a circle. His gaze roved over those who only watched. The man Albert had been trying to speak with observed the dancing with a slightly contemptuous smile on his face. Maybe dancing was considered unmanly in Sicily.

Now if only the abbot would arrive when he was due, the wedding could proceed with no further problems. Roger sighed and leaned back in his chair, well satisfied with his plans, and with himself. Except for a little niggling doubt about Chilcott that would not go away.

Chapter Nineteen

After the maidservants left Madeline, she put back on her purple gown and waited impatiently for the moment she could venture unseen from her chamber. It seemed hours, and in fact was approaching midnight before she deemed it safe enough.

Cautiously she peered out the door and down the corridor. The torches flickered from the chill breeze that blew from the upper walk. Below in the hall she could still hear the faint sounds of music and men's laughter. All of the female guests and servants would surely have retired by now. As for the men, they might stay in the hall until nearly dawn, celebrating. Roger's wine and ale were the very best.

With stealthy steps she crept along the corridor. She knew which chamber had been set aside for the bridegroom. For a moment she hesitated, wondering if what she was about to do was too dangerous to attempt.

Her heart decided for her and she hurried along the rough, uneven stones, keeping watch lest any sleepless servant see her and prayed that Dafydd, her glorious, foolish, reckless love, would not have locked his door.

When she came to his chamber, she didn't knock or make any sound. She simply slipped inside, to see Dafydd wakeful, standing by the window. He turned, simultaneously pulling out a dagger. Quickly she whispered his name. He stared, then, avoiding the carpet, he sprang toward her and enveloped her in his arms.

For a long moment, nothing else mattered. No danger, no fear, no wondering how it had come to pass. She was in his arms again, safe and loved. With fervent passion she kissed his lips, his eyes, his cheeks, laughing with joy. He took her face in his strong, capable hands and pressed heated lips to hers.

"Madeline," he murmured, pulling back so that she had to look at him, had to think and not simply feel. "What are you doing here? This isn't safe."

"Who are you to talk to me of safety?" she chided softly. "And what are you doing here, pretending to be Lord Chilcott? I thought you would be far away by now, safe in Wales."

"I couldn't leave you to marry someone else," he said, his eyes full of devotion. "You are not the only person capable of imitating others."

"But how—?"

"After I left you in the woods, I met some old friends of mine who were willing to help me. Your brother may find items missing from his castle, and Chilcott's not going to get his baggage back, but I thought it was a small enough price."

"You've managed to fool everyone, Dafydd," she noted happily. "But you had best take care you don't make a mistake." She glanced at the carpet. "You can step on that, you know."

"Truly?" he answered, shocked. "I . . . I wasn't sure what it was for."

"You did very well at dinner, though. I was most impressed."

"That's good. I thought I would go mad not being able to touch you. Or kiss you." He did so now, passionately. Then he gave her an aggrieved look. "What were you thinking, to marry Chilcott to save me? Did you think I would agree to such a thing?"

She laid her head against his chest. "I could see no other way. I might have guessed, though, that you would not let me have my way in this, too." She looked at him, her eyes twinkling. "I'm glad you didn't follow my plan this time, Dafydd. Tell me, how did you learn to be such a fine Norman?''

"I'm not sure I should be flattered to be called that," he answered pensively. Then he grinned. "I had a good teacher. My 'squire' was trained by the Normans. Him it was told me what to do."

"Guiseppe? Is he really from Sicily?"

"Not unless Powys has moved a considerable distance south. His real name is Owain."

"He looks very familiar."

"He should. He's the one took you from your brother."

She stepped back and stared. *"What?"*

"No need to look like he's come to assassinate you. He's hotheaded and bitter for his treatment, but not totally unreasonable. It was ransom he was after, not to hurt you."

"And the others, are they Welshmen, too?"

"They wanted to help, and they don't plan to leave empty-handed."

"It will serve Roger right."

"I thought you wouldn't worry about that. And if this plan goes well, we can all go home together, with no more need to steal."

She reached out and ran her hands up his arms, enjoying the feel of his strength through the soft velvet of his tunic. "I'm grateful to anyone who helped you return to me. But Dafydd, this is so dangerous!"

"Not having to tell me," he answered ruefully. "I've never been more frightened in my life than I was when I rode into that courtyard."

"You? Frightened?" For all his talk of risk and danger before, she had never associated it with fear. It had seemed more a matter of prudence than self-preservation.

"I'm surrounded by Normans here, and I confess I hate it. Believe you me, Madeline, I will be glad when we're well away."

"Where is Reginald Chilcott?"

"He is enjoying Welsh hospitality some miles from here. Alcwyn's men won't let him go till they know we're gone."

She took hold of his hands and looked up at him. "What do you plan to do? Can we leave this place tonight?"

"We're getting married tomorrow, remember?"

"Dafydd, is this a jest?"

"I assure you, Madeline, I am quite serious. Father Gabriel is arriving tomorrow at dawn for that very purpose."

"Father Gabriel? What happened to the abbot?"

There was a glint of humor in Dafydd's dark eyes when he replied. "Waylaid in the woods, poor man, by a band of terrible, fierce rebels. I...um...found Father Gabriel and wanted to ask him about you. When I thought of this, he agreed to give us the church's blessing, instead of Abbot Absalom. Besides, the abbot's met Chilcott, so we couldn't let him come."

Madeline had to smile, then she grew solemn. "Enough teasing. You know as well as I that we dare not stay in Roger's castle a moment longer than necessary. To do so would be folly."

"Don't you want to marry me, Madeline?" he asked softly.

"With all my heart," she answered, caressing his face.

"Good. Besides, if we run off tonight, Roger will come chasing after us again, and I, for one, am tired of that. So you marry Chilcott, just as Roger wanted. The happy couple leave to go home, only a message will come requiring a ransom for Chilcott and the abbot. By the time Roger finds them and guesses what happened, we'll be well away."

"What about the ransom?"

"No need to bother. There's more than enough for everyone in Chilcott's baggage, with a few things from here."

"Oh, Dafydd, it's...it's too incredible!" But she smiled, for despite her words, she believed his plan might indeed work. She would be his lawful wife, he her lawful husband, and there would be nothing Roger could do.

A burst of raucous laughter outside the door and drunken mumbles made them both start. "I had better go," Madeline said regretfully. "It wouldn't do to let anyone find us together, especially since I am not supposed to want to marry you."

"I knew that was why you were acting so cold toward me," Dafydd said, tugging her into his arms. "I've missed you so much." His lips met hers in a deep, passionate kiss.

Maybe she could stay, she thought vaguely. They would be wed tomorrow. No. If this plan was to work, nothing suspicious must occur, nothing improper. And although it was night, who was to say that someone might not stumble into the wrong room and find them together?

Slowly she slipped from his embrace. "I will see you in the morning," she said softly, moving toward the door. She glanced back at him with a warm smile. "Those clothes suit you, Dafydd. You look very much the Norman noble."

"Insulting me, you are," he replied with a low chuckle. "Go, if you must, and now, or I'll pick you up and carry you to my bed."

"The feather bed is the only thing I'm going to miss about this place." Madeline flashed him a glorious smile and was gone.

* * *

"Any troubles?" Dafydd asked Owain in quiet Welsh at dawn the next morning. He had left his chamber and made his way to the courtyard, where he had already arranged to meet with Owain to make sure the ruse was not in danger of being discovered.

"So far, all's well," Owain answered. "The castle servants seem in awe of the men, thinking them from so far-off a place, so the men have had little enough to do with them. Things went well yesterday, I thought, although you have to remember to wipe your lips more daintily. You rubbed at them too hard."

Dafydd grimaced. "I'll try to remember. Anything else I did wrong?"

"Well, try not to stare at her so much. You look like a dog expecting some meat tossed his way."

"Is it that bad?"

"To me, but then I know the situation. I don't think anybody else noticed."

"Not Sir Roger?"

"No. He was too busy keeping an eye on how much everybody was eating. He should be even more distracted today. I hear more guests are expected for the wedding feast."

"Thank God for that, I suppose. Any sign of Father Gabriel?"

As if in response to his question, there was a murmur of greeting at the gate, and Father Gabriel appeared, riding a donkey. Dafydd gave the priest a barely perceptible nod of greeting, and Father Gabriel responded in kind. He dismounted and bustled off toward the hall, his fingers anxiously twisting his hemp belt.

"Well, there is a relief," Dafydd said. "He had better calm himself, though, or the game will be over."

"Indeed." Owain winked at Dafydd. "If you will excuse me, my lord, I've got to rouse those Sicilians." He sauntered off toward one of the barracks, whistling softly.

Dafydd headed toward the hall, encountering Roger de Montmorency coming out the door. Dafydd had expected the man to be still abed, after his late night, and far from in a healthy state of being, after the amount of wine he had consumed. Roger, however, looked none the worse for wear. He smiled and said, "I've been looking for you."

"Oh?"

"I thought we should go through the dowry and the marriage contract together."

"Why?" Dafydd demanded arrogantly. He hoped he sounded insulted, rather than anxious. He had no knowledge at all of contracts, dowries and legal terms, nor could he read a word. "I apologize for the tardiness of the cart bearing Madeline's gifts. I was, perhaps, in too great a hurry to see my bride."

"I meant no offense," Roger replied.

"The loading of the dowry can wait until tomorrow, can't it?" Dafydd asked. "And we can peruse the wedding gifts and contract later."

"If you would rather."

"I would. Legal business always makes my head ache, and I would rather converse with your fascinating, beautiful sister."

"Anytime it will be convenient for you, then."

"Good. Now I am going to mass. I say, Roger, whatever's happened to the abbot? Nothing to cause a delay in the ceremony, I trust?"

"It seems he's fallen ill. A priest who was visiting here recently met one of the abbot's men on the road and returned to give me the news."

Dafydd looked startled and upset. "Well, as unfortunate as that may be for the abbot, surely you have a priest here to give the blessing?"

"Yes, but Father Gabriel has also offered to give the blessing. Have no fear, Reginald. There will be no delays."

"I assume I will see your charming sister in the chapel?"

"Of course. I shall walk with you."

Dafydd fell into step beside Roger, going over in his mind the ceremony of the mass that Owain had described, which was rather different from that of the Welsh church.

"My sister seems most impressed," Roger noted as they drew near a large stone edifice close to the hall.

"Does she? I gather, from some talk I heard, that she was somewhat reluctant to marry? Typical woman, I suppose. Weeped and wailed and made quite a fuss?"

"No." Roger hesitated a moment, then halted. "I will be honest with you, Chilcott. She ran away."

"Well, well, well. I gather some women take these little contrary spells. What did she do, hide in the orchard? Take refuge at the nearest inn?"

"No. After we were attacked by outlaws, she was saved by a Welsh rebel. She spent several days in his company."

"Indeed?" Dafydd answered, taken aback by Roger's confession, and his own reaction. He actually felt a measure of respect for the nobleman's honesty, because he felt the words had not been easy for him to say.

"Yes." Roger, too, looked as if Dafydd's reaction was unexpected. "She fancies herself in love with him."

"Now that *does* surprise me. She seemed most amenable to our marriage last night."

Roger cleared his throat and gazed at him intently. "She isn't a virgin, Reginald."

"Neither am I." He realized that Roger had anticipated a different response, and smiled cheerfully. "Well, to be perfectly honest, Roger, I think most women aren't, no matter how they act on their wedding night. Women are sly, sinister creatures. Beautiful and desirable, of course, but a man is a fool if he trusts one."

"You have voiced my own thoughts exactly!" Roger exclaimed softly, glancing around as others made their way to the chapel for mass. Then he fixed his shrewd dark eyes on Dafydd. "You are indeed a clever man. I could do worse for a brother-in-law."

It didn't seem much of a compliment, but it didn't really matter, Dafydd thought. "I cannot begin to tell you how happy I am to hear you say so."

"Yes, we were told—"

"Rumors and secondhand information can be so wrong," Dafydd remarked with a wave of his hand. "For instance, I expected to find quite the hardhearted blackguard in you, my lord."

"Really?"

"Indeed."

Roger barked another laugh. "My steward tells me you do not intend to stay after the wedding feast. I confess I mean to persuade you to stay, Reginald. It is not often I enjoy a man's company, but I will be sorry to see you go."

Although Dafydd found it impossible to like Roger because of the pain he had caused Madeline and himself, he nevertheless realized that under different circumstances, they might have been friends. Roger was harsh and stern, but not completely without qualities worthy of respect. All he needed, Dafydd thought, was a little less self-assured arrogance and a lot more humility. "I regret I cannot," he replied, with more sincerity than would have been possible even minutes before. "There is a slight problem with my estate in Sicily. I shall be unable to enjoy your delightful hospitality for as long as I should have liked."

"But surely you do not wish to spend your wedding night on the road? One night should not be too much time to tarry."

"No, really, thank you for your kindness, but I must insist—"

"*I* must insist, Reginald, for my sister's sake. She has had a difficult time recently, and I think to travel again so soon would not be wise."

Dafydd knew he was trapped. "As you say, Roger, one more night should not be too much of a delay."

Without any further conversation, they entered the chapel.

Dudley smiled happily as he watched the company gathered at the high table to break the fast. The great weight of suspicion that Lady Madeline was miserably unhappy no longer weighed on his kindly heart. To be sure, she had seemed reserved and far too serious when she had first arrived with Roger, but Dudley was certain that she must have been too tired and ill to be as he had remembered her.

Dudley thought of Lady Madeline's almost-husband with considerable approval. He had met many noblemen in his long life, and without a doubt, this Lord Chilcott was as fine as any of them. He had the bearing, the looks, the manners of a nobleman. For some reason, he was not in the hall at present, but that was just as well. When he was, all the maidservants acted like besotted idiots. He would have to speak with them, or they would be an embarrassment to this hall. Hilda, especially, whom he had more than once accused of setting her sights on Sir Roger himself, was taking far too long clearing away the fruit.

Mercifully, Sir Roger seemed too preoccupied with his sister and his guests to notice. And the other men in the hall, who had obviously stayed awake carousing far too long, didn't seem to even take note that food was being served.

Since there was much to do to prepare for the wedding feast, Dudley didn't linger over his bread. He got up, happily recalling that Lord Chilcott had been persuaded to stay at the castle after the ceremony. Nonetheless, Lady Madeline's goods had best be packed, for the most part.

A groom hurried into the hall and whispered into Dudley's ear. "When did he arrive?" the steward asked anxiously. "Never mind. It doesn't matter. Put him up in the barracks. Sir Hu won't mind, I don't think. He's brought ten men? That's eleven more for the feast. I'd best tell the cook and the kitchen servants. And we'll need another table. You see that the horses are bedded down properly."

Dudley rose and bustled off to greet Hu Morgan, his mind already full of the thousand little details necessary to make this wedding and the subsequent feast flawless.

Chapter Twenty

Hu Morgan stood in the great hall of Montmorency Castle waiting for Lord Trevelyan, so that he and his father-in-law could proceed to the yard in front of the chapel to witness the wedding ceremony of Lord Reginald Chilcott and Lady Madeline de Montmorency. His arrival here had been unexpected but necessary, for a messenger from King Henry's regent, William Marshal, had recently arrived with an urgent and confidential request for Lord Trevelyan to attend a meeting of the most powerful barons in southern England to be held in London. Lord Gervais was expected to attend, as well. The two noblemen would have to leave right after the wedding; however, so many guests, servants and soldiers were bustling about, their absence would scarcely be noticed.

As Morgan surveyed the hall, prepared and decorated with garlands of spring flowers and the colorful pennants of visiting nobles, he didn't doubt the two lords would be missing a fine meal and good entertainment, too. Well, such was the price of power. Fortunately, he could stay.

And although he would never have admitted it, Hu Morgan was curious to see if Lady Madeline would refuse to marry Reginald Chilcott at the last moment. His wife had implied that she might, for, she had said, that seemed like something Madeline would do—to go along with the wedding plans and then, at the very door of the church, thwart her brother's schemes. Liliana had been keen to come herself, but their son's slight cold kept her at home.

Just as well, Morgan thought with a wry grin. He did not have his wife's faith that Sir Roger would lose this battle of wills, and he would have been afraid Liliana might say or do something to prevent the wedding, which was none of their affair.

Lord Trevelyan appeared on the stairs. "I trust I'm not too late," he said with a smile. "Sorry to keep you waiting. This damnable tunic should be given to the paupers. No servant seems capable of managing the laces."

"I think most everyone is already outside waiting."

"Lady Madeline's still in her chamber. I can hear the women chattering like geese."

"What about the bridegroom?"

"Reginald has been waiting some time, I gather. That fellow's so anxious, I was surprised he left the chapel after mass to eat. I half expected him to stay there and wait for the ceremony. As for the bride—well, she led everyone a merry chase for nothing. Whoever that Welsh fellow was, he's forgotten now, I can tell you."

"What, she's agreed to the wedding?"

Lord Trevelyan snorted in a most unlordly manner. "Agreed? My God, I'll say she has. Tries to look like she's not, but any fool with eyes can see otherwise. Roger's been preening like a peacock to think he was right all along. He was arrogant enough before and there'll be no bearing him now, I daresay. Come, we'd best not tarry. I warrant this is one ceremony that will definitely start on time."

Together, they made their way through the crowd of soldiers and servants that stood nearest the hall to join the nobles waiting close to the church. Morgan could make out a familiar-looking priest at the door.

And then Hu Morgan got the shock of his life.

For there, standing on the chapel steps, large as life, wearing very costly garments of black and gold, and looking every inch the nobleman, stood the Welsh rebel he had left for dead. Before Hu could speak or even blink, however, the crowd parted and Sir Roger appeared escorting his sister, who looked as lovely and happy as any angel in heaven, toward the man who was expecting to marry her. The Welshman.

As Dafydd waited at the chapel doors, it occurred to him that he might feel somewhat similar if he had been waiting for his own execution. Better dressed he was, of course, but standing there on display for everyone to see. Still, no one seemed to suspect he wasn't Reginald Chilcott and he had only a little while left to maintain the ruse, just until he and Madeline were pronounced man and wife, really. If Roger tried to annul their marriage, Father Gabriel, standing beside him and nearly as nervous, would be able to confirm that the relationship had already been consummated, should Roger attempt to say otherwise. Everyone would believe Father Gabriel.

Dafydd pushed aside the one real regret he felt, that he was pretending to be someone else, as if he were somehow ashamed of his name. It was a very necessary deception, however, and they would still be married in the eyes of God.

Dafydd shifted slightly, looking over the assembly for Owain and the others, as well as Madeline. He spied Alcwyn's men at the edge of the gathering, keeping a watchful eye on everyone.

With a great collective exhalation, the crowd parted to reveal Madeline and her brother.

How gloriously beautiful she was, her eyes shining with love the most beautiful thing about her. With regal poise and her hand lightly on her brother's arm, she came toward him. He smiled, filled with such happiness that he could scarcely believe it, until someone in the motionless, hushed crowd moved, drawing Dafydd's attention from his bride.

He drew in his breath sharply. Morgan! Hu Morgan, standing there like an evil spirit come to destroy his happiness. While Dafydd stared, transfixed and horrified, their gazes met.

Dafydd knew it was over. Morgan recognized him. In another moment, Morgan would denounce him as an imposter.

With a great effort, Dafydd slowly turned to look steadily at Madeline, sick at heart to think they had come so close. Her expression clouded at once and she glanced nervously at her brother, who walked on unawares. But she realized something was wrong; she saw it in his face. Her eyes lost their love and became filled with desperation.

Surely Morgan was going to move at any moment, Dafydd thought with equal desperation. Identify him as a Welsh outlaw. Call out his men.

Still Morgan didn't move. What was he waiting for, Roger's arrival at the steps?

Madeline loved him. He loved her. They were meant for each other and no one should try to stop them. When she reached the steps, he would clasp Madeline to his side, draw his sword and fight their way out.

But he should be alone in this. He glanced at his friends and hoped they would guess what had happened and leave at once, without waiting for them.

Then he looked again at the crowd, many of whom might be hurt if a melee ensued, for there were several soldiers there, albeit standing idly for the time being.

No. He would not fight. They would not run. He was the equal of any man here, even to Lord Trevelyan, because he was Dafydd ap Iolo and Madeline loved him. He straightened his shoulders. At least everyone here would know who he really was. He would tell them, proudly and with no shame, and together they would face the consequences.

When Roger and Madeline reached the steps, Dafydd took a deep breath. "I am Dafydd ap Iolo," he announced loudly, expecting Sir Roger to look at him with loathing and call for his arrest.

The crowd reacted with shocked murmurs and whispers as Madeline gave a startled cry. She had seen Hu Morgan, then the proud determination in Dafydd's expression. She had hoped he would keep silent, for Morgan wasn't moving. But he was Dafydd ap Iolo, and proud to be so, and she was proud, too, that he would face her brother and speak the truth. No matter what happened, her brother would know that Dafydd was worthy of any woman who had the honor of his love, and she had never loved him more.

She let go of her brother and rushed to join Dafydd. Whatever happened, his side was where she belonged. They would have to drag her away and it would be to Roger's shame. Together they waited for Roger to call out the guard.

Roger . . . did nothing.

Except raise one eyebrow and quietly say, "Really? He certainly fooled me."

Madeline wasn't taken in by her brother's words for an instant. He had known all along. Somehow, he had found out. "You knew, Roger," she accused. "And yet you were going to let me marry Dafydd anyway."

"I suppose I should be flattered you think me so intelligent," her brother replied evenly. "But if that was so, do you honestly believe I would agree to let my sister marry a Welshman?"

"I love your sister and I want her for my wife," Dafydd said firmly.

"Madeline tells me she is besotted with you, too."

"I *love* him, Roger!"

Father Gabriel, wringing his hands anxiously, stepped forward and opened his mouth, but Roger held up his hand. "Spare me your assurances that he is a fine fellow," he said wearily. "I know a conspiracy when I see one." He fixed his cold eye on Father Gabriel, who cleared his throat awkwardly and then Hu Morgan, who simply shrugged. Madeline realized that neither man was particularly repentant, nor, more surprisingly, was Roger at all angry.

"And I can also see that Madeline could do worse—and better," Roger added with a scowl. "Still, I am tired of all this marriage business. Marry this Welshman, then, Madeline, and get it over with. These people are waiting."

"Roger, I..." Madeline whispered, searching for the words to express her gratitude and happiness.

"Bless them, Father, before I decide to have this imposter arrested after all," Roger growled, loath to think that all the people in the courtyard might now think him weak and sentimental.

Father Gabriel, with a nervous nod, did just that. When all was finished, the blessing and giving of the ring, pledges of faith and the kiss, the guests and crowd remained strangely silent. Roger supposed that the shock of the unexpected revelation that the groom was not a Norman nobleman undoubtedly accounted for much of their collective passivity, which lasted through the procession to the hall and Father Gabriel's blessing of the feast.

As the somewhat strained murmurs of the guests and glances at the couple continued, Roger muttered under his breath to the faithful Albert sitting beside him, "By God's holy rood, what's the matter with these people? We could be at a funeral mass. I'll be damned if I've spent all this money for such poor sport."

"I fear, my lord," Albert said somewhat warily, since he was also voicing his own opinion, "that they think you do not really approve of the match...?"

"Of course I approve, or they wouldn't be married."

"I know that, and you know that, and I'm sure Madeline knows that, but the guests are less sure, perhaps."

"Then, by God, I'll give them proof." Roger stood up abruptly and the few murmurings grew silent. "Dafydd ap Iolo!"

His new brother-in-law looked at him, for once taking his eyes from his bride. "Yes, Sir Roger?"

"Stand up."

"Roger, what...?" Madeline began. Roger held up his hand to silence her and waited while Dafydd got to his feet.

"Kneel," he commanded.

The Welshman's eyes narrowed and he crossed his arms defiantly. "Why?"

"God's blood, you look as stubborn as my sister. So I can knight you, you bloody fool."

Madeline's smile was delightful to behold, and there was a buzz of excitement among the guests. Hu Morgan's approval was quite obvious, not that his opinion mattered, and the other guests' expressions ranged from outrage to surprise to amusement. The gossips would have a fine time spreading this, Roger thought sardonically, and Baron De-Guerre might take his next action amiss. Then he looked at Madeline's shining eyes, and no longer cared very much about what anybody thought, even the baron.

Dafydd ap Iolo, however, was not smiling. "Why are going to knight me?"

"What do you mean, why? It's an honor!"

"I do not want to be a knight."

"Are you mad?"

"No. Would I not have to swear fealty to you?"

"Yes. For the estate I will give you."

"I do not want to swear fealty to any Norman, nor do I wish to be beholden to any Norman. Not even you, Sir Roger."

Roger raised his eyebrow speculatively. "Well, Madeline, he seems as proud as any Norman, I will say that for him."

"He has a right to be," Madeline replied evenly.

"Where do you plan to live, then?" he asked next, well aware that they were making a fine show, but determined to have an answer after this rude refusal.

"Wales."

"Roger, I hardly think this is the time—" Madeline protested.

"I do," Roger snapped at her. Then his gaze returned to Dafydd. "I won't have Madeline living in squalor."

His brother-in-law barely flickered an eyelid. "Do you think I would let my wife live in squalor? I have relatives who are every bit as fine and noble as you. I will find a home with them."

"Who?"

"Have you heard of the DeLanyeas?"

"You are related to Emryss DeLanyea?" Roger asked, taken aback to learn his new relation was so well connected. Emryss DeLanyea, half Welsh, half Norman, was famous in the border lands for being a just and capable lord. Even Baron DeGuerre spoke of him with admiration.

"Yes. Our grandmothers were sisters."

"Seems a tenuous connection," Roger noted.

"Not to the Welsh."

Roger reached out to take Madeline's hand and drew her up to stand beside her husband. "Then take her there. But I must have your promise that you will let me know how you fare, and perhaps even visit from time to time."

Both Madeline and Dafydd nodded their agreement. How happy they were, Roger realized. He had been wrong to try to come between then, although he might never see his younger sister again. Without stopping to think, and to everyone's surprise—including his own—Roger suddenly reached out and embraced his sister. "I wish you every happiness," he whispered in her ear.

When he drew back, he saw that her eyes were moist with tears, and her husband's eyes were also glistening. "Yes, well," Roger announced gruffly, "it's time to get on with the feast."

The guests cheered and then the celebration truly began.

"Why did you refuse Roger's offer of knighthood? Are you still angry with him?" Madeline inquired later that night as she brushed her hair.

"You seem to have forgiven all the trouble he caused rather quickly." Dafydd leaned against the sill of the window, watching her. How her luxurious hair seemed to glow in the candlelight! "He was going to marry you off, remember? You were quite upset about it at the time." His gaze strayed toward the bed and he noticed that the coverings had been drawn back invitingly.

"I can afford to be magnanimous," Madeline replied airily, setting down her brush and going toward him with a smile that was at once gentle and enticing. "Since I have the husband I want."

"He's not completely wicked," Dafydd conceded. "Just stubborn. Seems to be a family trait."

"Your family, too. I've never noticed that little mole beside your ear before," she said, rising on her toes to kiss it. "Won't you have to give an oath of loyalty to this DeLanyea?"

"That's different. I've never noticed how perfect the curve of your neck is." He kissed her there, sending shivers down her spine.

"Why is it different?" she whispered, playing with a strand of his hair.

"Because DeLanyea's more Welsh than Norman." Dafydd ran his hands through her dark locks. "Enough talk of such things," he murmured, lifting her in his strong arms. "It's our wedding night."

"And we're finally going to sleep on a proper feather bed," Madeline observed with a throaty, sultry laugh.

"Sleep is not what I had in mind."

* * *

The next morning, an exhausted but blissfully happy Dafydd ap Iolo was busy making the final preparations for departure in the courtyard of Montmorency Castle. As a wedding gift, Roger was providing them with two very fine saddle horses, as well as another horse to carry their belongings. The other Welshmen were in the stables, saddling their mounts and obviously relieved at no longer having to pretend to be Sicilian Normans. There had been some grumbles about the early hour of their departure, for they had been celebrating as only the Welsh do, and many looked ill and barely awake. A few of the hardier souls, who had never gone to sleep, were singing verse after verse of the same ballad, tears of laughter streaming down their cheeks.

Most of the Normans were still slumbering in the hall, having slept where they fell the night before. Only Dudley, ever responsible, was going about his business as usual, although, since he had already said his farewell to the newly wedded couple, his nose and eyes were as red as if he had downed as much wine as any man at the feast.

Despite Roger's generous request for them to stay with him longer, Madeline and Dafydd had been adamant about leaving. For Dafydd's part, he had spent quite enough time in Norman territory.

Dafydd made a final check to see that Owain had tied the pack onto the beast properly. There seemed to be quite a bit of baggage, considering, and there was one particularly large bundle....

"Going now?" said a cheerful voice in Welsh.

Dafydd glanced over his shoulder to behold Hu Morgan strolling toward him. "As soon as Madeline is ready, aye," he answered.

"Envious I would be, man, you going to Craig Fawr, if I didn't have a lovely wife and child to go home to."

"You know Emryss DeLanyea's castle?"

"Know it? Did Sir Roger not tell you? Emryss was my foster father."

"Ah—lucky you were, Morgan. Still, I can't help but wonder..."

"What I'm doing living in Norman territory? With a Norman wife? And fighting off outlaw Welshmen?"

"Yes."

"Well, the Norman wife you of all men should understand. I fell in love. As for fighting Welshmen, if they attack me, I fight back. As for the rest, as I told you once long ago, the Welsh have got to learn to live with the Normans. They're here to stay, man. And they're not all fiends, I think you'll have to agree."

"No, not all. I am tired of the fighting, too."

"After all, I think we've hit the best way to conquer the Normans. Marry them!"

They shared a companionable chuckle, and looked so self-satisfied that Madeline frowned a little as she joined them. "What is so amusing this morning?" she asked.

"Just a Welsh joke, my lady," Morgan said with a straight face. "I came to bid you a good journey. May God go with you!" An infectious grin lit his face.

Dafydd and Madeline said their farewells and Morgan walked jauntily toward the hall.

"What was he really doing?" Madeline asked as soon as Morgan was out of earshot.

"Congratulating us."

"Oh. That's all you're going to tell me, isn't it?"

"Yes."

"Oh, you...you..."

"Villain? Outlaw? Scoundrel?" He pulled her into his arms. "Welshman." He kissed her lightly on the lips. "Husband." He kissed her again, more leisurely. "Lover." This kiss was passionate.

"I hate to interrupt..."

They pulled apart and turned to see Roger standing a short distance away.

Roger de Montmorency, who Dafydd now knew had a heart after all, came closer. "You're certain you won't let me knight you?" he asked casually.

"Absolutely."

"Well, you *are* a proud, stubborn fellow. You two are going to have some battles, I foresee."

Madeline gave Dafydd a grin. "We've already had some. We find the peacemaking afterward makes up for the fight."

"I suppose I have just witnessed such an event? If so, I'm tempted to agree. When will you let poor Chilcott and the angry abbot go, you and your 'Sicilians'?"

"As soon as we get back to the others. You have my word."

"I confess I am not looking forward to putting up with either of them. Especially the abbot. I think I'll suggest to the baron that Father Gabriel would make a better leader for the monastery."

Dafydd grinned his approval, happy to think that the kindhearted Father Gabriel would be in charge.

"Roger, I'm truly sorry to be leaving you to deal with them. What are you going to tell the baron about the wedding and everything?" Madeline asked.

"Well, since your husband took it upon himself to make his revelations in such a public place, I can hardly keep it a secret. The baron will have to be mollified, but I believe I know a way."

"You do?"

"Baron DeGuerre wanted our family united to Chilcott's. That might still be possible."

"How?" Dafydd asked.

"I understand Chilcott has an unmarried half sister."

Madeline understood him at once. "You mean *you* will marry for the sake of this alliance?" she demanded.

"Some of us are not so particular about our future mates," Roger replied coolly.

"But Roger—!"

"Dafydd ap Iolo—really, that's an outrageous name, Iolo. I trust you won't give it to your son, Madeline."

"Roger, we are speaking of your marriage."

"No, we're not."

"But—"

"Will you kindly control this wife of yours? I have no wish to discuss my future matrimonial prospects. I came to say goodbye."

"And me going to ask you for advice on controlling your sister," Dafydd said mournfully.

Madeline glared at both of them. "You're going to let this matter be ignored?"

"Yes," her husband and her brother answered together.

"Listen to me, Madeline, for once," Roger said, his tone soft and unmistakably sincere. "It doesn't matter a whit to me who I marry, and my idea of marriage has never been based on any notion of love. If it wasn't Mina Chilcott, it would be someone else I don't particularly know or care about, and that's fine with me." His voice returned to its more usual cynical tone. "Dear sister, look at all the trouble this *love* of yours has caused."

"Dafydd, make him understand."

"No, Madeline," Dafydd said slowly. "He's got to make his own decisions."

Madeline realized that although she was dismayed by Roger's seemingly callous attitude, Dafydd was right. She had fought for a long time to make her own choices, and if she did not agree with Roger, she could not force him to change his mind. "Oh, very well," she conceded at last. "But I hope you'll be as happy as we are."

"I doubt that," Roger replied. "You two are so delighted with each other, it's embarrassing. I think you should get out of here at once, before you give my men ideas and they start traipsing over the countryside seeking wives."

Despite his cavalier tone, Madeline wasn't fooled for a moment. "We'll send you word when we arrive at Craig Fawr," she said softly after Dafydd helped her mount her horse.

"Good."

"Farewell, Roger." Dafydd swung up into his saddle. The other Welshmen came out of the stables, mounted and ready to leave. Dafydd signaled Owain to lead the way through the gates.

"Take good care of my sister, Welshman," Roger warned.

"I will. You have my word on that."

"And don't let her have her way all the time. She's spoiled enough as it is."

"Roger!"

"I think she's perfect," Dafydd said.

"This love must be a powerful thing, if you think Madeline's perfect."

Madeline nodded. "It is, Roger. It's a wonderful, astounding feeling. I hope you discover that for yourself someday. Goodbye, brother."

"God go with you, sister."

Madeline and Dafydd rode out of the gate, pausing to wave once more at Roger, who stood alone in the courtyard. "Sorry to be leaving him?" Dafydd asked when Roger marched out of view.

Madeline turned to her husband with tears in her eyes and a lovely smile on her lips. "I would be, if I were going with anyone else but you, Dafydd."

His gaze faltered. "You're giving up so much, Madeline."

"I have everything I ever wanted," she replied seriously, then she gave him a comically lascivious look. "And Roger gave us a feather bed, too," she added, nodding at the large, mysterious bundle tied to the packhorse.

Dafydd ap Iolo threw back his head and laughed. Madeline joined him, and soon the sounds of their happiness echoed along the road leading north into Wales.

* * * * *

Author Note

Sometimes, when I'm very lucky, a character pops into my head who is so complete and so exciting that I have to stop, take a deep breath and wonder what the devil is going on. That happened when I was writing *The Welshman's Way*. The moment Madeline collided with her brother, Sir Roger de Montmorency, I knew I had a character who was going to be something special.

However, *The Welshman's Way* was not Roger de Montmorency's story. He had to wait until I had finished his sister's book. He's not the most patient of men, and so, to be honest with you, that's really why he got knocked over the head. It was my way of preventing him from taking control of Madeline's book the same way he wanted to control her life.

The one major worry I had about Roger's story was his heroine. Roger is rather overwhelming, to say the least. What kind of woman could not only deal with him, but ultimately match him in strength, bravery and, yes, arrogance?

Then in rode the soaking wet, bedraggled but unbowed Mina Chilcott, and my dread dissipated.

I hope you enjoyed *The Welshman's Way*, and look for *The Norman's Heart* in the spring of 1996.